ROMAN SPRING

Recent Titles by Sally Stewart from Severn House

APPOINTMENT IN VENICE
CASTLES IN SPAIN
CURLEW ISLAND
THE DAISY CHAIN
FLOODTIDE
LOST AND FOUND
MOOD INDIGO
POSTCARDS FROM A STRANGER
A RARE BEAUTY
A TIME TO DANCE
TRAVELLING GIRL

ROMAN SPRING

Sally Stewart

severn House

This first world edition published in Great Britain 2005 by
SEVERN HOUSE PUBLISHERS LTD of
9–15 High Street, Sutton, Surrey SM1 1DF.
This first world edition published in the USA 2005 by
SEVERN HOUSE PUBLISHERS INC of
595 Madison Avenue, New York, N.Y. 10022.

British Library Cataloguing in Publication Data

Stewart, Sally
  Roman spring
  1. Italy - Fiction
  2. Love stories
  I. Title
  823.9'14 [F]

  ISBN 0-7278-6227-8

Typeset by Palimpsest Book Production Ltd.,
Polmont, Stirlingshire, Scotland.
Printed and bound in Great Britain by
MPG Books Ltd., Bodmin, Cornwall.

One

She'd underestimated the lunchtime traffic snarl-up as usual, set out too late for her appointment with a man who probably didn't tolerate fools gladly. The taxi raised her hopes by inching forward round Trafalgar Square, then stopped again; there was nothing to do but watch the fountains' spray blowing in the wind. They needed sunlight, she thought, and so did Landseer's poor old lions crouched there miserably with rain streaming down their flanks. If Paul Costello hadn't changed his mind by the time she got to meet him she might soon swap this grey city for sunlit Rome. Then again, knowing his reputation, she might decide not to work for him; but success often made other people snide, and it would be nice to discover that reputation had lied. John Wyndham, her boss, liked him and he didn't often make mistakes.

In the Strand at last, the cabbie – driven mad, she supposed, by the daily ordeal of trying to ferry passengers around the capital – suddenly lunged across the oncoming traffic and, unscathed, pulled up in the forecourt of the Savoy. A minute or two later she was being shown to a table in the restaurant – led there by the head-waiter himself; the man she'd come to meet apparently merited that amount of attention. He stood up, frowning at her and not holding out his hand. On his feet he was tall enough to look down on most other people and she suspected him of preferring it that way. He looked formidable and at the moment very cross – only due to hunger, she hoped.

'Clio Lambert, I take it.' It wasn't a question but she nodded anyway, about to apologize for being late. 'You were supposed to be here twenty minutes ago – are you always unpunctual?

The apology died on her lips, and she could see that visions of sunlit Rome had been sadly premature. 'I'm on time more often than not,' she answered calmly, 'but the traffic was even worse than usual.'

She didn't even, he noticed, try to turn away wrath with a smile. Most women he met went to some trouble to please – it was an effort he'd come to expect – but this girl didn't seem inclined to make any effort at all beyond smiling at the waiter who was holding out a chair for her.

A brief assessment didn't tell him very much; she was slender, quietly dressed, and her short, dark hair, expertly cut, framed a face that wouldn't stand out in a crowd. So far so acceptable; but he expected a reaction of some kind to himself and got only the very unacceptable impression that she was judging *him*. His publisher friend, John Wyndham, had let English humour get the better of him when he recommended her; she wouldn't do at all.

Impatient to get the meeting over, he waved away the waiter's offer of a menu. 'I'll have a fillet-steak – rare – and a salad. The lady can order for herself.'

Clio smiled again at the waiter. 'The lady would like oeufs florentines, please, and some Evian water to drink.'

She waited for him to walk away, then looked across the table at her surly host. The common knowledge about him was that he was an American of immigrant extraction, Italian, obviously, given his name. A string of hugely successful thrillers had made him very rich, and either his rather handsome, bearded face or his graceless manners had led women to dance too much attendance on him.

Clio watched him glance at his watch, and decided that *she* preferred to be the one to declare the meeting a waste of time.

'Shall I save you the awkwardness of having to say that I don't suit?' she suggested kindly. 'It needn't matter from your point of view – there are plenty of good research assistants for you to choose from.'

She was right, of course, but he was irritated with her all over again. A woman had no right to be so brutally direct – where was the feminine guile and subtlety a man was entitled to expect? But he surprised himself by resisting the temptation to shout, and answered instead with a question of his own.

'Does it matter from *your* point of view if I agree with you? Why even consider a spell of hard work in Rome? I suppose there's someone here you're running away from – a husband or lover you don't want any longer, maybe?' But he doubted if she'd had either, and the disbelief sounded carelessly in his voice.

'No husband,' she admitted. 'No lover either at the moment, and no other ties to keep me in London. My parents divorced when I was a child. One of them now lives in Los Angeles, the other in Geneva. I'm very unattached except for some elderly relatives in Somerset.'

It was matter-of-factly said, but he glimpsed the loneliness she'd probably had to contend with that explained her self-containment. Given no choice, she'd learned not to air or share her emotions. He didn't normally concern himself much with other people's feelings but, aware that she'd registered his jibe a moment ago, he briefly regretted it.

'You still haven't explained why *Rome* had appeal,' he pointed out in a milder tone of voice, 'except that I know you're a linguist as well as an editorial assistant.'

Clio waited while their food was brought before she answered him. 'I've spent the past six months wrestling medieval Italian into English – John Wyndham was kind enough to suggest that something a bit more up-to-date might make a welcome change.' She eyed him for a moment, weighing her chances of a snub for what she was about to say next. 'But I was curious as well. Your readers will be expecting another highly charged, highly sexed thriller; why offer them instead a slice of recent Italian history that might not appeal to them at all?'

3

His shoulders lifted in a careless shrug. 'Who cares what they're expecting? They don't have to read what comes next.'

'But *why* does it come next?' she persisted.

'Because I'm going to set some records straight, nail a few lies while the people who got damaged by them are still alive.' He began to demolish his steak with the energy she supposed that he devoted to any task in hand, but he suddenly laid down his knife and fork. 'It won't be popular or comfortable – the truth never is. All the more reason, now I come to think of it, for someone like *you* not to be involved. I'm sorry I didn't realize that sooner.'

He'd managed to increase her curiosity, but he'd also confirmed that the offer of a job had been withdrawn. She doubted if it was because she'd arrived late. Paul Costello had judged and found her wanting for some other reason. It was hard not to feel piqued, but he *had* apologized. In return she had to try to be helpful instead.

'I take it that you're familiar with Italy . . . know that trying to set any record straight will be one of the minor labours of Hercules?'

His dark eyes were now fastened on her face, attention fully held for the first time since she'd walked in. 'Meaning what, precisely?'

'That the Italian word "*storia*" means story in English as well as history. The truth you hope to find will have been buried by now under ship-loads of *documenti*; some genuine but most of them not. Nothing is ever quite what it seems there, and your search for reality is likely to become just as futile as Pirandello's strange plays suggest!'

'Difficult but not futile,' he insisted grimly. 'You might not believe it but I'm a patient man when it comes to getting what I want. I'll dig the truth out in the end.'

'Even if it damages other people than the ones that matter to you?'

'If necessary, yes.' He finished off his steak, then stared at her across the table. 'I was right to think you wouldn't do for the job – apart from anything else you'd be far too squeamish.'

She wondered what the 'anything else' might mean, but decided not to ask. 'Blame my sheltered upbringing,' she agreed solemnly instead, 'mostly at the hands of Great Aunts Hester and Henrietta, and the Cathedral Choir School at Wells!'

'Jesus Christ,' Paul Costello muttered, for once intending no blasphemy. 'Life with two old maids and three church services every Sunday; no sex before marriage, and afterwards only for procreation, not pleasure. No wonder you're . . .' But he thought better of finishing what he'd been about to say and signalled to the waiter instead to bring them coffee.

The odd meeting was nearly over, and there wasn't the smallest likelihood of it happening again. Clio didn't regret that, but she was intrigued enough by what he hadn't explained to chance another question.

'You still haven't said why it matters to an American to get at the truth about Italy.' She saw him ready to refuse and hurried on. 'It's not just idle curiosity – I'd like to know, even though it doesn't concern me now.'

His dark eyebrows almost met in another disapproving frown. 'For all you're so quiet-sounding, you're like a terrier at a rabbit-hole, persistent as hell.' Then he gave the little shrug, more Latin than American, that she'd seen once before. 'My father, Enrico Costello, emigrated to New York soon after the war to join an uncle who was already there. He'd had enough of Europe by then, but he raised me on the stories of what happened in Italy. His brother Giorgio was a Partisan, killed on his twenty-fourth birthday in a German reprisal raid. The men and women of the *Resistenza* were heroic then, but that's not what "history" says about them now. The neo-Fascists who wormed their way back into power after the war saw to that. Now do you see why I'm going to rewrite their lying version?'

Clio nodded, unable to repeat her fear that he would find it next to impossible. 'Yes, I see,' she said instead. 'I wish you luck, Mr Costello, and I hope you find the right person to help you.'

She stood up, holding out her hand; obliged to do the same, his fingers gripped hers for a moment, then released them. But he didn't seem inclined to trouble himself with anything more in the way of a goodbye, and she walked quickly out of the restaurant. He watched her go, surprised to find that his hand still retained the feel of hers. It would soon fade, of course; there was nothing memorable about Clio Lambert, except that glimpse he'd had of a small child growing up lonely.

She walked into her sitting room two evenings later as the telephone was ringing. Hester Woodward's voice, sounding less imperious than usual, travelled along the wire. She belonged to a generation that had always transmitted its messages in elegant handwriting, and her telephone conversations were brief and to the point.

'Clio, your great-uncle wanted to speak to you, but I asked him to let me do it – he's very upset.'

'Why upset, Aunt . . . is something wrong with—?' It was as far as she got before she was interrupted.

'Henrietta is also distressed, but otherwise quite all right. I'm telephoning about your grandfather, I'm afraid. He suffered a very serious stroke yesterday and died during the night. Could you . . . could you possibly come down?'

Shocked as she was, Clio still heard the rare quaver in her great-aunt's voice, and answered at once. 'Of course I'll come – I'm so sorry, Aunt dear. I'll be there tomorrow morning.' She glanced at her watch and changed her mind. 'In fact I'll come now – the rush will have gone. But don't wait up; I'll let myself in and see you in the morning.' About to end the conversation a minute or two later, she thought of something else. 'Have you rung my father or shall I do that?'

'I tried; as usual, of course, he wasn't there. Your stepmother promised to let him know – he's in the Galapagos Islands at the moment. So thoroughly inconvenient.'

It only needed mention of Peter Lambert or his current

6

American wife to make Hester sound more like her usual dry self. Also as usual, Clio tried to put in a word for her father. 'He has to go where he's sent, Aunt Hester . . . wherever a cameraman is needed.'

'The fact remains that he's always doing what *he* wants,' said Hester unanswerably. 'Now, drive carefully, if you really mean to set out in the dark. I shan't tell Henrietta; it will only worry her.'

With that, she hung up, leaving Clio to think sadly about the old man who had just died. She'd liked her grandfather very much, and never blamed him for the fact that his son had wanted so little to do with his family. Peter Lambert hadn't even bothered very much about his daughter either if it came to that. The chances were that he'd make no effort to fly over to his father's funeral, and she already knew that Grandfather Mark had named her in his will because he'd told her so.

She packed clothes warm enough to defeat the room temperatures her great-aunts reckoned it healthy to live in, and stopped on her way out of the house only long enough to explain to her friend and landlady on the ground floor why she was hurrying off to Somerset.

Once clear of London, she could make good time; the M4 was nearly empty of traffic, and it was still not quite midnight when she drew up in Vicars' Close, her home for almost as long as she could remember. The night was very cold but fine and, before letting herself into the house, she sat for a while looking at the great Gothic church across the stretch of frosted grass where her grandfather's funeral service would certainly take place. The Cathedral of Wells was part and parcel of their lives, dear, and always beautiful; but now mysteriously so, with moonlight washing its golden stone to silver.

When she went downstairs the next morning her great-uncle, Edward Woodward, was the only member of the family there. Coffee was on the table in front of him, but he wasn't eating

7

anything. He looked suddenly older than his eighty-three years, Clio noticed sadly, and more rumpled than usual, as if the shock of Mark Lambert's death had upset the care he normally took in facing the world.

'Clio, my dear,' he said as she walked into the room. 'Hester promised you'd come as soon as you could, but I'm afraid you must have left London in the dark this morning.'

'It was last night's dark,' she admitted, kissing the top of his head as he sat down again. 'I'm so very sorry about grandfather, Uncle Edward – I know he was your oldest, bestest friend.'

'Don't be too upset, Clio – my friend died as he would have wanted to – quickly and without any fuss.'

Then Edward relapsed into silence, a gentle scholarly man whose only separations from Wells had been enforced, by school and college and wartime service in the army. Mark, he was remembering now, had come home before him, invalided out soon after the invasion of Normandy had begun. Edward had spoken once to him, but never to his own sisters, of the horrors seen when his regiment had liberated a concentration camp in the closing stages of the war. Since then he'd been content with the life of a small-town solicitor, a bachelor sharing the family home with his spinster sisters, apparently serene but still haunted by the evil that his fellow human beings were capable of.

But there'd been young Clio eventually, to bring joy into the house, preferring in some miraculous way to stay with them rather than with her more exotic but separated parents. Looking at her now, for all that she was dark-haired like her father, he could see her grandmother – the vivid, golden girl who'd been his youngest sister. Antonia had escaped from Wells by joining the ATS. She'd come back and married his friend Mark at the end of the war, but she hadn't stayed long after their son was born. Edward had known that she would run away again. They'd never discovered where she'd gone, and nearly fifty years on he still privately grieved over what might have happened to her.

8

He surfaced at last from a wave of memories and smiled at the granddaughter Antonia had never seen. 'Tedious legal work to do, I'm afraid, my dear. But Mark knew it was useless to make your father his executor, and I could easily have died before he did!'

Suddenly close to tears, Clio managed to smile instead. 'You aren't allowed to die for years and years; you've got to stay here.' She was about to ask him what she must do first when her great-aunts walked into the room – Hester, tall, thin, and ramrod-straight still, and Henrietta, her younger, smaller twin, still conscious of the fact that she'd arrived into the world twenty minutes too late to ever assert herself over her sister. Predictably, she wept a little to see her great-niece but didn't question how Clio suddenly came to be there; she thought she knew.

'Dearest, knowing how much we needed you, I expect our guardian angels brought you down!'

'Helped by the contraption on wheels parked outside,' Clio smilingly agreed, long-accustomed to her great-aunt's flights of fancy. Aunt Hetty still had a reasonable grip on reality, but she managed to combine it with a world of her own imagining in which the messengers of heaven and hell usually played leading rôles.

Hester Woodward's greeting was more prosaic. 'I heard you arrive, my dear, but thought you'd need to go straight to bed. Was it very inconvenient to come down?'

Clio shook her head. 'I'd have come anyway, of course, but I'd just finished a long piece of work and I had some leave due. There's no problem about staying until after grandfather's funeral.'

'Not arranged yet,' Hester said briefly. 'We wanted to discuss the service with you.' She frowned across the table at her sister. '*After* breakfast, Hetty, please; not now.'

The command silenced them all for the moment, but while they obediently handed each other toast and butter and marmalade Clio decided that what she'd long suspected about her great-aunt was true: Hester had loved Mark Lambert, and

9

come nearly to hating the sister who had married and then deserted him. She never spoke of Antonia, as Edward and Hetty still did, and firmly disapproved of the son Antonia had left Mark to raise on his own.

It explained a lot about her, Clio thought sadly. She'd been heroic in fact – nursed her elderly parents, made a comfortable life for Edward and Hetty, and been kind in her own cool way to a small child who'd needed taking in; but bitterness had eaten into her during the long, unfulfilled years. Now that Mark Lambert was dead, her strongest feeling was probably pure and simple anger at the waste of it all.

Searching for something that she could bear to say, Clio asked a question of Edward Woodward. 'It's your old firm, I suppose, handling grandfather's affairs? If so, at least I know where to find them.'

'Yes, my dear; William Carstairs is waiting to hear from you, but you'll find that everything will be very straightforward.'

And so it proved, Clio discovered, when she went to see the solicitors that morning. There were no problems and no untidy loose ends – Mark Lambert had died as he had lived, a methodical, considerate and generous man. His funeral service in the Cathedral a week later was simple and moving, attended by his many friends but not by his son.

'Too selfish – always was,' Hester snapped after Peter Lambert's wife had telephoned to explain that he couldn't come.

'Too tied-up perhaps,' Edward bravely tried to suggest. 'How can we understand the sort of pressures a man like that, so much in demand, has to work under?'

'Someone that desirable can make his own terms, I should have thought.' Hester glared at her brother. 'Face the truth, Edward, your nephew would rather forget his English relatives altogether. I dare say he even speaks like an American now.'

'Surely not, dear,' Hetty put in distressfully. 'The poor things sound so . . . so unmusical!'

The typical comment made Clio smile – Hetty had given piano lessons in her younger days and was reckoned by the family to have an 'ear' – but all the same her great-aunt had used an evocative word, bringing vividly to mind the large American who'd berated her at the Savoy for being late. He'd have got some other victim lined up by now for the thankless task of helping him in Rome. Aunt Hetty's guardian angels had been working overtime perhaps in seeing to that.

With the funeral over and Mark Lambert's will made known, no one seemed surprised that he'd left his pleasant house on the outskirts of Wells to Clio. His books went to Edward, and some quite valuable paintings to Hetty; Hester's share was his small portfolio of stocks and shares. It seemed to Clio a sadly impersonal bequest, but her uncle said otherwise when they'd gone together to the house to do some clearing-out.

'Mark couldn't have thought of anything better, because she has a very good financial brain that she enjoys using. Buying and selling, usually quite rightly ignoring the advice of her broker, gives her enormous pleasure!' Edward put down a leather-bound volume of Dickens that he'd been absent-mindedly stroking, and stared at Clio's pale face. She was going through her grandfather's bureau and not enjoying the job very much, he thought.

'Don't feel that you're trespassing,' he said gently. 'It has to be done, just as you'll have to decide that the sensible thing to do is to sell this house. Mark would have expected you to.'

'I know ... it's just that ...' But what it was exactly she didn't say, and went doggedly back to work instead.

She'd reached the deep bottom drawer before she pulled out a box-file tied up legal-fashion with red tape. It was labelled by a single name, 'Antonia', and she untied the tape with fingers that trembled slightly. This surely was a trespass if anything was, and yet who else but herself should properly take care of whatever her grandmother had left behind?

The box contained a strange assortment of bits and pieces: some old-fashioned jewellery that Antonia had obviously despised, an ivory-handled fan that her Victorian mother might have used, two heavily tarnished, silver-backed hairbrushes, and a lovely small *Book of Common Prayer*, bound in faded crimson calf and inscribed with the date of her confirmation. It seemed the saddest of the things she'd decided to leave behind.

Clio leafed through the tissue-thin pages, seeing the familiar words; then something unexpected fell out into her hand. The photograph was of a group of people she didn't recognize, except for the golden-haired laughing girl in the centre of the group. That, surely, was an adult version of the child whose studio portrait still stood on Uncle Edward's desk in his bedroom? Next to her was a handsome young man with one arm around her shoulders. On the back of the snap were scrawled the words – 'Me and darling Filippo, Rome 1944 – the rest don't matter!'

Clio studied the photograph again: it was grainy and badly faded, but she felt certain that it had been treasured, carefully hidden long ago, and lost track of by mistake. She took it across to her uncle and held it out to him.

'I didn't know my grandmother went abroad during the war – surely that *is* her, isn't it?'

Edward stared at it, and then at the writing on the back. 'Antonia's untidy hand,' he agreed unsteadily, 'she was always in a hurry, wanting the next big adventure to arrive! Yes, I think she did end up in Rome – came back to England from there.' When he returned the photograph to Clio he tried to smile, but his face was now a mask of sadness.

'My dear, may I ask something? Keep this if you want to, but don't show it to Hester or Hetty – I think it would upset them even now, for all sorts of reasons that I won't go into.'

She knew that he wanted her *not* to ask what they were, but simply to understand that the past was better left alone. It was time to let the events of more than fifty years ago rest in peace.

'I *will* keep it, please, along with the rest of Antonia's things,' she said, 'but I agree that no one else need know about them. Now, we've done enough for today – shall we go home and have a well-earned cup of tea?'

He nodded, smiling more easily at last as she lovingly swathed him in his thick scarf and overcoat, and led him to the cold, falling dusk outside.

Two

She was intercepted by Hetty on her way out the following morning.

'Come to the Cathedral with me, dearest, please. A new young organist is being put through his paces, and I was his first music teacher years and years ago! I want someone else to hear him as well.' She saw that Clio was about to refuse, and her small face crumpled with disappointment. 'There's no point in asking Hester – she pretends that all organ music sounds the same to her. It can't be true, of course – she just likes to tease me when she's feeling out-of-sorts.'

'One piece I'll listen to, Aunt Hetty,' Clio relented. 'Then I *must* get back to Grandfather's house; there's still a lot to see to there.'

Mindful of the Cathedral's arctic chill, she borrowed one of Edward's thick scarves for herself, inspected her aunt's various layers of clothing, and then led her across the green to the great west door. The audition was already under way because a glorious surge of harmony that could only belong to Johann Sebastian Bach met them as they walked in. The pupil was doing his first teacher more than proud, and already Hetty's small figure seemed to be visibly swelling with pride.

Twenty minutes later the recital came to an end and content, if now half-frozen as well, they got up to leave. At the same time a large figure rose from a seat several rows behind and stood waiting for them. It seemed familiar, but for several confused moments Clio couldn't be sure she was in her right mind in identifying it as Paul Costello. But it *was* him, and she had to suppose that he was there by intention, not chance.

14

'Aunt Hetty,' she said a trifle breathlessly, 'may I introduce a visitor from New York – this is Mr Paul Costello. My great-aunt, Henrietta Woodward,' she added, completing the introduction.

Hetty held out a small, mittened hand, not sure what to make of the large stranger now looming over her. 'I hope you enjoyed the Chorale, Mr Costello – so wonderfully uplifting, don't you agree?'

'The very word,' he answered her, carefully not looking at her companion. 'I'm sorry I missed the beginning of it.'

Aware that, once started on a musical discussion, her aunt couldn't be stopped, Clio touched her cheek gently. 'Darling, you must go home and thaw out while I march our visitor briskly round the Cathedral. Will you warn Aunt Hester that we'll be over soon, needing *very* hot coffee?'

Hetty agreed that she would, bowed with dignity to the American despite her assortment of odd draperies, and trotted away down the aisle. Clio settled again in the nearest chair as if she had nothing else in mind but to stay there for a while.

'You're supposed to be showing me round – shouldn't we get started?' Paul Costello suggested.

Clio stared up at him, shaking her head. 'If you came to see the Cathedral you don't need me to walk about with you – it's a holy enough place to speak very eloquently for itself. If for some strange reason you came to talk to me, I'd rather *sit* and listen. You could tell me, first, how you come to be here.'

'It wasn't very difficult,' he said, resigning himself to the chair beside her. 'John Wyndham – my friend as well as publisher – was already prepared to release you for a few weeks as a favour to me, and he gave me your address. When I called there a helpful woman told me why you'd left London in a hurry; she even gave me your Somerset address. I decided to come in here first, not being sure of polite calling-hours in these parts.'

'That's the "how" bit out of the way; now the "why",' Clio suggested. 'You must have told John Wyndham you still needed an assistant.'

15

'I did; he suggested an agency who offered me eight candidates in all. Most of them I didn't like, the rest I didn't even dislike – worse in a way; there has to be *some* reaction to a person you're going to work with – which of course made me think of you.'

Clio considered this afterthought for a moment, wishing that she knew what it meant. 'First impressions are usually right,' she finally suggested. 'Ours, I thought, were that *we* didn't suit, either.'

Paul Costello swivelled round to look at her more directly. 'My first impression of you wasn't right at all, or else you're different here because you're on home ground.'

'*You* seem just the same to me.' It was his turn to consider what had been said, and she considerately studied the distant roof while he did so.

Eventually, instead of answering, he pointed towards the high altar. At the transept crossing two great inverted arches, one apparently resting on the other, dramatically supported the weight of the central tower.

'Cunning idea, that – I suppose those arches are modern!'

'They *were*, six hundred years ago.' But, in case she'd been unfair, she suddenly smiled at him. 'That was a statement of fact, not a put-down!'

'I'm at a disadvantage here,' he admitted, 'but I've just remembered that it's where *you* went to school.'

Rather to her surprise, she heard no resentment in his voice, and wondered whether her first impression had been correct after all. 'You can't compete with the Woodwards here, I'm afraid. Aunt Hetty's father was principal organist and choirmaster for about a hundred years, and before that *his* father was the Cathedral Dean.' Then she stood up, ending the conversation. 'Before we turn to blocks of ice, there's something else you ought to see.'

She guided him through the side aisles and stopped at the foot of a time-worn, stone flight of steps; shallow, curving and beautiful, they swept up to the medieval chapter house, whose perfection required no comment. Paul Costello didn't even try to make one – and it was another good mark she had to award him.

Finally, on their way out of the church, she stopped in front of a simple wall-tablet inscribed to the memory of Captain John Woodward, M.C.

> *Deeply loved by his family and*
> *by the men he led into battle.*
> *1892–1916*

'He was William – the organist's elder brother,' Clio explained, 'slaughtered in one of the terrible Somme battles.' Then she pointed at a small posy of snowdrops that stood beside the tablet. 'My great-aunts still come each week to bring fresh flowers. I'm glad John Woodward isn't forgotten.'

They walked in silence towards the door they'd come in by until her companion suddenly spoke again. 'You remember your dead quietly with flowers; we make a song and dance about ours. Is that what you're thinking?'

Blinking in the bright winter sunlight outside, Clio shook her head. 'No, I was still wondering why you're here. You don't have to say, of course; just decide whether you can face meeting all three of my elderly dears at the same time!'

The frown she was beginning to miss – so far he'd scarcely seemed like himself at all – now reappeared. 'God dammit, why do you need telling again – isn't it obvious I'm here to offer you the job? I leave for Rome on Monday. You can have today to think about it, and a week to sort out your life if you decide to come.'

'If I refuse, what will you do then?' she asked gravely.

'Find someone there, I suppose. It's my problem, not yours. Now, before I drive back to London, where's that hot coffee you asked for?'

'Just across the road,' she managed to stammer above the turmoil in her mind. 'It's where the family have always lived, in Vicars' Close.' She saw him register the beauty of the row of ancient houses but again he didn't comment on them. Then,

as they reached the front door, she remembered something
else. 'I'm afraid they won't have read any of your books.'

'I should be disappointed if they had,' he observed calmly,
leaving her with the impression that he might have just won
that round.

An hour later she saw him off again, with a promise to telephone her decision to the Savoy. But the visit hadn't been a
success, and she wasn't surprised to find that he was perfectly
well aware of it.

'I hope you noticed that at least I was *trying* in there?' he
suggested.

She nodded, her rare smile in evidence for a moment. 'There
are limits to the extent you can be expected to tone yourself
down! It wasn't a problem for Uncle Edward, but you're a bit
too much for Hester and Hetty, I'm afraid.' She hesitated a
moment, then added something else. 'Thank you for not talking
about the job; they'd have been upset if I hadn't mentioned it
first.'

He stared at her consideringly – she wasn't in any way
arresting but he was surprised to find himself thinking that it
would be a pity not to see her again. The chances were, though,
that she *would* turn the job down. 'I hope you'll make up
your mind on your own account, not let that elderly trio do
it for you,' he suggested. 'They're interesting to meet, but I
expect you know they're not in touch with the real world at
all.'

Then, without waiting for a reply, he lifted his hand in a
token wave of farewell and strode down the path. It had been
an unnecessary journey, she thought; he could more easily
have telephoned to offer her the job. If he'd lingered long
enough she might have asked why he didn't; but it was too
late now. She closed the front door, suspecting that his visit
would be treated as if it hadn't happened at all. It was the way
her great-aunts usually dealt with anything that disturbed them.
But when she returned to the sitting room Hester had clearly
decided to make her opinion known.

'I didn't quite take to Mr Costello, my dear. Is he ever likely to call again?'

'I think you can be sure you've seen the last of him,' Clio answered calmly, 'but I'm sorry you didn't enjoy the meeting.'

'Interesting man, though,' Edward put in tactfully. 'At least, I found him so.'

'Oh yes, certainly interesting,' Hetty hastily agreed, 'but there . . . there *was* rather a lot of him.' She thought about this for a moment. 'I suppose we aren't accustomed to people being quite so large and . . . and magnetic.'

Once again she'd landed on the right word, Clio thought, but Hester objected to it with sudden fierceness. 'Nonsense, Hetty – he's an American. They make a fetish of size; I suppose it comes of living in an enormous country. Thank God we don't.'

It sounded so unpleasantly smug that Clio was for once provoked into arguing with her. 'We can't take any credit for that, Aunt Hester – this happens to be where our forbears were. And, as it happens, Paul Costello's family originated in Italy.' It was a mistake, of course, because Hester Woodward had strong opinions about the Italians as well; and her pitying smile said as much – they were not oversized perhaps, but definitely unreliable.

Clio found herself goaded into saying the very thing she'd meant *not* to say. 'He wants me to help him research a book he's writing about Italy. It would mean working with him in Rome for a month or two.'

She half-expected some cries of protest but not the shocked silence that now seemed to settle on the room. Unusually, Hetty was the first to find her voice. 'Not *Rome*, dearest?' she quavered, and there was distress in her voice that couldn't be smiled away.

'What's so wrong with Rome, Aunt Hetty?' Clio asked gently. 'It's one of the most historic cities on earth, and it's stuffed full of beautiful things.'

'Papist and dangerous – that's what wrong with it,' Hester snapped, and got up to leave the room. But she halted at the door, and spoke again in a different tone of voice. 'Don't accept Mr Costello's invitation, my dear; we'd be much happier knowing that you were in London.'

'I promised I'd think about it,' Clio had to answer. 'I must do that before I decide.'

Hester hesitated – not something she made a habit of – then nodded, and walked out. It had been a strangely tense few moments, but Clio made an effort to smile at the others' anxious faces.

'If I did go, it wouldn't be for ever, you know! But right now I must finish clearing up at the house. Don't wait for me for lunch, please.'

She let herself out, thinking what an unexpected morning it had been. Why, most strangely of all, had Paul Costello changed his mind about her? She'd placed him as a man who made decisions and stuck to them. But there was her family's strong objection to him to ponder as well; there'd been nothing in his manner for them reasonably to take exception to. She also remembered moments when *she*'d had to reassess him, but they weren't enough to convince her that they could work painlessly together; it was probably better on the whole to agree with Hester that she should stay in London.

By mid-afternoon there was nothing left to do; she'd made the inventory requested by the solicitor, collected her grandfather's remaining papers and tidied up the house. When probate had been granted would be time enough to finally decide whether she wished to sell it or not. She was taking a last look round – a last sad farewell to Mark Lambert, it felt like – when a knock sounded at the front door. Her great-uncle stood there, his white hair ruffled by the wind as he punctiliously lifted his hat.

'Thought I'd come and keep you company,' he suggested. 'It's sad working here on your own.'

'I was just saying goodbye to Grandfather,' Clio answered gently. 'Why don't we do that together?'

They made a little tour of the house and ended up in the pleasant book-lined room that Mark Lambert had used most.

Clio wandered to the window to stare out at the garden, bare now except for bright patches of gold where winter jasmine and hamamelis shone in the sunlight. 'It will be more of a wrench to part with the garden than the house,' she said with regret. 'Grandfather had made it beautiful for every season.' She turned to smile at the old man who'd come to stand beside her. 'I'm sure he'd say it won't be wasted – someone else will come and love it in their turn.'

Edward Woodward nodded, then cleared his throat, hesitating over how to phrase what he had made up his mind to say. 'Clio, my dear – about that work Mr Costello wants you to do: I expect you were a little taken aback by the girls' reaction to it this morning.' The 'girls' were eighty-one but, two years younger than himself, it was always how he'd referred to them.

Clio tucked her hand through his arm. 'Aunt Hester *was* a bit fiercer than usual,' she admitted, 'but I'd have done better not to bring Paul Costello to the house.'

'It was nothing to do with Mr Costello,' Edward insisted gravely. 'What upset her, and Hetty too, was the mention of Rome.'

Clio stared at his face, recognizing from its withdrawn expression that his mind was back in the past. 'You said the photograph of my grandmother would upset them too,' she suddenly remembered. 'What *is* it about Antonia and Rome that they find so distressing?' He hesitated again, and she gave his arm a little squeeze. 'Tell me, please – I think I ought to know.'

'You should have known years ago in my view,' Edward confessed, 'but Mark agreed with my sisters that what was past was past, better not revisited.' He released himself from her hand and went to sit in the armchair that had been his whenever he and Mark had spent an evening together. It seemed easier there to go on with his story. 'Antonia was in Rome almost as soon as it had been liberated from the Germans – she drove American generals about in their staff cars, I think. We heard from her occasionally – the city itself was in a bad way, but she sounded happier than I'd ever known her.'

'Because of "Filippo"?' Clio put in quietly, remembering the name on the back of the photograph.

'Yes, I think so. We didn't know that at the time, of course – just imagined it was the excitement of all that she was living through. Then, just before Christmas of that year, 1944, she suddenly arrived home, looking desperately unhappy and rather ill. Her army career was over – she wasn't well, she said.'

'I suppose I can guess why – was she going to have a child?' Clio put it into words for him, knowing that he would find it hard to say.

Edward nodded. 'It was soon obvious, of course – a scandal then, especially in Vicars' Close, though perhaps you can't appreciate that now. Mark Lambert was already home – he'd been wounded early in the year and invalided out of the army – and I think he'd grown up loving Antonia. He asked her to marry him, and by the time Peter was born it was generally accepted that the child was his son.'

Clio pondered the story for a moment, thinking how much it made clear things that had always puzzled her. 'My father knows, doesn't he?' she suggested.

'Yes, Mark told him when he was eighteen, although Hester was against it even then. Mark was right: the boy had to know; but from then on he seemed to feel that he could live his life more happily if he more or less forgot about us. Mark never complained, good man that he was.'

'Saint that he was, I think,' Clio exclaimed. 'How *could* Antonia have gone, leaving him to bring up a child who wasn't even his own?'

'She was desperate,' came Edward's sombre answer, 'but without knowing her you can't possibly understand. She was the most alive human being you could ever meet – beautiful, of course, but warm and loving as well. Grateful as she was to Mark, she felt suffocated by the quiet, provincial life he offered her. The note she left behind suggested that she was going to friends in America. Since she would never come back, he was free to get the marriage annulled. He never did, because he never stopped loving her; never stopped hoping he'd see her again.'

'*Did* she go to America?'

'We had to assume so. Unlike Hester, she found Americans very engaging; and I'm sure they must have been entranced by her.'

'What about Filippo – did she never speak of *him*?'

'Once, to me, but never to the girls. His family was aristocratic, princely even, and he was required to marry a rich contessa, not the unendowed daughter of an English cathedral organist. Filippo had seemed to share his family's view that she'd tried to trap him into marriage; that was why she came home.'

'Poor Antonia,' Clio murmured. 'I have to feel sorry for her after all, but what a sod the Italian must have been.'

Edward looked startled by a word his sisters probably didn't even know, but he managed a rueful smile. 'Your actual grand-parent, I'm afraid, my dear, even so.'

'Unfortunately true!' she had to agree, but her chaotic thoughts now centred on Hester Woodward, who'd not only had to watch Mark Lambert marry Antonia, but knew when her sister abandoned him that she could never take Antonia's place – apart from a marriage that hadn't been annulled, the tables of consanguinity would have forbidden it.

'Poor Hester,' Clio murmured this time, without explaining why.

It was Edward who finally broke the silence in the room. 'What about Mr Costello, Clio – is Rome now a place you'd rather stay away from?'

She answered slowly, relieved to discover that she was at last sure of what she was going to do. 'I thought I was on the point of turning his offer down. But I shall accept it after all.'

He nodded as if it was what he'd already guessed. 'To show your great-aunt that she can't run your life?' he suggested half-seriously.

Clio shook her head. 'That might have something to do with

it, but mostly it's because of the odd coincidence that I'm offered the chance to learn what Rome was like when Antonia was there – it's the very time Paul Costello is going to write about.'

'We were wrong, of course,' Edward said, as if talking to himself. 'The past is never dead, whatever we do to bury it.' Then he tried to smile at the girl who stood watching him – so like yet *not* like Antonia. 'Let's go home, shall we?'

Three

A week later she boarded an Alitalia flight, expecting no improvement in Rome on the miserable January weather she was leaving behind. Paul Costello had morosely confirmed on the telephone the night before that London wasn't the only city drenched in rain. He'd sounded ill-tempered altogether. His rented apartment, though grand, lacked the comforts any right-minded American took for granted, and the overweight lady who came to clean couldn't be discouraged from singing loudly while she worked. Clio decided that she'd been wise to insist on a two-week trial; chances were that the hired assistant would turn out to be just as incompatible.

He'd been right about the weather, though. Emerging from the plane at Fiumicino was like walking into a waterfall; rain didn't fall gently on Rome with the quality of mercy. There'd be no free taxis while it lasted; but even as she hesitated over which airport bus to take into the city, her eye caught sight of a man holding up a sign. Her name was written boldly on it and, to aid identification, someone had also sketched an outline of the twin towers of Wells Cathedral. It made her smile, and immediately the man moved towards her.

'Signorina Lambert? My cousin Paolo couldn't come himself; I am here instead – Luigi di Palma, at your service,' he said in English that was accented but fluent.

She smiled again, touched by an unexpected piece of thoughtfulness that made the miserable day look suddenly brighter. 'If you're here to save me heaving my luggage on to a bus, I'm deeply grateful to you, Signor di Palma.'

'Luigi, please,' he corrected her gravely. 'Of course I am

here to drive you to your *pensione*. We shall place your . . .
I forget the English word . . . your *valigie* near the exit. It
will take a few minutes only to find the car and bring it round.'

She watched him competently drape himself with her
luggage and select a spot near the door where she was to wait.
Then he headed out into the downpour, raincoat collar turned
up but dark head bare. He'd called himself Paul Costello's
cousin but there was no family likeness that she could see.
His manner was unexpected too; polite but reserved as well.
No inspection, admiring or otherwise, and no smiling desire
to make a good impression on a woman he was meeting for
the first time; very un-Italian in fact.

She waited until they were in the car, heading north-east-
wards into Rome, before she thought conversation was needed.
'I didn't realize Mr Costello had relatives still living here. I
suppose your mother and his father were sister and brother.'

Luigi di Palma nodded. 'That is how it was,' he agreed.
'There were four children; my mother was the youngest.'

Clio let another mile or two go by, aware now that if they
weren't to drive in silence she'd have to prod her companion
into talking.

'Your cousin learned about the wartime years from his
father,' she remarked at last. 'But perhaps your mother was
too young to remember them clearly.'

'She was fifteen when the war ended – she remembers,'
Luigi insisted briefly. But, afraid of having sounded too abrupt,
he went on, 'I know why my cousin is here – we've talked
about the book. It needs to be written, signorina.' A stoppage
in the traffic ahead allowed him to glance at her. 'But I hope
you realize that Paolo is half-Italian. If things don't go well,
I'm afraid there will be some shouting and swearing.'

Clio thanked him for the warning – kindly meant, she
assumed – but doubted whether it was necessary. Paul Costello
might ride rough-shod over anyone who seemed to invite such
treatment, but he wasn't likely to waste powder and shot on
battles he couldn't win by force – she had him down as a clev-
erer man that that.

'An author and his assistant at least have to be able to tolerate each other,' it seemed safe to say. 'If we can't do that, I'll admit defeat and go back to London!'

'Then I shall wait and see.' It sounded ominous, but Luigi had turned his attention to the road again, and she now let him drive undisturbed.

Already they were nearing Rome. Even without the thickening traffic to tell her so, she recognized its familiar landmarks ahead. Then they crossed the Tiber – a mere brown stream in the dry months of summer, and still not a very impressive river even now. In the Piazza Venezia she tried to avoid looking at the Vittorio Emanuele monument, deplorably grandiloquent when it should have been grand. Time hadn't toned down its glaring whiteness and probably never would. But now they were threading through narrow streets that properly belonged to Rome, a harmonious jumble of honey-coloured stone, faded red stucco and terracotta roofs.

Finally, Luigi stopped in front of a shabby-looking antique shop in the Via Margutta. The sign over the door indicated that the Pensione Pinciana could be found on the first floor.

'It looks not very good,' Luigi said doubtfully. 'Maybe we should find somewhere else for you to stay.'

Clio shook her head. 'No need, I'm sure. I've been here before, and Signora Rollo is still in charge – I've spoken to her on the telephone.'

Arriving breathless with her luggage at the top of a flight of worn stone steps, he had to agree that she was right. The *pensione* looked clean and comfortable, and the middle-aged woman who greeted them seemed delighted to welcome back a *signorina inglese* whom she insisted she remembered very well.

Clio thanked her chauffeur warmly but he waved her gratitude aside, bowed courteously and went away. Since it seemed more likely than not that they would meet again if he was in touch with his cousin, he might have been expected to say, however untruthfully, that he looked forward to it. But her uncomfortable impression was the reverse: if he could avoid her in future, he would.

27

It was a puzzle she had to put aside because the *padrona* was waiting to conduct her upstairs. Shown to a pleasant room on the floor above, she looked out of the window at an aerial view of neighbouring roof-tops and little secret gardens, and discovered that the day was ending well after all; what she could see of the sky was now a tender, rain-washed blue. The early winter darkness would soon set in, but if she hurried she could make it in time to see the view from her favourite vantage-point. She explained this in Italian to Signora Rollo, who nodded as if it was exactly what she'd been expecting to hear.

'Always English ladies must take walks,' she pointed out. 'We Italians, we stroll a little – *fare la passeggiata*, you understand – but *walk*, never!'

'Too energetic, or too unfeminine,' Clio agreed ruefully. 'I expect it's all the games we had to play at school.'

Ten minutes later she was where she wanted to be – on the terrace at the top of the Pincio, leaning over its balustrade. Rome lay spread out below her with, away to the west, St Peter's dome silhouetted against a delicate winter sunset. As always, there were church bells ringing – the evening Ave Maria now, before the final '*ora di notte*' signifying that another day had ended.

Looking out over so ancient a city, it seemed natural to think about the past. Imagination couldn't paint for her what it had been like at the end of a bitter war; but Antonia had known. Because of *her* presence here Clio Lambert – who wasn't properly a Lambert at all – was a tiny part of it as well. The man who'd begotten and then repudiated his child was likely to be dead by now. She would probably never know who he'd been, any more than she would learn what had happened to her grandmother. But the fact remained that some tinge of Roman blood was in her own veins; to that extent, at least, Edward Woodward had been right – the past wasn't over.

She walked slowly back to the *pensione* again, content for the moment just to grow reaccustomed to a city that still felt unfamiliar – voices, street signs, murderous traffic that showed little inclination to stop at red lights and none at all at pedestrian crossings; everything needed getting used to again before she had to face the ordeal of working with Paul Costello.

But, back in her room, she was getting ready to go down to supper when the telephone rang and she heard his unmistakable voice along the line.

'Luigi di Palma left you at the *pensione* an hour ago; couldn't you have stayed there? I've been trying to ring you.'

'I thought I started work tomorrow,' she pointed out calmly. He'd probably share Signora Rollo's opinion of the mad English habit of taking walks, so better not to mention where she'd been. 'Thank you for arranging the lift for me from the airport,' she said instead. 'It was much appreciated.'

'Don't mention it. Now I suppose you need feeding as well. If there's anything to eat in that place you're in, it will only be an indigestible mound of pasta. You'd better come round here.'

'Thank you but I've already accepted the *padrona*'s offer of *saltimbocca alla romana*. The cook is her sister, and she can leave most four-star hotel chefs standing.'

With a suggestion of gritted teeth he was heard to speak again. 'Then perhaps you'll do better than I shall. I'll see you at nine a.m. tomorrow, *sharp*, if that isn't too much to ask.'

She put the phone down, having promised to be on time. Either something was upsetting Mr Costello's normal sunny temper or this was the cantankerous frame of mind in which he always worked. It was hard to remember at the moment why she'd decided to come at all.

But downstairs in the dining room, eating her delicious supper, which, as the name suggested, did indeed 'jump in the mouth', optimism returned. Rather to her surprise the room had a pleasant sprinkling of other guests even though mid-January was a time when few tourists came to Rome.

She was being brought coffee when a man at another table closed the book he'd been reading and sauntered over.

'The *signora* thinks you might agree to drink your coffee with me. Patrick O'Connor is the name.' But the engaging smile and easy manner also proclaimed his nationality.

29

Suddenly aware of feeling lonely, she gestured to a chair and he sat down. 'Clio Lambert,' she responded, 'from London.'

He grinned and glanced round the room, then at her. 'I've nothing against the priesthood, you understand, but in this part of the world they're all certain to be male!'

There *were*, she now realized, a number of clerical collars to be seen. 'What brings them here – a special occasion?' she asked.

'It *is* for them – they'll have booked an altar months ago, to realize a lifetime's ambition to say mass in St Peter's. Go there early any morning and you'll see them scurrying across the *piazza* carrying their little attaché cases!'

'You aren't one of them,' she suggested, 'but you seem to know a lot about them.'

'I'm a roving correspondent for the *Irish Times*, here to report on the state of Italy in this year of grace. I've covered Milan, Venice and Florence. After Rome I can go home.'

'Interesting but wearing work – having to take in impressions all the time, as well as facts if you can find them!'

'The problem in a nutshell,' he agreed ruefully. 'Truth's like the hydra-headed monster here – you think you've got hold of it and then another version, the exact opposite of course, turns up looking just as good!' He waved the problem aside and smiled at her. 'I hope *you're* staying for a while.'

It was an invitation to talk about herself, but even if she'd been inclined to do that to a chance-met stranger, she thought her employer was entitled to tell his own story if he wanted to.

'I'm here to do some research,' she admitted briefly, ' – not on my own account; for someone else. It's for a book he plans to write.'

'A brandy while you tell me about it?' the Irishman suggested.

Clio shook her head. 'No brandy, thanks. It seems to have been a long day and I must start work in the morning. I'll say goodnight instead, Mr O'Connor.'

'Pat to my friends. I hope we can dine together tomorrow – I hate eating alone.'

She smiled but didn't commit herself; the gleam of approval in his eyes did a woman's self-confidence no harm, but she was wary of men whose social speed was quick-quick when hers was definitely slow. A lesson learned from long ago had been too painful to be forgotten; she couldn't help now but distrust charming men. He sensed her withdrawal and accepted it with the easiness that seemed to be his hallmark.

'*Buona notte, signorina!*'

She replied in kind and walked out of the room. Tiredness had set in, and she remembered with gratitude that her bedroom didn't face the street. It would be quiet there, and she'd be able to sleep – no mean achievement in Rome.

Four

She timed her arrival at the Palazzo Soria carefully the following morning – no need to be early, but she wasn't going to be one minute late. With time in hand, though, she could loiter on the way. Miss Babington's English Tearooms, established in the nineteenth century, were still going strong, and the Anglo-American bookshop just off the Piazza di Spagna was something else she would almost certainly be needing. The great upward sweep of the Spanish Steps looked bare for the moment – no flower-stalls but no tourists either; and Bernini's Barcaccia fountain quietly chattered to itself in the middle of the square, as it had for the past several hundred years.

The *palazzo*, almost next to the one that housed Spain's Embassy to the Vatican, wasn't hard to find. Inside, the custodian directed her to the second floor. She was greeted there by an amply built, smiling woman who introduced herself as Lucia. The *signore*, she said, was talking on the telephone; would the *signorina* please to wait in the *salotto* while she got on with her work; then she resumed her dusting to the strains of '*Mio caro babbo*' delivered *con amore e fortezza*. Clio applauded at the end of it, before approachinng the matter as delicately as she could. The friendly conversation was just over when Paul Costello walked in. She'd forgotten quite how large he was, but at least he seemed to suit the size of the room.

'Good morning,' he said grimly, by way of welcome. 'Keep your coat on, I should; the central heating is more often off than on. I've got an office of sorts set up for you.' He led her along the hall to a small room at the back of the building. It was adequately equipped, if not luxurious – desk, filing cabinet, telephone and computer ready for use.

'This is yours,' he said. 'My bedroom's large enough to house my office as well.'

If that had also been set up, he'd used the past week to good purpose, she realized. Things didn't normally happen so fast in Italy.

'Another table would be useful – to spread books and papers on,' she suggested after a glance around. He nodded, accepting it as reasonable. 'I see you've made the acquaintance of the charming Lucia – she's been in particularly fine voice this morning.'

'I complimented her,' Clio said, doing her best not to smile, 'but I also thought to mention that you were weak in the head.'

'You did *what*?'

She winced at the shout – Luigi di Palma had been right about that – but tried to soothe. 'In Italian it only means that you suffer from bad headaches and need the rest of us to be quiet. I'm afraid she may still madden you by creeping about on tip-toe, but it was the best I could do.'

It was touch and go whether he roared at her again; then to her great surprise a smile she hadn't seen before changed his face to something unexpectedly pleasant.

'I suppose I should be grateful,' he agreed at last. 'But I shall tell you again what I said at Wells – you practise a very neat deception on other people; there should be a warning notice. Now, I'm afraid you have to come into my bedroom if we're to make a start.'

She decided to ignore a note in his voice which was surely meant to disconcert her; he was, as even Aunt Hetty had noticed, a very magnetic man, but she could be entirely sure that his only interest was in her ability to help him.

For the next hour he laid out, with lucidity and skill, the task in front of them and the way in which he intended to tackle it. Occasionally she made a comment, asked a question that he considered carefully, but on the whole she was content to listen. He was a professional writer, organized and highly intelligent; there might be problems ahead, but there'd be pleasure too in the challenge of keeping up with him.

'No disagreements so far?' he asked, uncannily reading her mind. 'Not yet, thank you!' She hesitated, then risked something he *might* take exception to. 'Your cousin Luigi was polite and very helpful, but it was obvious that he didn't approve of me. We're strangers, so I assume that it's the English he doesn't like?'

Costello remembered the directness that he'd met in her before; she didn't believe in beating about the bush. 'I looked you up – Clio turned out to be the Greek Muse of History. How much do you know about Italy's post-war years?'

'A fair amount,' she answered cautiously.

'Well, your people were pretty much in charge here after Rome was liberated – it was called a "British sphere of influence". Luigi's father, Mario di Palma was a lifelong friend of Palmiro Togliatti, the leader of the Communist Party after the war. They reckoned the British allowed the Fascists to creep back into power – at their expense.'

'If true, perhaps because the Cold War was already starting. What was there to choose for evil between Hitler or Joseph Stalin?'

'Not all Communists are mass-murderers,' he pointed out. 'Men like my uncle believed in the principles of true universal brotherhood; men like him led most of the Resistance groups and they were quietly shunted aside. Memories are long here, I'm afraid.'

Clio made a little gesture with her hands, abandoning the argument. 'I'm here to work, not offer you my own opinions, so I'll go and make a start.'

She'd almost reached the door when his voice halted her. 'If you feel brave enough to meet the rest of the di Palma family, my aunt has invited us to dinner tomorrow night.' It felt like a gauntlet thrown down, and she was bound to pick it up.

'I'll look forward to it,' she said, and left the room.

The rest of that day passed peacefully – Costello, helped by family connections, delving into the history of the Garibaldi Brigades which became the Resistance movement, while Clio tackled municipal records. This, to her great pleasure, required a visit to the Town Hall, once the Senator's Palace, on the Capitoline Hill.

In the *pensione* dining room that evening she wasn't surprised to have Patrick O'Connor ask if he might join her. They lingered over dinner, arguing about favourite places in the city. For him it was the misty, colonnaded piazza of St Peter's early on a summer morning, with the fountains playing but not a single tourist coach yet in sight. Clio's choice was the Campidoglio at night, with Marcus Aurelius and his glorious horse bathed in moonlight.

'We'll never change each other's view,' she concluded at last.

'No, but we could look at them both together, just to convince ourselves that we're right! Shall we start with your choice tomorrow night?'

Again she was conscious of being hurried, and she had no wish to loiter with him in the moonlight, as if waiting to be kissed. Worse, he'd insist on talking too, and her conviction was that if Michelangelo's lovely square was silent enough, she might one night hear the old horse whinnying to his rider.

'Not tomorrow, I'm afraid,' she answered, 'and after that I don't really know when I'll be free – it isn't a nine-to-five job.'

His quick smile reappeared, rueful this time. 'I think that was a gentle "get lost, Mr O'Connor" I just heard! I can take a hint, Clio, but I'd like to know why. It wasn't a very dangerous invitation!'

'Of course not,' she agreed quickly. 'It's just that talking to you is a pleasure, but it's the only pleasure I want.'

'Truthful and to the point! What shall we talk about, my cautious friend?'

She smiled her rare wholehearted smile, then looked serious again. 'I assume you were given this assignment because you already know quite a lot about Italy. What do *you* think happened after the war – did we make some awful mistakes here?'

'Probably, if by "we" you mean the British; but that's with hindsight, of course. At the time, in the middle of chaos of every kind, who's to say what could have been done differently? You still can't even get a universal opinion here about Mussolini. For some he was the devil walking, for others a man ahead of his time, dragged into joining the Nazis because he had no choice.'

'And we'll never know the truth – is that what you're saying?'

He nodded, wondering why the truth seemed to matter to her so much. It wasn't the sort of dinner conversation he usually had with an attractive woman, and she *was* attractive; no doubt about that. Not obviously so – a man needed to be close up to see her unobtrusive kind of beauty, and she didn't encourage close encounters.

'I tried to warn the man I'm working for,' she went on thoughtfully, 'but I don't think he believed me. Americans tend to assume that everything can be had, even the truth, if they work hard enough for it.'

'Then Italy may defeat him,' Patrick O'Connor agreed. 'Now, what about that brandy you refused last night?'

She dressed with care for dinner the following evening, dithering over playing for safety or cutting a dash. But a family gathering suggested discretion rather than dash, and she settled for a simple suit of black velvet that not even the most conventional Roman matron could object to. Asked by Costello not to keep the taxi waiting when he picked her up, she was ready in the hall, but it was Luigi di Palma who walked in. He smiled very pleasantly, hostility to the Anglo-Saxons apparently put aside for the time being.

'Again it is I, not Paolo,' he said in his careful English. 'He had another guest to collect. She is a family friend who has just returned to Rome from New York.'

Clio followed him downstairs, to his own car again, and

left him to concentrate on the traffic while she looked at the Italians' genius for night-time floodlighting. The Piazza Navona was a perfect example of it – each of its three fountains dramatically lit – but Luigi turned out of it into a neighbouring lane and pulled up at a relatively new block of flats.

'My mother grew tired of living in old buildings,' he explained with a smile. 'She insisted on modern comfort when my father died!'

Mirella di Palma had good sense as well as excellent taste, Clio decided a few minutes later. Her apartment on the top floor was spacious and beautiful, and its roof-top terrace provided a stunning bird's-eye view of Rome. She was a white-haired, elegantly dressed matriarch, courteous enough to her nephew's hired English helper, but reserving real warmth for the woman who walked in soon after them with Paul Costello.

Introduced by Signora di Palma, she embodied the ultimate perfection of Roman chic, Clio acknowledged to herself. Francesca Cortona wasn't strictly beautiful – nose a fraction too long, chin a mite too prominent, and her hands were ugly! But apart from being supremely elegant she had the kind of sexual allure that didn't come naturally to Englishwomen.

She greeted her fellow guests, with an accent acquired in the US, then directed a teasing smile in Costello's direction that spoke of a very close relationship between them. 'An *English* assistant, *caro*? You didn't mention that in New York.'

'I didn't know,' he answered calmly. 'The arrangement was only made in London a week ago.'

Francesca Cortona's glance now assessed Clio – her suit a good enough Chanel copy, but only a copy of course; her *poitrine* too small; in fact she was too thin altogether. A woman needed curves, not angles.

With the round of introductions completed, Clio most liked the look of Luigi's elder brother, a tired-faced doctor called Matteo, whose wife looked gaunt and unhappy. The remaining couple were Mirella di Palma's daughter and son-in-law, Lorenza and Gino Forli. Lorenza was probably younger than her brothers, her husband about their same age. They looked what they were – rich, well-groomed socialites, who saw nothing in their cousin's assistant that seemed worth noticing – no sign of wealth, none of the *bella figura* that they set such store by, and it was irritating that they couldn't even criticize her among themselves because the *Inglese* unusually spoke Italian.

It was a relief to find herself seated between Luigi and Matteo at the dinner table, safely out of conversational range of the others. She wanted, in fact, to talk as little as possible herself; it was more interesting to watch a group of people who were typical of their kind – well-heeled and well-fed, as their English counterparts would be, but noticeably better looking. The only puzzlement was to match that with what she knew of their family history – had they all abandoned Mario di Palma's austere brand of Communism? Absorbed in this train of thought, she was jerked out of it by a question from Matteo.

'You find us interesting, *signorina* . . . or should I say bizarre?'

Colour rose under clear skin, bringing her face to life. 'How rude of me – to sit here making assumptions that are probably wide of the mark. But it's true that I like watching people!'

It made him smile, and she saw in his face a fleeting likeness to his cousin. 'From something Paolo said, I gather you have only met him recently. Shall you like working with him?'

'I don't know yet,' Clio answered honestly. 'It's probably just as well though, that I'm only on trial at the moment.'

'*Povera ragazza* – as uncertain as that!' She heard sympathy in his voice and deduced that, like her great-aunts, he found his cousin overbearing.

She would have liked to ask whether he shared his brother's prejudice against the English, but with Luigi sitting on the other side of her it seemed a difficult subject to broach. Instead, she said politely how well-maintained were the records she'd been working on during the day.

'You sound surprised, *signorina*,' he said, with a gleam of amusement in his face again. 'Don't you know about our army of bureaucrats – why should they not at least keep our paper mountain in order? It seems to us that they do very little else!'

'Italy *is* changing though,' she insisted, as if it was something he'd just denied.

'Because Brussels sees to it that we obey at least *some* of the rules, and we've managed to propel certain areas of the country into the twenty-first century. We're an industrial nation now, and quite a successful one – yes, that is certainly a change.'

'Not one that you like, though?'

He gave a little shrug that again reminded her of Paul Costello. 'It would be foolish to dislike prosperity, but it comes at a certain cost, I'm afraid.'

It was a conversation she'd have liked to continue, but Francesca Cortona claimed his attention, reckoning that he'd ignored her for the *Inglese* long enough. The meal wound its leisurely way – antipasto, then pasta with tiny clams, followed by rosemary and garlic-flavoured lamb, all served by a white-gloved manservant. She took small helpings of the rich food, hoping not to be noticed; but Signora di Palma spoke to her suddenly across the table.

'You eat too little, *signorina*, but perhaps you don't care for Italian food?'

'It's delicious,' Clio assured her quickly, 'but my supper at home would be one dish and a piece of fruit; I'm afraid we've mostly lost the habit of enjoying meals at leisure.'

'How strange,' said her hostess. 'Don't tell me it's the same in America, Paolo?'

'Worse, Mirella,' he answered blandly. 'We eat too much but we eat it very fast – no finesse at all.'

'Barbarians!' But she gave him an indulgent smile, and Clio reckoned that the *signora* had decided to be forgiving where her half-American nephew was concerned; he brought the family a certain fame after all.

It was Lorenza's husband, Gino Forli, who then brought up the subject of football – Italy's 'beautiful game'. He'd just

Sally Stewart

come back from Milan, where English supporters had behaved even worse than usual at a match. 'Tactless of me to mention it, *signorina*,' he said insincerely to Clio. But Lorenza chipped in as well to underline his message.

'A pity about some of your tourists, too, I'm afraid – such scruffy-looking men and ill-dressed women; scarcely a fair English rose in sight!'

They weren't indifferent to her after all, Clio realized, but deliberately set on making her feel uncomfortable.

'I'll apologize for all of them, hooligans and dowdies alike,' she said quietly. 'But they don't represent the entire United Kingdom, you know.'

Lorenza's smile was sweetly pitying. 'I hope not – *too* depressing if they do.'

'On the other hand, there are things they *don't* do,' Clio went on, suddenly roused to defend her race, 'like shoot people out of hand without a fair trial, then string them upside-down in the street for a mob to howl round and desecrate.'

Silence fell in the room – the *Inglese* had just made the unforgivable social gaffe – raised the ghost of arch-Fascist Benito Mussolini. Costello was still trying to think of something to say when Matteo suddenly deserted his family, and smiled at her.

'Well done, *signorina*, to remind us of things *we* should certainly feel ashamed of.'

Conversation was somehow resumed, but the evening seemed never-ending. Clio was on the point of suggesting that she should find a taxi outside when Costello got to his feet. It seemed that Luigi could most conveniently see Francesca Cortona to her home; he himself would return his assistant to the Via Margutta.

As they stepped out of the overheated apartment building into fresh, cold air Clio looked up at the star-lit sky and gave a deep sigh of relief.

'*I*'d like to walk back to the *pensione*,' she said. 'There's no need to deliver me – I know the way.'

'You won't, nevertheless, walk by yourself. Even a soft slob

40

of an American can stagger that far, provided we go slowly enough of course.'

His tone of voice ruled out any argument, and she simply fell into step beside him, disinclined for any more talk. There'd been enough conversation for one evening.

'Tough going tonight?' he finally asked, out of what sounded more like curiosity than concern.

'I've known friendlier dinner parties,' she admitted, 'but your aunt has done her social duty now. The *signora* needn't feel obliged to invite me again – probably wouldn't anyhow.'

He glanced down at her and saw the glimmer of a smile. 'I rather liked her as a matter of fact – she's a cross between Aunt Hester and Lady Catherine de Bourgh – *Pride and Prejudice*, you know,' she added helpfully.

'I *am* acquainted with the lady; you aren't the only one who reads.' They walked a little way in silence, then he spoke again. 'At least you made a hit with Matteo. Isabella is more used to seeing him fall asleep over family dinners – he works in a busy hospital all the hours God sends. Now, what shall we say about Lorenza and Gino?'

'As little as possible, please.' Clio noted that it left Francesca Cortona unaccounted for, but that was probably just as well. The Italian woman was clearly on terms with Costello that didn't need to be discussed at all. Instead, Clio broached the subject uppermost in her mind.

'I can't make sense of your family. You said that your uncle was a Communist idealist, and I suspect that both Matteo and Luigi still are. But their mother lives in something approaching luxury, and Lorenza and the ghastly Gino hark back to the decadent *dolce vita* lifestyle of the 1960s. All they have in common is a shared dislike of the English, perhaps excluding Matteo.'

Costello didn't answer immediately. 'I can fill the picture in a bit,' he said at last. 'Mario di Palma certainly disapproved of the money that Mirella inherited. While he was alive she simply let it accumulate; now she enjoys using it. She still hates the Fascists (Italian *or* Germans) who killed her brother,

41

but she hates the Communists as well for ever enticing him into becoming a Partisan. Lorenza and her creep of a husband have the apartment below her, paid for of course by Mirella. Gino is smart but work-shy, and he has expensive aristocratic relatives and friends. Luigi suspects him of being a neo-Fascist, probably with good reason.'

'Matteo asked me if I found his family bizarre,' Clio replied thoughtfully. 'I should have said yes.'

'You *did* get intimate with him; he's normally far more reserved than that.' Then a wave of Costello's hand dismissed the subject of the di Palmas. 'Is the *pensione* bearable? Luigi seems to think it's full of visiting priests.'

'Not quite,' Clio corrected him primly. 'I have a charming dinner companion – a visiting Irish journalist. Perhaps you should meet him. He's investigating present-day Italy.'

'Thanks, but I'll stick with my own investigations, and you're supposed to stick with yours, not get led astray by passing journalists, however inviting.'

'Patrick O'Connor was only a suggestion; you needn't sound so tetchy about him,' she suggested.

'He's already erased from my mind,' Costello said untruthfully. They had reached the entrance to the *pensione* now, and the light above the door showed him the amusement in her face. It revealed something else too that he realized he'd been slow to appreciate. She wasn't anywhere near being conventionally beautiful, hadn't the obvious allure of Italian women like Francesca and Lorenza. But she had a spare, delicate grace that was all her own and, once noticed, it couldn't be easily forgotten. The Irishman *had* obviously noticed her, and that, for some reason, was irritating.

'By the way,' he said suddenly, 'in case you feel inclined to throw the name of Mussolini in my family's face again, perhaps I should mention something. The Piazzale Loreto where Il Duce was strung up was the place where Giorgio and his friends were shot.'

Before she could find anything to say, he went on himself. 'I'll see you in the morning, provided Mirella's clams haven't

been the death of me in the meantime.' Then he nodded goodnight and walked away.

At any other time she'd have been amused by an American's
inbred distrust of foreign food, but now she was too shocked
by what she'd been provoked into saying. No doubt Mirella
assumed that she'd been as hurtful as she could; and no doubt
it was why Costello had brought her back, instead of going
off with Francesca. He couldn't leave Luigi with the task of
giving his assistant a few more of the tragic facts of family
life.

Five

Costello had already gone out when she arrived the following morning, but Lucia greeted her with a beaming smile, knowing what their arrangement now was – if the *signore* wasn't in the *palazzo* she could sing to her heart's content.

'Signor Costello, he tell me *you* like music, *signorina*.' She considered Clio thoughtfully for a moment. 'The voice is low – you are mezzo or contralto, I think; we would go well together.'

Clio visualized them jointly warbling away – murdering the duet from *Madam Butterfly* perhaps – with Costello harpooned by the noise outside the door. Regretfully she shook her head.

'My singing days were long ago; now I'm afraid you wouldn't hear me at all.'

She knew already about Lucia's children and, from what had been proudly said of their age and talents and amazing beauty, guessed that the Italian woman was perhaps a few years older than herself.

'Lucia, your grandparents must have been newly married at the beginning of World War II. Did they live here? Were you told anything about the way things were?'

'They weren't in Rome, *signorina* . . . they're dead now, but they were *contadini*, you understand – people working the land; my parents also. *They* still live in the same village out in the Campagna. Many people left and came to the cities to find work, like me; but for my father the *paese* where he was born is where he means to stay.'

'Life is less hard there now?'

'*Certo* – fresh running water, electricity, even a *televisione*

44

they have! But I know they were close to starving at the end of the war – most of what they grew was taken to feed the German soldiers. The war was all wrong for Italy, my grandfather used to say – a terrible mistake that Mussolini led us into; but the poor man didn't know what else to do.'

'If you still visit your parents could I go with you one day?' Clio suddenly asked. 'I should like to meet them.'

Lucia's gentle face flushed with pleasure. 'Of *course*, but I shall have to warn them – the house is always shining, but Mamma will want to clean it all over again for you!'

It was agreed that Clio would be told when all the necessary arrangements had been made; then they would take a bus out to the *paese* together. Lucia went happily back to work, now making a spirited solo attempt on the Grand March from *Aida*.

Clio's own task was the laborious one of collating lists of post-war government politicians. She was frowning over some of the names when Costello walked in, and she was interested enough in what she was doing to be able to put aside the memory of the previous evening.

'Do children play the game of musical chairs in America?' she asked, and then explained because he looked blank. 'They walk round a line of chairs, but each time the music stops a chair gets taken away; the child who can't find a chair is out of the game, and the last one left in, wins. It's the game these politicians played, except that no chairs were ever taken away; they just kept changing places!'

'And probably still do.' Costello helped himself to coffee from the tray Lucia had brought in; he looked preoccupied rather than ill-tempered, so it seemed safe to risk another question.

'Successful interview this morning?'

'Not from my point of view. Getting information out of these people is like getting blood out of a stone. Without the di Palma name to use as a battering-ram I'd be getting nowhere fast; they don't *want* the truth out in the open.' He frowned at Clio but made an admission she didn't expect. 'You *could* say "I told you so"; I should have listened more carefully in London.'

She said something else instead. 'Whoever you found so obstructive this morning has almost certainly been taught what happened at the end of the war – men who'd been Partisans were victimized because they were Communists as well. Over the years since then they've been blamed for terrorist bombings they probably knew nothing about; they're justifiably mistrustful now of even being identified. But it's also true that *their* Liberation committees settled a lot of old scores very bloodily when they had the chance. So of course people try to hide the truth here – it's always incredibly painful.' She hesitated a moment, then added what else needed to be said. 'Did . . . did your aunt think I *meant* to hurt her last night? Could she possibly have thought I knew?'

'God knows *what* they think,' he said violently, 'or even if they think at all. They feel instead, react, live on their emotions most of the time.'

'Your father was one of them,' she pointed in an unsteady voice. 'You should be able to understand them better than I do.'

'I'm an American, not a bloody mixed-up hybrid who can't decide where he belongs. Is that *clear*?'

'Perfectly, and shouting doesn't make it any clearer.' Clio stood up, distressed by their being so sharply at odds again. 'There are messages and queries on your desk. I'm going back to the town hall for more records; I'll be working there for the rest of the day.'

She half-expected him to give a different instruction, just to remind her which of them was boss; but the telephone rang in his room and he was obliged to go and answer it. With the door left open, his end of the conversation was audible as she walked along the hall.

The caller seemed to merit a change of voice – he sounded suddenly amused now by something that had been said – and from his reply it was clearly Francesca Cortona he was talking to. The morning's frustrations were being smoothed away by a woman who'd probably learned in her cradle how to manage men. Clio resisted the strong inclination to slam the door as she went out, and allowed herself a brief call at Miss Babington's on the way to the town hall; damn espresso coffee for once – a calming pot of properly made English tea was required before she tackled any more municipal archives, or any more Italian emotions.

That evening Patrick O'Connor wasn't waiting for her in the *pensione* dining room – just when his company would have been welcome. She decided it was probably her own fault for having made her withdrawal so obvious the night before last, but that only made her feel worse, not better.

She was doggedly swallowing the last of her supper, and counting up the hours to bed-time, when a small figure dressed in clerical black stopped beside her chair. It was the silver-haired old priest who habitually sat in the same corner table – a resident, Clio had guessed, because the staff took such affectionate care of him.

'*Permesso, signorina?*' He waited politely, with his head cocked like an expectant robin's, then bowed when she smiled at him. 'I am still known as Monsignor Fiocca, though long retired from active service in the Church.'

Settled in a chair facing her across the table, he glanced round at the other diners with a look of innocent glee. 'There are few advantages in growing old, but at least I may now dare to approach a young lady and have her smile at me because I'm so ancient and harmless!'

'Ancient' was the word, she thought, looking at the lined map of his face, but age hadn't diminished him – he still looked very intelligent, as well as humorous and kind.

She introduced herself as a visitor from London – a working visitor, not a tourist.

He nodded as if it was what he expected. 'I also know about you that you speak beautiful Italian, and that this evening you're feeling a little troubled, *signorina*. Explain to me, please, the work you are doing.'

He spoke with gentle firmness, and she recognized it as a habit acquired over years of asking for his flock's confessions.

'The research itself isn't a problem,' she said, having briefly outlined what she was there for, 'I'm trained to do that. But . . . ' She broke off suddenly and started again. 'Monsignor, do you believe there's such a thing as absolute truth?'

He didn't answer at once, and she went on herself, anxious to make him understand. 'I think you must have lived through the war years – you know what happened here. Partisans killed Germans whenever they could, *knowing* that innocent civilians would be killed in return. So even though they sometimes suffered cruelly themselves, were they heroes, or murderers of their own people? Twenty years on from then there were terrible bombings, carried out by men who thought they had no other means of protest against injustice and corruption. Were *they* right, or wickedly wrong? How are we ever to decide?'

The old priest answered with another question. 'Are you afraid that Mr Costello will represent only his side as being right . . . in correcting what he sees as lies will merely create different lies?'

She nodded, knowing that it was her problem in a nutshell. Costello wanted *his* truth, or rather the truth as his family saw it.

'Then nothing will be gained by writing his book,' the monsignor said gently. 'History must be written by someone whose only ambition is to reach the truth. Is Mr Costello not intelligent enough, or humble enough, to realize that?'

'He's intelligent enough for anything; his humility is more open to question! He sees his book as a crusade *against* deception.'

'Then he is misguided, and you must try to make him understand that.'

Clio smiled ruefully at the idea; surely a wandering lamb had a better chance of persuading a marauding lion that it wasn't hungry than she had of influencing him one way or another. But the priest had one more thing to stay.

'In an ideal world we *could* be sure about absolute good

and evil, but as things are we must settle for much less; admit that life seems to require adjustments and compromises. Because although we sometimes manage to behave like disciples of Christ, we are much more often sinful!'

His face suddenly creased in a charming smile. 'Enough discussion for tonight, my child; you look tired, so I shall say goodnight. Put your anxieties aside now and sleep peacefully.'

She watched him walk out of the room – carefully, as the very old walk – and felt glad that Patrick O'Connor hadn't been there after all. He was a very pleasant man, but he wasn't wise and holy. Her conversation with Monsignor Fiocca hadn't solved her problem, but at least she now saw clearly what the problem was: the longer she and Paul Costello worked together, the more their views would diverge. *She* hoped for truth; he was bent on vengeance. Better, therefore, to suggest that she went home now. Sooner or later, after some more fierce disagreement than they'd already had, he'd fire her anyway. With that settled in her mind, she might even do what the kind old priest had suggested – sleep peacefully.

Sunday, a non-working day, intervened before she needed to face Costello again, but he was already in her office as if waiting for her when she went in the following morning. She expected him to point out that she was three minutes late, but he had a different complaint to make.

'It must be even colder outside than it is in here – your nose is red.'

'Thank you for mentioning it. The weather *is* freezing but fine – you won't need your galoshes if you're going out.'

An unexpected smile touched his mouth for a moment, and she found herself wondering why it looked so attractive – the contrast, perhaps, of very white teeth against the crisp silver-grey of his beard.

'You're reminding me again that I'm an effete American, made flabby by soft living and terrified of eating anything that hasn't come sealed and vacuum-packed!'

She didn't answer, being too busy thinking how cussedly

perverse life was. He was required to shout some unreason-
able command at her, to be overbearing, objectionable –
anything but the humorous, human man he'd suddenly become.

'How did you get through a wet Roman Sunday at the
pensione?'

The question was even more unexpected and disconcerting,
and she stared at him in astonishment when he went on.

'I should have done something about that; I'm sorry.'

He saw from the expression on her face that confusion was
now complete. Probably without meaning to, she was making
it clear that, while his normal behaviour could be taken in her
stride, she had no idea what to make of him now. It might
have helped to admit that he'd intended ringing the *pensione*
to see if she sounded lonely, but good intention hadn't survived
an invitation from Francesca to spend the day with some of
her sophisticated friends. They'd got back very late, but still
he'd felt an unusual twinge of guilt about Clio Lambert.

'I went to church,' she finally said, by way of answering
his question, '– Santa Maria in Aracoeli; I wasn't allowed to
take Communion of course, but at least I could admire the
Bambino Santo. Then I spent the afternoon at the Keats
Museum. Altogether a wet Roman Sunday passed very pleasantly.'

'Rounded off, of course, by dinner with your Irish friend.'

'No, he's been called back to Ireland – his father is very ill
in Dublin.' Clio hesitated for a moment, then went on. 'I've
made another friend at the *pensione* – an elderly monsignor
living there in retirement. I should like you to meet *him*.
Digging the past out of official records is one way of recon-
structing history, but talking to people who have it within their
own living memory is important, too.'

Paul Costello looked unconvinced. 'Thank you for the idea,
but I can guess what a priest's interest in talking to a lapsed
Catholic like me would be – be entirely professional, I expect.'

'Father Fiocca talks to someone worse – a protestant heretic
who is still officially excommunicated by his Church!' She
saw no interest in Costello's face still, and understood that she

was now about to provoke the very row she'd been hoping for.

'Why refuse actual experience that's likely to be more authentic than most of the records we're trawling through? Is it because it's easier to select what you want from them, and ignore anything that doesn't fit your theories?'

No hint of a smile now; his frown was back in place. 'Exit harmony – I thought it wouldn't last long! You have a bloody nerve, *signorina* – I'm not "selecting" anything as far as I know – simply unearthing hard *facts* with even more patience than I thought I had. I've assumed that you've been doing the same; so in what way are my theories being fitted up?' She didn't answer immediately, and her pale face made him speak more quietly. 'All right – so I've got to shouting again, but it's the effect you have on me. Now *explain* what you said.'

She remembered being told by the priest to try to make him understand, and struggled with an hysterical need to laugh. But that would make matters worse because, unexpectedly, she sensed hurt as well as anger in him.

'In London you spoke of nailing lies,' she began, rather unsteadily. 'The official version of events had to be corrected for posterity. It sounded all right then.'

'So what's wrong with it now.'

'Nothing, if the version you want to put in its place is entirely accurate. Will your version say that Italy was largely liberated by the blood and sacrifice of many thousands of mostly Communist Partisans, whose only ambition was to rid the country of the Germans?'

'It will say *something* like that,' Costello agreed grimly. 'It's what the facts say.'

'*Your* facts; what about the others that claim many so-called Partisans leapt on board only when liberation was no longer in doubt; that they drew German punishment on whole villages and then disappeared themselves; that their real allegiance was to Moscow, not to Italy at all. Shouldn't your book at least mention those possibilities too?'

She wasn't sure what to expect, a roar of anger, even some

51

physical rough-handling – he was easily capable of that. But after a silence that hung heavily in the room he spoke almost mildly.

'You're on trial, remember, I could still fire you.'

Clio took a deep breath. 'I was going to save you the trouble anyway by resigning. I decided last night that it's what I ought to do.'

She shot a glance at him that told her nothing of what was in his mind – his face was expressionless and, instead of looking at her, he now seemed engrossed in staring out at the traffic hurtling round the piazza.

'You don't like crass Americans – is that it?' he asked at last. 'We sometimes forget to say please and thank you, we raise our voices, and reckon nowadays that it's *we* who own the earth.'

'It's *none* of those things,' she insisted unevenly. 'Last night the old priest said that history should be written by someone whose *only* ambition is to reach the truth. You understandably want the story of Giorgio di Palma and his friends, and all that came after it, to be told in your own way; but I agree with Monsignor Fiocca. That's why I should go home.' Costello had turned to look at her now, and she tried to smile at him. 'Our first impressions *were* right, I think!'

He walked towards her and before she could guess his intention and step back out of reach, clamped his hands on her shoulders; she could feel their warmth through the wool of her sweater. He was too close, too big, too male altogether . . . too magnetic, dear Aunt Hetty would say.

'I should like you to stay,' he said quietly. 'I can't promise that you'll approve of the book I finally write. But it shall be as truthful as I can make it. Will that do – for you *and* the old priest you're obviously going to plague me with from now on?'

She freed herself so that she could breathe more easily. 'Will it do for the di Palmas, and all the other families who are concerned? You're writing it for them, not for me or a man you don't know.'

'I can't answer that; we shall have to wait and see.'

She smiled suddenly, remembering something. 'That was the phrase Luigi used when we were driving back from the airport; he'd "wait and see" he said, whether you and I managed to survive together – I'm afraid he seemed doubtful!'

'We could try to prove him wrong,' Costello said, 'even if you do offer to resign once a day or *I* keep threatening to fire you. Now shall we get on with some work?'

She nodded, and he walked out of the room. Her shoulders still remembered the feel of his hands – but not for much longer, she told herself. Soon the day might become entirely normal.

Six

Their officially declared truce hadn't had time to fall apart before Costello said he was going north for a few days. Clio expected it – traditionally left-wing workers in the large factories in Turin and Milan had been the mainstay of the Garibaldi Brigades from the beginning; he had a lot of checking-up to do there.

But the morning he was due to leave there *was* a surprise. Francesca Cortona was at the *palazzo*, with her luggage in a heap by the door. She was obviously making the journey as well. While Costello made last-minute telephone calls she wandered into Clio's room, supremely elegant as usual, and insolently at ease. Her eyes assessed last winter's roll-neck sweater and tweed skirt, and measured them against her own faultless rig.

'Trouser-suits are not chic in London?' she enquired innocently. 'Such a pity, *signorina* – they're so "now", as we say in the fashion world here.'

'I'm sure they are, but I expect I'm more "then" than "now",' Clio suggested. Something more in the way of conversation seemed to be required, so she asked the obvious question. 'Are you going to help with Costello's interviews?'

Could the suggestion be malicious? Francesca wondered. Was she supposed to look like a woman who chatted to Communist agitators? Probably not; the *Inglese* wouldn't know how to use that sort of weapon.

'I'm a fashion journalist,' she replied, 'not an interrogator of individuals who are better left alone. Forgive me if it does you out of a job, but I want Paolo to forget this family matter.'

She inspected polished fingernails for a moment and then smiled at Clio. 'Fortunately there are shows I must attend in Milan. Convenient, *non è vero*? I shall be able to amuse him after working hours!'

'Nice for you both,' Clio agreed politely, wishing with all her heart that he'd come and take his helpmate away. They belonged to the same world, where wealth and glamour ruled. Francesca was right to believe that it was ill-judged for him to have strayed out of it; he didn't fit among the men and women he was now going to try to get on terms with.

'You'll be glad to finish your work and go home,' Francesca said suddenly. 'I'm afraid we Romans don't make strangers welcome – unkind of us, no doubt, but there it is.'

She sounded so pleased about it that Clio saw no reason not to agree with her. 'I'm told the explanation is that you've had too many strangers to contend with – all of them barbarians! We've been luckier; no invaders to speak of for a thousand years!'

It was the moment Costello chose to walk into the room; he couldn't help thinking that since even Clio seemed pleased to see him, it was a pity he'd missed their conversation.

'*Cara*, why are you wasting my assistant's expensive time?' he said to Francesca. 'We ought to be on the road by now.' Then it was Clio's turn. 'I hope I've left you enough to get on with?'

'More than enough, especially as I'm taking a day out to share Lucia's visit to her parents.' She saw objection in his face and went firmly on. 'We agreed, I thought, that authentic memories would be valuable.'

He managed to swallow what he'd been going to say. '*Something* of the sort we agreed, but I shall be the judge of what's authentic. Now, try to stay out of trouble till I get back.'

A moment later they were gone, and she could draw a sigh of relief and settle down to work. But the *palazzo* seemed suddenly very empty, and it was necessary to insist to herself that she wouldn't rather have been beside Costello in the car.

There was no question of being interested in the man himself, of course; it was only that sharing in his work in Milan *did* appeal to her.

The girl who *was* seated in the car was remembering what he'd just said. '*Amore*, there was no need to warn your assistant – I doubt if the *povera ragazza* could get into trouble if she tried.'

Costello turned towards her and she saw him smile. 'Sweetheart, what a comfort you are – I'm glad she's got you fooled too!'

It wasn't the reply Francesca expected and after a moment she tried again. 'She's impertinent – calls you Costello. I think you should get rid of her.'

'One of us will almost certainly sack the other before we're through,' he agreed. 'Now, let me drive in peace, please – we've got a long journey ahead of us.'

Content now, she merely rested her hand on his knee to remind him that she was there.

Two days later, tempted by winter sunshine that was rare in Rome, Clio took her lunchtime sandwich into the ruins of the Forum. She was sharing it among several hungry cats when a quiet voice interrupted the feast.

'A mistake, if I may say so, *signorina* – you'll soon have dozens of them here!'

She looked up to find Matteo di Palma smiling at her. The bright sunlight fell on his face and thinning hair too clearly. He couldn't yet be middle-aged, but she saw a man who seemed to have set youth and hope aside as things that weren't recoverable.

'Is this the best lunch-break you can manage?' he wanted to know, settling himself beside her on a convenient chunk of marble column. 'It's cold, and not exactly comfortable.'

'I know, but I like this place empty of visitors – at least, in one way I do,' she corrected herself. 'The truth is, of course, that it *ought* to be crammed with people and noise. Now it's simply a haunted ghost of itself.'

Matteo looked around the ruins with a rueful smile. 'I used to come here as a schoolboy, trying to imagine what it would have been like – golden roofs shining in the sun, painted statues, toga-ed Romans, and sightseers from every province of the Empire come to stare at the wonder of it all. Now, like the rest of my fellow citizens, I simply walk through it because it's a convenient short-cut – sad, is it not?' He didn't wait for her to reply, but went on himself. 'My cousin is in Milan, Luigi says, and you are here alone. We should do something about that.'

'There's no need,' Clio insisted. 'I've work to do, and in any case I'm not lonely.'

'Because you are used to being on your own?'

'Partly that, but also because I don't feel lonely here.' She hesitated, not inclined to tell Antonia's story, even though it would have been easier to share it with him than with anyone else she knew there. 'I'm afraid we're not exactly personae gratae any more, but like a lot of English people, I feel at home in Italy . . . feel comfortable here.'

Matteo's face was rueful. 'You're thinking of my mother's dinner party. Don't let Lorenza and Gino upset you. My guess is that you know the history of this country; your eyes are clear enough to see all the things that are wrong with it – the corruption that we now take for granted among the people in power, the incompetence of an army of petty officials, the huge gap still between north and south, rich and poor.'

She could hear, now, the voice of Mario di Palma talking through his son – an idealist tortured by wrongs he could do nothing about.

'I know all those things exist here,' she agreed quietly, 'but they exist everywhere else as well. They can't be ignored, but nor can all the things that are wonderfully *right* with Italy: the warmth and kindness of its ordinary people; the imagina-tiveness that makes a work of art out of everything, even a display on a fish stall or the flowers you buy from a girl in a florist's shop; and of course the sheer visual beauty that stops you in your tracks everywhere you look.'

Matteo smiled at her. 'I think you *do* belong here, more than my cousin does. Paulo is a true American – physically big and also big in spirit, but he can't help feeling impatient with tired old European countries that can't forget their past and live in today's world!'

Clio shook her head. 'The past *isn't* dead for him either – it's why he's here.' She stuffed the empty lunch bag in her pocket and brushed crumbs from her skirt. 'I must get back to work, but I hope you've got a day off.'

'Officially, yes; but there are one or two small patients I want to see. They slip back a little if I take my eye off them. May I walk you in the direction of Paolo's apartment first?'

'Thank you, but my route is just up there,' she pointed towards the Campidoglio. 'I'm going back to the town hall.'

She held out her cold hand and had it grasped in both his warm ones – for a little longer than it should have been. But before she could feel uncomfortable about that, he released her and walked away, a slightly bowed, dejected figure. She wanted to call out something that would make him turn and smile, but he chose a path she didn't expect, and in a moment was out of sight.

The outing with Lucia took place the following day. It entailed a bus-journey south-eastwards across the Campagna to the Alban Hills – enjoyable in itself as soon as the city suburbs were left behind – while Lucia explained with pride that the Pope's summer residence at Castel Gandolfo wasn't far from her parents' farm; in fact she made the Holy Father sound like a near and valued neighbour.

Her family home was just as Clio had visualized it – a simple stone farmhouse whose outside staircase had once led to the living rooms up above; now, the beasts were housed in a separate barn instead of below them on the ground floor.

Lucia's father, Pietro Nenni, was a small, wiry man, still nut-brown even in winter. He smiled shyly at the English visitor, but left conversation to his wife. Maria was simply an older version of her daughter – plump, laughing, and kind.

Everything had to be seen, house, outbuildings, animals and orchard, before they could sit down to Maria's idea of a simple lunch – pasta, *scaloppine al marsala*, gorganzola cheese and fruit. Clio was conscious of the time ticking away, but nothing could be allowed to interrupt the flow of hospitality – '*hai bisogna di mangiare*', Maria insisted whenever her guest's appetite looked like faltering. But at last a chance mention of Pietro's father gave Clio her opportunity. Did they know about his life as a young man – had he ever described the time when the Allied armies and the *Resistenza* were slowly driving the retreating Germans northwards?

There was a little pause before Pietro answered. ' My father *wrote* about those things, *signorina*,' he said with a touching note of pride. 'You're surprised, I expect. Men like him had little schooling; some of the older ones couldn't read or write. My father was different – he wanted to learn, and we had a good priest who taught him.'

Clio scarcely dared ask her next question. 'You . . . still have what your father wrote down?' How unlikely that was. They'd have had to light a fire with it in those desperate days, lost it in the destruction going on all around. But she saw Pietro nod his head.

'It's in a notebook upstairs. You could take it away to read – Lucia will bring it back.'

Clio smiled at him gratefully. 'I shall take the greatest care of it, Signor Nenni.' But there was still one more question to ask. 'Perhaps Lucia has told you about the American writer we both work for. He is collecting material for a book about those times. Your father's diary would be an enormous help to him.'

Pietro looked anxious, and she thought she could guess what he was going to say. 'There are names mentioned, you understand – people whose families are still here.'

'If I promise that nothing will be used without your permission, will you at least allow Signor Costello to read the diary?'

He stared at her for a moment, and finally gave another little nod; if the *Inglese* promised, he would trust her. The notebook, originally intended for school exercises, was brought down and carefully wrapped. Then, thanks and good-byes said, it was time to set out to catch the bus back to Rome. Installed in their seats, Clio smiled gratefully at the woman beside her.

'It's been a lovely day, Lucia, thank you for taking me.'

She was excited at the prospect of reading the diary, but her thoughts lingered on the couple they'd just left – not yet old, but probably aged beyond their years by a life-time of hard physical labour. There were still plenty of country men and women like them caring for the land, but thousands more – especially the young ones – had given up and turned themselves in a single generation into urban people.

'What will happen to the farm?' she asked suddenly. '*You* live in Rome and your husband isn't a farmer.'

'Pappi will stay until he dies,' Lucia's normally cheerful face grew sad as she thought about it. 'My brother emigrated to Australia – said there was no life worth having in Italy; imagine that, *signorina*; what foolishness! But it means that the farm will be sold. Some rich man will buy the land and use it to grow vines that make him richer still. He won't care that Nennis took care of it for two hundred years, and made it beautiful.'

'Perhaps *your* sons . . .?' Clio suggested hopefully, but Lucia shook her head.

'They think only of computers, and an easier life than tending land and livestock. Always here in Italy it was the *famiglia* that mattered, but not any more. I make them visit their grand-parents, but they don't understand each other.' Then she shrugged and smiled. '*Ma, nondimeno, sono buoni ragazzi.*' Yes, they were good boys.

Clio parted company with her at the bus station and walked

slowly back to the *pensione* with her head full of the day's events. Most important of all was the precious notebook in her bag; memories didn't come more authentic than the ones Pietro had entrusted to her. After Maria's feast she would have been happy to miss supper altogether and start working on them, but Monsignor Fiocca now looked for her in the *pensione* dining room and would be anxious if she didn't appear. Then her thoughts strayed northwards to Milan. The working day would be over there by now – time, no doubt, for Francesca to entice Costello's mind from the 'communist agitators' he'd gone to meet. If he'd been at the *palazzo*, she'd have suggested going there to work the following morning, even though it was a Saturday. As things were, she decided to tackle the notebook in her room at the *pensione*, once the usual weekly telephone call to Vicars' Close had been made. This morning it was Hetty who answered, a treat she rarely got, because Hester insisted that she wasted time and money on telling Clio things that weren't important.

'You *sound* well, darling,' she suggested now, knowing that it wasn't – as her sister would suggest – a stupid thing to say. Appearances were important too, of course; but much could be learned from voices, and in any case how could she look at Clio when the dear child was miles and miles away.

'*I*'m fine, Aunt Hetty, but I want to know about you.'

All was well in Vicars' Close, it seemed, except that Hester was cross with herself for catching a cold that would prevent her attending the following morning's service in the Cathedral. But there was one item of news to report – *good* news, Hetty suggested; at least she supposed it was, even though they all knew Hester's opinion of her nephew.

'You mean it's to do with my father, Aunt Hetty?' Clio patiently enquired, knowing that the news itself might now get lost in a familiar discussion of Hester's views.

'Yes, dearest – didn't I say? He's coming to London quite soon, on his way to Italy! Now, isn't that extraordinary – that you should *both* be there?'

Clio agreed but decided not to point out that Italy was a

big place and Fate could still easily refuse to bring father and daughter together. Instead, she promised to ring again the following Saturday, and put down the telephone, wondering about her father's visit. If it should happen that they *did* meet – and for once he might even make an effort – she'd have to tell him that she now knew that Mark Lambert hadn't been his father or her grandfather. But she put the problem aside, and took out of its wrapping the notebook Pietro Nenni had given her.

She could see soon enough that deciphering it wouldn't be easy – cheap paper, faded ink and crabbed handwriting presented their own difficulties, but she was soon discovering another one as well. Pietro's father had not only known dialect words she wasn't familiar with, but – perhaps as a safeguard against other people trying to read what he'd written – he'd also invented his own kind of code; once certain words and phrases had been used, they were repeated only by their first letters. Making sense of it was going to be a piece of fascinating detection, but first she must go out in search of a dictionary that would include the dialect words she didn't know.

When she came back an hour later with the dictionary she needed, and a detailed map of the area the notebook covered, a parked car outside the *pensione* looked vaguely familiar. A moment later she walked upstairs to find Luigi di Palma talking to Signora Rollo.

'*Ecco la signorina*,' she said with a broad smile, glad to have insisted that he should wait, because she knew her guest was certain to be back within *pochi, pochi minuti.*

'I was hoping I might take you out to lunch,' he said in his formal way. 'I telephoned, and they seemed to think you wouldn't be gone long.'

She was tempted to refuse, thinking that Matteo had asked him to look after her, but while she hesitated, Signora Rollo accepted on her behalf, unable to believe that an invitation from a personable male wouldn't be welcome to any right-minded young woman. The *padrona*'s pointed glance then fell on her off-duty jeans and anorak; something better was obviously needed.

'I *was* going to work,' she admitted with a smile, 'but, thank you – lunch out sounds more fun! I need five minutes to put these things in my room and make myself more presentable.'

Seven

When she reappeared, in a navy pleated skirt and scarlet blazer, it occurred to Luigi that he liked the way she dressed – not, as his sister and Francesca did, to be noticed and admired, but with a simple good taste that he found pleasing.

'I Tre Scalini, in Piazza Navona, I thought,' he suggested when they were settled in his car, 'or is it a restaurant you know too well already?'

'I've heard of it,' Clio said, 'but not been there; in any case I'm always happy to be able to look at Bernini's fountains!'

'We need a table in the window, then; it should be possible at this time of year.' He put the car in gear, and she didn't bother him with any more conversation; even in the city's comparative winter emptiness a motorist in Rome needed all the powers of concentration he could get. But when they were installed at their table in the restaurant, she said what was on her mind.

'It's kind of you to entertain me like this, but I did tell Matteo that I wasn't in need of being looked after!'

Luigi's face, never allowed to give much away, now looked completely blank. 'Matteo? It was because my cousin was going to be in Milan that I thought you might be lonely.' A slight frown replaced the blankness. 'Do I gather that you've seen Matteo recently?'

'We bumped into each other in the Forum one lunchtime,' Clio explained, wondering why Luigi's question should make her feel defensive. 'I was feeding the cats, *he* was using the Sacred Way as a short-cut!' Perhaps it wasn't the question, though, but the memory of Matteo holding her hand as if he didn't want to let it go that worried her a little. There was another troubling memory, too – Isabella di Palma's unhappy face the night of her mother-in-law's dinner party.

'Your brother works too hard and . . .' She hesitated over how to go on, and Luigi finished it for her.

'. . . and perhaps neglects his wife, you think, while he mends other people's children?'

Clio nodded, aware that she was straying into places where she had no right to be.

'Then I should tell you the truth,' Luigi decided reluctantly. 'Isabella was a happy, contented woman except for one thing – she desperately wanted a child. Miscarriage followed miscarriage until Matteo said that for the sake of her health they could try no more. She blames him for that, but she needs him more than ever, and she's terrified that some other woman might now take him from her.'

Clio answered with the directness Costello might have told his cousin to expect. 'Isabella needn't fear *me*, you know. I'm not equipped to lure married men from their wives, nor do I have the smallest inclination to try to. Matteo and I met by chance, we talked for a few minutes – about the state of Italy! – and went our separate ways.'

'My brother's *bête noire*, the state of Italy,' Luigi admitted wryly. He would have liked to apologize for a suspicion he hadn't put into words, but he wasn't in the habit of expressing his feelings and Clio Lambert, for all her gentleness, made things more difficult by being different from the women he was used to.

'Have you and my cousin decided that you *can* tolerate each other?' he asked instead.

She smiled at the reminder of their airport conversation. 'We manage, with frequent disagreements – I won't put it higher than that! Is this visit *your* first meeting with him?'

'No, I've been several times to stay with the Costello family in New York. My uncle Enrico – Paolo's father – regularly tries to persuade me to move there; apparently lawyers get very rich in America! But Matteo has never wanted to be anything but a doctor, so it was left to me to carry on my father's firm here.'

Clio debated whether or not to risk a comment he might resent, but decided that since it was no more sensitive than the rest of their conversation had been, she might as well. 'You have a slightly unexpected brother-in-law in Gino Forli.'

No offence was taken it seemed; in fact he smiled at the word she'd used. 'Unexpected – yes! My mother didn't – still doesn't – entirely share the ideology she married into; she's intelligent enough to see that my father's vision of society is probably unattainable this side of Heaven. But she understood that at least it was something to strive for. Lorenza merely thinks it's insane to share what we have with people who have less.'

'Is that Gino's view too?'

'It's the view he gave her. She fell in love with his looks, and his aristocratic connections. The di Palmas are definitely middle-class; Lorenza liked the idea of moving into a higher social bracket.'

The conversation was interrupted by the arrival of food, and while they ate they talked of other things. When music was mentioned, Clio admitted to an education at a Cathedral choir-school, and then made him laugh with a description of Lucia's vocal talent and Costello's reaction to it.

'If I'm honest I have to admit that all she does is make a cheerful noise,' Clio finished up, 'but the important point is that she loves everything she tries to sing. If I could see any way of arranging it, I'd take her to Milan before I go home, to give her an evening at La Scala that she'd never forget.'

'We can't quite match *that* quality here, nor that of the San Carlo in Naples,' Luigi had to confess, 'but there *is* opera in Rome. May I take you one evening – I have to say that I'd rather take you than Lucia!'

She thanked him, and reckoned that for a reserved, anglo-phobe Roman lawyer, he was unbending rather well. Luigi di Palma might not have his brother's shy charm or Costello's force of personality, but he *was* intelligent, perceptive, and kind enough to bother with the tiresome female his cousin kept wishing on him.

The leisurely midday meal was almost over when he surprised her with a sudden question. 'What would you like to see now – Michelangelo's Sistine Chapel ceiling, the Villa Borghese – newly and very well renovated! – the Catacombs even? The choice is yours, *signorina*.'

No half-measures about Luigi di Palma, she reflected; asked to entertain her, he was performing the chore handsomely. She didn't have to think long about her answer.

'If you can really spare the time, I'd like to go to the Protestant Cemetery.'

'Do I make a guess at the grave of John Keats?' he suggested, smiling at her.

'Hackneyed, I know; practically a rite of passage for most English visitors. But I've never managed to get there. It's a long trudge on foot, and Rome buses are not for faint-hearted foreigners. We haven't quite got the nerve to fight our way to the front the moment we get on, in order to get off in time!'

Luigi agreed that Roman elbows, honed to the right degree of sharpness, were needed; then he asked for the bill to be brought and they were soon outside again. By car the journey didn't take long, out through the Aurelian Walls by the Porta San Paolo, but on the way Luigi pointed to the strange stone pyramid they were passing, which he explained housed the tomb of a long-dead magistrate called Caius Cestius.

'That sums up this extraordinary city,' she commented. 'Not just centuries rub shoulders here, but millennia! Everywhere you walk there's a layer of history beneath your feet, and then another and another layer below that!'

'Republic, Empire, Dark-Age tyranny, Papal States, Kingdom – more or less unified – and Republic again; you can't say we haven't given everything a try!' Then his smile faded. 'Matteo would tell you that we're an ungovernable people. Every system falls apart sooner or later, and we simply raid what one system leaves behind to build the next one.'

'Put like that it sounds quite sensible,' she said thought-fully, and made him laugh again.

The cemetery when they reached it was an oasis of peace and quiet in a noise-ridden city. Even birds might live here unscathed, she thought; its seclusion would deter the most determined Italian hunter. They quickly found the grave they were looking for, and Clio stood staring at it, thinking about the doomed young man who'd lived briefly in the house by the Spanish Steps.

'His name *wasn't* "writ in water" after all,' she said, pointing to the sad epitaph he'd chosen for himself. 'But dying at the age of twenty-six, with so much still to do, how could he have known that?'

She wandered on at last, too deep in thought to notice that they were now in a section of more recent burials. But Luigi had fallen behind to look at something, and she turned round, waiting for him to catch up. Because of that she saw what she would otherwise have missed. It made no sense . . . couldn't be anything to do with her . . . but oh, dear God, it *was*. The stone slab was as simple as the message engraved on it:

Antonia Lambert
1923–1951
R.I.P

The words swam in front of her, and she ducked her head to ward off faintness. Behind her, a long way off it seemed, she heard Luigi call out.

'Clio, is something wrong? Are you not well?' He came to stand beside her and saw her white face and trembling lips. 'What is it . . . tell me, please.'

She pointed to the gravestone and he read the name. 'Not someone you knew,' he said gently. 'You're much too young.'

Clio shook her head and finally managed to say something. 'No, I never knew her, but she *was* my grandmother.'

Luigi led her along the path to a wooden seat, and took

hold of her hand. 'The stone is the end of her story; how did it begin?'

'She came here towards the end of the war, as part of our liberating forces, then returned to England, married, and had a child – my father in other words.' That was the easy part to tell, and Clio managed it calmly. But it became harder after that, because she couldn't tell it all, even now. 'She married a very nice man, but she couldn't survive in his quiet, humdrum life – probably never would have done, but the excitement of the war years made it all worse. She abandoned home and family, and was never heard from again. It seemed that she'd gone to America – to one of the US Army friends she'd made. The note she left behind said that there was no chance of her ever coming back.'

'But she returned *here* instead,' Luigi said slowly. 'She might have gone to America, but she didn't stay there either.'

'I doubt if she did anything else at all but just come back to Rome.' Clio was quiet for a moment, remembering the lonely grave she'd been looking at. Antonia's name had been enough to take in then, but there'd been something else, scarcely noticed at the time. She got up and walked back to make sure; no, she hadn't dreamt it – there *was* a small posy of narcissi at the foot of the stone. The flowers were fresh, and must have been put there recently, surely by someone who had known Antonia.

She walked back to Luigi, and stood looking at him. 'How do I find out about such things? We have a registry of births, marriages and deaths at home. Is it the same here?'

Luigi nodded. 'Of course, but your grandmother died fifty years ago, at a time when things were still chaotic here after the war; I can't promise you that the records were being properly kept.'

'Someone knew her . . . her death had to be reported, and funeral arrangements made. Whoever did that surely had to identify themselves?' Clio turned to him with her eyes full of tears. 'I must find out if I can.'

'Of course,' he agreed gently. 'But will you let me see what *I* can do? A lawyer has a better chance, I think.'

She could see the sense of that and didn't argue. 'I'll have to let her brother and sisters know that her grave is here. *Not knowing what happened has always deeply troubled them.*' She tried to smile at the man who was watching her with such kind concern in his face. 'I'm being a terrible nuisance, I'm afraid, and you're being so very nice about it.'

'My niceness now consists of taking you back to the *pensione*! You are beginning to shiver with cold.'

She nodded and walked with him back to the car. It seemed a long time ago that they'd arrived to search for nothing more disturbing than the grave of John Keats. Outside the *pensione* again, he sat looking at her for a moment, as if undecided about leaving her, but she managed a proper smile this time. 'I shall ask Signora Rollo for our present English help in times of trouble – a soothing cup of tea! Thank you again for your kindness.'

He waved her thanks aside, promised to set enquiries on foot as soon as he could, and drove away once she was safely inside the building. They'd spoken of the beginning and the end of Antonia Lambert's story, but he felt sure that in between there'd been a lot that hadn't been mentioned, and he was interested enough in Clio herself now to want to find out what it was.

Her letter to Vicars' Close arrived a week later. The Woodwards were still at the breakfast table when the mail was delivered, but Edward always waited until afterwards to deal with it. He enjoyed opening the occasional letters that still came, and a definite ritual had to be observed because that was part of the pleasure – sitting at his desk overlooking the garden, not tearing the envelopes but slitting them neatly with his silver letter-opener. He rather pitied the people whose correspondents only used the new-fangled methods of communication; life had lost much of its previous finesse, he was inclined to think.

He left until last, because it looked the most interesting, an envelope with a foreign stamp – Italian – and surely the handwriting was Clio's. Odd that she should be writing; her weekly telephone calls kept them in touch. He stopped to consider *that* for a moment. It was one of the things about old age that he enjoyed – there was time, now, to give a little thought to any matter. Then, with the letter finally spread out in front of him, he read what Clio had written.

He read it again, more slowly; but not because its news seemed unbelievable. They'd agreed between them long ago that Antonia had settled for what one of the American generals she'd met could offer her. It was a legend meant to comfort them, but he'd never accepted it in his heart of hearts – wealth, comfort, security weren't the things that had appealed to her. He would have staked his life that she'd gone back to Italy, looking for her lost love, and he'd grown certain over the years that she was dead. It had to be the reason they'd never heard from her.

He put the letter down, and picked up Antonia's framed photograph. But instead of her lovely, smiling face he saw the gravestone Clio had described – so lonely it must look; the poor darling girl should have been with them where she belonged. At last, letter in hand, he went in search of his sisters. He knew where they'd be – at this time of the morning Hester would be studying the financial columns and castigating the Chancellor for the state of the economy; Hetty would be deep in gardening catalogues. He often teased her about imagining she was another Gertrude Jekyll, but the truth was that she had an instinctive knowledge of which plants would thrive together and, thanks entirely to her, their garden was the envy of Vicars' Close.

Both sisters looked up when he went into the room; Edward didn't normally leave his study so soon. Anxious to break the news now, he spoke more abruptly than he meant to.

'You must both read Clio's letter, but first I'll tell you the important thing – she has found Antonia's grave in Rome. Our poor girl died *there* in 1951.'

For once Hester gestured to her twin to take the letter first. She had more to think about than Hetty, even understood the desperation that would have driven their sister back to Rome;

71

and she had to acknowledge to herself at last that her own life *hadn't* been ruined by Antonia. Mark Lambert had loved the wrong woman, that was all.

Her turn came to read Clio's letter, and then she put an arm round Hetty's shoulders in a rare gesture of affection. 'I'm glad we know,' she said quietly.

'But we still know so little,' Hetty cried. 'How *could* Antonia have died, unless there was an accident of some kind? She would only have been twenty-eight in 1951. Look at *us* – still alive now!'

'There's nothing wrong with that,' said Hester, with something of her usual sharpness.

Edward held up his hand, asking for silence. 'Listen, my dears. We know very little at the moment – Clio explains how difficult it is to trace records of fifty years ago, when much of Italy was still in ruins. But she has friends helping her. If they can discover something more, she will let us know. We must just be patient.'

Again it was Hetty who put another anguished question into words. 'What are we going to say to Peter? Have you forgotten that he's coming here in three days' time? Antonia was *his* mother.'

'We know that,' Hester snapped. 'If Edward agrees, we must show him Clio's letter.' But the sight of her brother's sad face made her phrase her next remark more gently. 'Shouldn't we admit that Antonia's son probably won't be very interested in what happened to her? He never forgave her for . . . for all sorts of things.'

There was no reply to this, but after a moment or two Hetty found something else to say. 'Poor dear Clio – what a shock for her!' Then tears suddenly began to trickle down Hetty's cheeks. 'I wish we *didn't* know. We could have gone on thinking that Antonia had a happy life wherever she was, but I don't think that was true; something sad happened to her.'

'I think so, too,' Edward agreed quietly. He knew already what he was going to do. While Clio was still there to show him where to find Antonia, he was going to say goodbye to her. He'd been to Rome, but only as a young man. He could remember Mussolini's black-shirted young men striding about as though the city belonged to them . . . a different world then, in those years before the war came to change everything.

First, he'd have to write to Clio; time to tell the girls when it was all arranged and too late for Hester to try to persuade him not to go.

Eight

It had been a tense week, in Clio's view. She thought she had an excuse to be on edge, waiting to hear from Luigi; but what accounted for Costello's strange frame of mind? Nothing seemed to have gone wrong with the private part of the Milan visit. He and Francesca spoke to each other every day on the telephone, and Lucia reported – with a slightly disapproving note in her voice – that some mornings his bed at the *palazzo* hadn't been slept in. But he said very little about the meetings he'd gone to take part in, except that they'd been quite interesting.

It seemed a tepid phrase to use, as if he'd grown bored with what he was doing; but when Clio suggested this after several rather silent days she got shouted at for her pains.

'I may be confused, frustrated, even a little angry; I am *not* bored. Is that clear?'

'If you say so,' she agreed quietly. 'You don't have to explain *why* you're these things if you don't want to.'

'Quite right, any more than I expect you to tell *me* how my cousins seem to know more about you than I do.' She stared at him, not sure what she was expected to say. 'Gino Forli often lunches at I Tre Scalini,' he explained smoothly.

'Luigi di Palma invited me out at *your* request,' she reminded him with some heat. 'I suppose Lorenza's charming husband was also hiding behind a column in the Forum when I bumped into Matteo. What exactly is Signor Forli's rôle – family spy?'

'At least I've got you all fired up as well,' Costello said, as if something had been achieved. 'I don't like to be the

74

only one that's mad.' But he no longer sounded angry, only strangely regretful, and she wished very much that she knew what had happened in Milan. Had Francesca persuaded him that what he was doing there was a waste of time? Had he come round to regretting that he'd ever begun to dig up the past? Something had changed, because even Pietro Nenni's diary, that she'd transcribed so carefully, had been glanced at and put aside.

'Luigi was kind enough to drive me to the Protestant Cemetery,' she suddenly decided to explain. 'We went to look for John Keats' grave, which of course we knew was there. But we also found something totally unexpected – my grandmother, Antonia Lambert, had been buried there fifty years ago.'

'Luigi, discreet lawyer that he is, didn't mention that.' Costello forgot that he didn't expect to be told anything. 'You'd no idea her grave was there?'

Clio shook her head. 'It's a long story, not of interest to anyone outside my family, but Antonia left her husband and small son in Somerset not long after she'd returned there from Rome at the end of the war. She was thought to have gone to America, but never heard from again. Luigi is using his legal contacts to try to discover who arranged for her burial. It was a long time ago and he isn't very hopeful.'

'But you are?' Costello asked curiously.

She gave the rare smile that he found himself watching for nowadays in case he missed it. 'Here's your chance to laugh at me, but I don't care. The odds against my stumbling across Antonia's grave were so enormous that I believe it *wasn't* just chance. Unless we live to a ripe old age we probably don't see the patterns that life makes, but I'm sure this is part of our pattern – Antonia's and mine – and I don't think it's finished yet.' There was silence in the room until Clio herself spoke again. 'You haven't laughed – why not?'

'Because it doesn't strike me as funny.' Costello hesitated, then went on more diffidently than usual. 'I think I came across a pattern of my own in Milan. I told you that it's where Giorgio Costello was shot, with fourteen other men. German soldiers carried out the murder – they were in control then in Mussolini's so-called Republic of Salò in the north – but the men were betrayed by fellow Italians.'

'Did you find out who they were?' Clio asked.

Costello hesitated. 'Not precisely, but very much involved was a secret Fascist organization called Decima Mas. A leading light of that was a patrician by the name of Prince Massini – he and his family had been supporters of Mussolini from way back.'

The story ground to a halt again, until Clio prompted him with another question. 'Does it matter that they were involved?'

'I'm afraid it does, because Lorenza's husband is related to them.' Costello's face was now a mask of despair and she knew why his appetite for investigating the past had been blunted so suddenly. It had nothing to do with Francesca at all. 'Gino's mother was a Massini before she married Giancarlo Forli – how is that for one of life's messier patterns?'

Now it was Clio who had to search for something to say. 'You can't assume that Gino knows anything about it,' she finally managed to suggest. 'The Massini you're talking about would have belonged to his grandfather's generation. People can't be held accountable for the sins of their ancestors – at least, not unless they deny that they *were* sins.'

'The Massini I'm talking about *was* his grandfather,' Costello said grimly, 'and there's a very good chance that Gino does deny they were sins. Matteo has always believed that he's a secret neo-Fascist.'

Another silence hung heavily in the room until Clio asked the only question left that mattered. 'Where does your book stand now – will you go on with it, or not?' He didn't answer for so long that she went on herself. 'It was to be a correction of the way history has been written since the war. The necessity for that hasn't changed.'

He stared across at her and she found it hard to remember

a time when she'd thought his face either expressionless or arrogantly self-willed. She was seeing him clearly now, a tough but not insensitive man who would hesitate after all to use the truth to damage other people.

'You said to me once, quite early in our acquaintance, that the truth – if ever I found it – would be too painful, because it was never going to be quite what it seemed. I discovered in Milan that you were right. My heroic Partisans repaid with interest the atrocities that had been committed against *them*. Before civilian government was in place again at the end of the war, their Insurrection Committees were in charge and terrible things were done to their opponents. Tell me where that leaves my "correction of history"!'

'You search out all the truth you can, and write *that* – as impartially as possible,' she said.

'Simple,' he agreed with a wry smile. 'I might have known you'd have the answer for me.'

'It's not my answer; it's Monsignor Fiocca's, but I'm sure he's right.' Clio hesitated for a moment, then went on. 'While you're deciding what to do, you *could* look more closely at the diary Pietro Nenni lent me – it might restore your faith in the value of what you began.'

'And you'd like to remind me in any case that I wasn't properly grateful for all the work you've done on it!'

'That also,' she agreed, getting up to leave the room.

She'd got as far as the door when his voice halted her. 'By the way, it was Luigi who told me you'd met Matteo again, not Gino. It's intriguing that *both* my cousins seem to have forgotten that they don't trust the English!'

'Perhaps they've decided that we're not as black as we're painted,' she suggested solemnly, and saw Costello smile.

'Could be!' Then he grew serious again. 'I hope Luigi *can* find out about your grandmother. The elderly trio I met in Wells were – what? – Antonia's brother and sisters?'

Clio nodded. 'I've written to Edward – he's the one who's missed her most. My guess is that he'll want to come and visit her grave. Then Hester will insist that because he's too old to travel alone – he's her senior by all of fourteen months – *she* must come too, despite her strong misgivings about Rome.'

'Too pagan for her?'

'First pagan and then Papist – what could be worse?!'

Costello laughed out loud, his own family problems put aside for the moment. 'Let me guess the rest: Hetty can't be left on her own, so *all* of them will descend on Rome.'

'More to the point, they'll descend on the *pensione*, where Hester will lock horns with Monsignor Fiocca over the dinner table, and Hetty will agonize about not being able to wind spaghetti round her fork as the Italians do!'

'I can't miss it – you'll have to invite me, too.'

'So that you can laugh at them? I don't think so.'

The amusement was wiped from his face and they were back to glaring at one another. 'Godammit, Clio, what do you take me for?' he nearly shouted again. 'I'd enjoy them, not laugh at them. There *is* a difference.'

'So there is,' she agreed after a moment. 'I'm sorry.' Then she was allowed to walk away to her own room.

There were papers on her desk that needed attention, but for the moment she had other things to think about. The most trivial she considered first – Costello's unexpected use of her name. It was a small milestone in their odd working relationship, and she supposed that she had her friendship with Luigi to thank for it.

Then there was Francesca. She shared Costello's bed and must surely have been told about his discoveries in Milan. Had she used them to reinforce her view that he should abandon what he'd set out to do? It seemed very likely.

Lastly, Clio came to thinking about herself – her glib solution to his problem had been that he should simply write the truth. But the truth wasn't simple at all, especially if it meant splitting his own family apart. That evening she took the dilemma to her old friend, knowing that it would be safe with him. With the bare bones of it laid out in front of him, she reminded him of what he'd said.

'The historian's duty is to write the truth, but what if that hurts people who are still alive? Should the good historian only write about things that are long past? And if he does, will the bad historian's version of events become the accepted truth?'

He smiled at the medieval picture she conjured up – the Good Historian surrounded by a flock of cherubim, the Bad Historian being consumed by the fires of Hell – but he understood how serious her questions were.

'Your author friend has uncovered parts of the truth that he doesn't like,' the priest suggested gently. 'Shall he hide them again for mercy's sake, or go on with what he set out to do?' Clio nodded but didn't interrupt, and the Monsignor slowly answered his own question. 'I think your American must consult his family. They might agree to be sacrificed. If not, he must either proceed in spite of them, or wait for some other historian who isn't personally involved to write the truth instead of him. There *will* be such a person in the end; there always is.'

'So it won't matter too much if *he* gives up?' Clio asked anxiously.

'Only to him, perhaps,' came the quiet reply, and she could see the truth of that as well.

It seemed as the days passed that Costello had at least postponed making his great decision. She didn't ask again what he intended to do, but simply got on with her own work of patiently checking sources, and translating the officialese that defeated his rather basic knowledge of the language. She heard nothing from Luigi – apart from a note to say that he'd set enquiries going, and would contact her as soon as he returned from visiting a client in Naples. If Matteo continued to walk through the Forum, she didn't see him there or anywhere else in her frequent trudges through the city in search of information.

She was still working in her room one evening when Costello returned from visiting a retired member of the Communist party that Luigi had put him in touch with.

'What's so fascinating about official records that you're still here at long past office hours?' he asked ungratefully.

'The information they can't help containing. Look at this, for example: by 1960 all but two – *two*, mark you! – of the provincial Prefects, the local Governors in other words, were the same as in Fascist times, and so were almost all of the *Questori*! No wonder people with different views – like Mario di Palma – despaired of ever seeing anything change.'

Costello nodded. 'What else gave birth to the Red Brigades except despair? But now, for God's sake, go back to your *pensione* . . . no, on second thoughts I'd better buy you dinner instead – you look hungry.' He smiled at the look of doubt on her face. 'It's all right – I'm a free agent; Francesca's covering some fashion shows in Paris!'

The invitation now seemed more, not less refusable, but Costello saw her hesitation and took exception to it. 'I was offering you dinner – not a night of unbridled sexual licence; what's to get up-tight about in that?'

'Nothing, of course,' she finally agreed. 'Nowhere smart, though; I'm not quite dressed for it. The best I can do is comb my hair.'

Out in the piazza a few minutes later, he hailed a cab and asked the driver to take them across the river to Trastevere – the quarter whose inhabitants still liked to claim they were the true old Romans.

'It's *getting* spoiled,' Costello said as they trundled across the Ponte Garibaldi. 'Too many visitors come here looking for "atmosphere"; but you can still find authentic bits that only the locals know about.'

The bit he had in mind was a small piazza approached by a lane so narrow that they had to abandon the taxi and walk to it. There was a *trattoria* tucked into one corner whose tables would probably spread out into the road during the hot nights of summer. Now, at the beginning of February, its customers were still content to eat indoors.

'It doesn't look much,' Costello said as they walked towards it, 'but the food's good, and the wine comes from the family vineyard out in the Campagna.'

'I even like the look of it as well,' Clio answered truthfully, wondering whether Francesca allowed herself to be brought there – on the whole, she thought not.

The patron greeted Costello like an old friend and recommended the roast suckling pig.

'Forget your scruples,' Costello said, smiling at Clio. 'It *will* be as good as he says! Now, a glass of golden Frascati to whet your appetite while we wait.'

Looking at him across the table, she realized that he at least was content there, untroubled by the lack of what it clearly didn't have – smart décor, expensive table-linen, and too-obsequious waiters. She'd taken it for granted that success had bred in him a taste for such things; perhaps the other assumptions she'd made weren't anywhere near the truth either. Unaware of being studied herself, she wasn't prepared for the question he suddenly fired at her.

'What happened to you? I know some of the facts – parents' divorce, and new marriages that didn't seem to include you; unnatural childhood in a cathedral close with elderly relatives – but you've been out of that for a good ten years at least. Why are you still an oddity among today's anything-you-can-do-I-can-do-better young women?'

The word 'oddity' stung her into a confession she hadn't meant to make. 'I shed my upbringing very quickly – almost as soon as I went to Oxford.'

'Let me guess. You fell in love, went to bed with the wrong man, and decided to keep the rest of us at arm's length from then on. Is *that* all?'

'Put like that, it doesn't sound much – just every cloistered female's story when she steps out into the real world armed with a very shaky hold on the facts of life and no practical experience at all of the opposite sex. Yes, I fell in love and, yes, I chose the wrong man. It took me quite a while to discover what everyone else knew – that *he*'d only gone into it for a bet, because his friends reckoned that he wouldn't be able to shake the puritan principles I'd been reared by! It was a very painful introduction to reality.'

'Quite enough to have to deal with,' Costello agreed almost gently, 'but your student days are long gone, and you've had time to discover that we come in all shapes and sizes, and some of us are better than others.'

'I do know that now. I've all the friends I want in London, and they come from both sexes.' She took a sip of wine, and then suddenly smiled. 'Your turn now; I'm out of the confessional box.'

'A childhood much less lonely than yours – family means something even for Italians who are half-American. I have three sisters; being the only boy, I was in clover. My father joined his uncle, who'd started from nothing and set up a chain of restaurants. Thanks to them, I didn't even have to starve in a garret while I learned the craft of writing.'

Clio examined his face for a moment. 'I think something went wrong though.' She expected what she'd said to be brushed aside but, as if her own confession required a similar effort from him, he went on with his story.

'I married young – I was twenty-three, Teresa was nineteen. We were besotted with each other's bodies; didn't know, didn't care, what the rest of us amounted to.' His voice was rough now, but made so by pain, not anger. 'Success *is* a double-edged sword. Teresa couldn't cope with it at all. She came to dread the next book launch, the next round of parties in the unreal world of money and celebrity that we got sucked into. I was enjoying it, of course, never understanding that somewhere along the way we'd lost each other.'

He stopped talking and Clio gently prompted him. 'So your marriage fell apart?'

'You could say that. I was being made much of in Hollywood when my wife killed herself and our unborn son in New York. I hadn't even known that she was pregnant. It was a long time ago – twelve years to be exact – but it still feels to me as if I killed them both.'

'You didn't know about the child,' Clio managed to point out. 'It might have been different if you had.'

'Maybe. Who knows?' He stared at her shocked face, and shook his head. 'Don't look so sad. I'm not in the habit of telling this story, and God knows what possessed me to unload it on *you*. Now, here comes Marco with our food. Smile at him, or he'll think you don't like his restaurant.'

She did as she was told, and even ate the pork that was as delicious as Costello had said it would be. They spoke of easier things, and it wasn't until the meal was over that she suddenly reverted to the reason they were in Rome at all.

'Have you made up your mind about the book? I should let John Wyndham know whether I'm soon going to be back in London or not.'

'I spoke to him last night. We go on as planned, gathering material. That *must* be done while there are still people alive who remember what happened. It remains to be seen who gets to write the book in the end – me or someone else.' A faint smile touched his mouth for a moment. 'And before you ask your next question, yes, I do realize that our trial is long gone. I can go on putting up with you if you can do the same for me. Do we have a deal?'

She considered this, then nodded. 'I think so; in any case, I don't want to leave Rome just yet.'

'The mystery of your grandmother's grave, or a growing attachment to my cousin Luigi! Either way, nothing to do with me. Shall we go now? Francesca will be ringing soon and I shouldn't like her to think I was out *enjoying* myself.'

A taxi was summoned, and ten minutes later he waited only long enough to see her inside the front door before he said a brief goodnight and went away.

She climbed the stairs slowly, too tired to move any faster. The shared meal had been a mistake; they now knew things about each other that they hadn't needed to know. Would he amuse Francesca with the story he'd been told of his *Inglese*'s pathetic love affair? If so, she'd make it obvious with a pitying smile when they next met. But his own tragedy had been so much worse that it scarcely mattered whether the Italian woman knew or not that Clio Lambert had come a cropper on her first ride out into the arena where men and women played their dangerous gladiatorial games.

Nine

The following morning no reference was made to their Trastevere visit beyond a polite enquiry from Costello as to whether Marco's rich *porchetta* had resulted in a sleepless night. She was able to smile cheerfully at him.

'Nothing does – it's Americans who are always so worried about what they eat abroad.'

'That's what I find so irritating about you; I never get the last word.' But he said it mildly, and didn't scowl at her again until he wanted to use the telephone and couldn't because Luigi was calling her from his office.

'I stayed to listen,' Costello explained brazenly, when she'd put the receiver down, 'because it obviously wasn't a romantic assignation my cousin was making. Do I gather that he's found out something about your grandmother?'

Clio nodded, staring at the address she'd scribbled down. 'Luigi has been in Naples but some information was waiting for him when he got back this afternoon. My grandmother died of *polmonite,* pneumonia in English, at the Fatebenefratelli Hospital on the Tiber Island. The hospital records still exist. Her body was released for burial to undertakers whose name Luigi was able to give me. They're in the district we were in last night. Back in the 1950s I dare say it was quite a lot rougher than it is now.'

'Almost certainly, I should think. Do you want to go and see the undertakers?'

Clio shook her head. 'Luigi still insists on being helpful. He thinks a foreigner might get very little out of them; an Italian lawyer has a much better chance.'

Costello was silent for a moment. He could have pointed out that his normally shy, reserved cousin was involving himself in her affairs to a surprising extent, but there was nothing permanent about that, of course. Before long she would be back in London, and Luigi would return to his self-contained, bachelor existence. It was more important to make her think of something else.

'I know you're hell bent on completing your pattern, but have you considered that Antonia might never have got in touch with her family simply because she didn't *want* them to know what had happened to her?' Clio didn't answer straight away, so he went on himself. 'Whatever it was, half a century's gone by since then. Might it not be better to leave her past alone?'

She shook her head, now certain of what she was going to say. 'I can't – it *isn't* over and done with yet. You see, there were fresh flowers on Antonia's grave. I need to know who is putting them there.'

'Probably an elderly friend who remembers her with affection; why should it be any more important than that?'

'Because I know *something* of what happened here. The man I still think of as my grandfather died a few weeks ago, and Uncle Edward and I were at his house, clearing things out. I found a photograph of Antonia and a man whose name was written on the back of it – "darling Filippo, 1944". Then Edward told me the truth – she'd arrived home pregnant, dismissed from the army before the war ended. Can you imagine the disgrace in Vicars' Close? She married Mark Lambert, who brought up her son as his own, even after she abandoned them both! I feel sure that she came back here to find the real father.'

'You said the name on the stone was Antonia Lambert; so even if she found him, she couldn't have married him,' Costello pointed out. 'But it would be nice to think that Filippo, aged gent that he must now be, is still putting flowers on her grave.'

Clio's thin face broke into a smile at last. 'That's what I'd like to be able to tell Uncle Edward.'

'Am I going to be kept informed as well, or is only Luigi allowed to be involved?'

She stared at him for a moment, disconcerted by what had sounded like a note of jealousy in his voice, but he made haste to recover himself. 'I'm a writer, remember? Professionally interested in what, in our crude way, we like to refer to as human nature in the raw!'

She nodded and would have ended the conversation, but he suddenly spoke again. 'My cousin is a very nice man, by the way – you wouldn't need to fear that *he*'d be likely to hurt you.'

'Oh, I know that,' she said, and walked out of the room.

She climbed the *pensione* staircase that evening anticipating a meal that might be dull if Monsignor Fiocca was out visiting a clerical friend, but would at least have none of the emotional turbulence of her dinner with Costello. The thought of the old priest made her smile – he'd explained how much pleasure it gave him to be acquiring, rather late in life, the reputation for being something of a ladies' man! Her smile faded as she walked into the hall. Signora Rollo was talking to a man whose identity she must already have guessed – because father and daughter resembled each other, same build, dark hair, and crisply modelled features.

'*Ecco la signorina*,' said the *padrona*, and tactfully disappeared.

'*Buona sera,* Clio,' Peter Lambert greeted her. 'I hope the aunts told you I was coming.' He sounded English still, but life in California had made other differences apart from adding a sun-bronzed patina to his skin.

She kissed him Italian fashion on both cheeks, wondering whether he was staying long enough to offer her dinner. They hadn't met for over a year, but she knew better than to expect that she came high on his list of priorities. 'They told me you were coming,' she agreed, 'but not when.'

'They didn't know. I had the choice of stopping to ring you or missing the plane. It had to be the plane – I'm off to Sicily in the morning.'

'Katherine's well, I hope,' Clio said politely, 'and the children, too?'

'They're fine; send you their love, of course.'

Of course, they always sent their love, along with Christmas and birthday cards, and small expensive gifts that she never knew what to do with. Katherine was meticulous about remembering such things.

'I hope you've told Signora Rollo if you're eating here,' Clio said next.

'I told her we'd be eating out. When you've tidied yourself up we'll have a drink here, to keep her happy, but we can do better in Rome, I hope, than eat *pensione* food.'

She didn't waste time pointing out that they probably couldn't, at least in this *pensione*. For her father the setting would be all wrong in any case. 'I'll be down in ten minutes,' she said instead, and left him staring with an expression of acute pain on his face at Signora Rollo's choice of pictures on the walls.

She took no more than the time she'd asked for to change into a thin cashmere sweater and velvet skirt, add a touch of lipstick, and emphasize her eyes with liner and eyeshadow. He had high standards where appearances were concerned, and now, of course, that made more sense to her than it had before. He was the son of an Italian, after all. When she went down to the hall again he was pouring the chilled white wine that the *signora* had brought. He raised his glass in salute.

'You look well, Clio; Rome obviously suits you, and so does your rig. Most women who choose to wear that shade of green shouldn't!'

'Why Sicily?' she asked with a smile of thanks for the unexpected compliment.

'Location shots for a film that's going to make use of the classical sites – Agrigento, Taormina, Syracuse. I'm looking forward to it; plan to do some photographic work on my own account as well while I'm there.'

'It sounds exciting.' Clio sipped the wine he'd poured for

her, and then asked a different question. 'Did you get down to Somerset, or were you only passing through London?'

'I went for one night – which is about as much as I can stand of Vicars' Close. Edward seemed to think he needed to apologize for Mark Lambert's will, but that was quite unnecessary; I'm glad *you* inherited Mark's house. I certainly wouldn't have wanted it.'

Clio stared at her father, wondering whether this was the moment to touch on even more delicate matters. She decided that the moment would do as well as any other.

'Uncle Edward finally told me what you knew long ago,' she said bluntly. 'I suppose it explained your . . . determination to have little to do with . . . with anyone in Wells.'

'Explained, but didn't excuse! Mark Lambert was a good man who treated me more kindly than even most blood fathers would have done, and I figuratively spat in his eye! I *think* that's what you are not quite saying.'

'Yes, it is,' she agreed quietly.

'You're right, of course, and the truth is that I'm sorry I left it too late to tell *him* so.' It was such an unexpected admission that Clio found nothing to say for a moment, and her father went on speaking. 'Edward also let me know that you've found my mother's grave here in Rome. I haven't time to go and see it, and I don't know that I would in any case.' He smiled at his daughter with a rueful but defiant air that came as another surprise. 'I know what you were brought up to say every night – "Forgive us our trespasses as we forgive those who trespass against us"! But I still haven't forgiven my mother for deciding that I didn't matter in her life.'

Clio thought of something that was better left unsaid, but the man watching her read it in her face.

'You, on the other hand, did forgive me and *your* mother for deciding that you could be safely dumped on elderly relatives, out of our way.'

'There were those daily prayers,' she pointed out with a faint smile, wondering how many more surprises this strange meeting would spring, 'and my elderly relatives are very dear.'

'It was hard on you all the same,' Peter Lambert commented, 'and I hope our failure hasn't put *you* off marriage.' Then, with a glance at his watch, he announced that he was hungry having, as usual, refused the squalid lunch tray offered him on the flight to Rome.

They went to the sort of restaurant he felt at home in – Al Vicario's, with its candle-lit international cuisine and clientèle – and it wasn't until they were drinking coffee at the end of the meal that he suddenly referred to what she was doing in Rome.

'Did Hester get it right? She kept insisting that you're working here for Paul Costello on some historical research. It didn't seem to be his sort of thing at all.'

'Nevertheless it's what I'm doing, but it sounds as if you know him,' Clio suggested.

'Enough to be surprised that you seem to be surviving unscathed. I've met him in Hollywood and in New York. He has the reputation for knowing exactly what he wants when it comes to turning one of his books into film. Producers who have their own ideas, not to mention over-indulged actresses, don't like him at all; other authors get browbeaten in Hollywood, but not Costello!'

Clio nodded, not surprised. 'We snap at each other from time to time, but I shall be sorry when the work is finished – it's a challenge keeping up with him.'

'But why a rehash of past history? If it weren't for his name and huge following, a publisher probably wouldn't even look at it.'

'I don't think that would worry him,' Clio pointed out. 'He's doing it to set the record straight, and because his family were involved. But the problem now is that they don't all seem to have been involved on the same side.'

'Then it's almost certainly ill-advised. Much better not to drag into the light of day things that should be kept decently hidden.'

Clio gave a wry smile. 'Speaking of which, a cousin of Costello's here is making some enquiries for me – about my grandmother's death. If you're very strongly against our doing it, I should have to ask him to stop; but it seems important to me.'

Peter Lambert shrugged. 'My dear girl, do what you like. It strikes me as pointless, even macabre, but I shouldn't dream of stopping you.'

She stared at him for a moment, thinking how little she understood him. 'You had an Italian father – wouldn't you at least like to know who he was?'

'You're making an assumption. Rome was full of men in 1944 – Americans, British, Germans even, to name but a few, besides a lot of war-shattered, half-starved Italians. If you want the unvarnished truth, I'd rather *not* know which of them fathered me.'

He was right, she realized; her assumption *had* been made on the flimsy evidence of a photograph and a name scribbled on the back of it. Out of that she'd woven a pattern that Luigi's findings might completely destroy. It was time to stop talking about Antonia. Instead, she asked her father if she could see whatever photographs he took of the Greek temples in Sicily.

'I've got an exhibition in mind – provided they're good enough,' he said with a small nod to modesty. 'If you're prepared to make a trip to New York, I'll send you an air ticket.'

'An offer I can't refuse,' she agreed, smiling at him.

They parted company a little later at the door of the *pensione*, and she was left with the memory of a more amicable meeting than usual with her father. It had been another surprising evening in fact – Rome was making a habit of them.

She heard nothing from Luigi until the following afternoon; then he rang to ask if she could meet him for a drink. It was all he could manage before a legal function that evening. Indeed she could, because she knew from his voice that he had news for her.

In her anxiety not to keep him waiting, she set off too early for the Caffé Greco in Via Condotti, but it was no hardship to wait for him in one of the city's legendary meeting places. Here since the eighteenth century had come not only the local intellectuals but a stream of visiting writers and artists as well, and by the look of the evening's clientèle they still did. She had ordered a glass of wine when Luigi hurried in, resplendent in formal evening dress for the dinner ahead. He seemed so shyly pleased when she said he looked splendid that she supposed his female acquaintances didn't normally pay him compliments.

'I'm being a nuisance, I'm afraid,' she went on to say, 'but truly I *am* grateful for all your help.'

'I don't know this word "nuisance",' he answered with a charming smile, 'and *I*'ve become as interested in Antonia Lambert as you are.'

'You found something out?'

'Well, yes. I called on the undertakers this morning – fortunately it's a line of work that tends to run in families, so there'd been no change of ownership in fifty years. The Ruffolis are still there, although of course the present head of the firm is the son of the man who arranged your grandmother's burial. The important thing was that their records are intact, so he could turn up the entry for me quite quickly.'

'Was it a man who made the arrangements with them?' Clio asked quietly. 'A man called Filippo something or other?'

Luigi shook his head. 'It wasn't, I'm afraid. The name Ruffoli gave me belonged to a woman – Luisa Caetani.' He saw the expression on Clio's face, and touched her hand briefly in an unexpected gesture. 'I'm sorry if that's a disappointment. This is the address that was given for her, but forgive me if I ask you not to expect too much. If this lady was older than Antonia she could easily be dead by now. There's no one by that name listed in the telephone book.'

'She might have married,' Clio suggested; 'she might even have left Rome.' The address written on the piece of paper Luigi had put in front of her was the Vicolo di San Rufina – Travestere again. 'I won't go this evening; a daytime visit would be better from a stranger, don't you think?'

Luigi was strongly tempted to say that she shouldn't go at all without him, but she was right – a call at night was '*non si fa*', something not properly done; and he was overwhelmed with work during the day.

'It's in a rough part of the city,' he pointed out instead. 'Take a taxi there, please, and ask the driver to wait for you.' She was touched by his concern for her, and promised that she would. 'Now you must leave,' she added, smiling at him. 'I'm sure your fellow dinner guests are too important to be kept waiting.'

He reluctantly agreed, apologized for not being able to accompany her on the five-minute walk back to the Via Margutta, but waited long enough to pay for the wine she'd been drinking. Luigi di Palma was a throwback, she reflected, to a time when both sexes took it for granted that one of men's prime duties in life was to take care of women.

The following morning she arrived at the *palazzo* to find a note from Costello. He would be out all day; in his absence she was to work hard, not skip lunch, and knock off at a reasonable hour. It was a typical message that made her smile, but it didn't change her intention to go first to the address Luigi had given her. She'd admit afterwards that for one day she hadn't worked hard enough.

Luigi's advice not to search out the Vicolo di San Rufina on foot had been good, she discovered half an hour later, when even the cabbie had to scratch his head a good deal, and finally ask for directions from two passers-by. They arrived at last in a narrow street untouched by any trace of new prosperity – the tall grim houses, obviously divided into small apartments, looked in the last stages of what could be reckoned habitable. Any remaining optimism dwindled as Clio walked inside No. 51, and looked at the names listed on a grubby notice on the wall. There was no lift, and she climbed a filthy staircase to the third floor, thanking God that she hadn't come at night. She wasn't frightened – in all her walking about Rome she'd met with no discourtesy, much less any trouble – but she was aware that her heart was beating faster than usual, and her hands felt clammy.

Her tentative ring at the door-bell produced no response; she forced herself to try again much harder, and visualized the sound echoing through empty, perhaps untenanted rooms. She was about to turn away when the door suddenly opened, and she found herself looking at a slatternly young woman of about her own age. That in itself was a shock. In her experience so far, Rome was a city of women who prided themselves on their appearance, no matter what their circumstances were, and she was accustomed to seeing well-groomed and attractive girls emerging from even the shabbiest row of houses.

'*Buon giorno, signorina,*' she began hesitantly. '*Cerco una donna che si chiamo Luisa Caetani. Conosce il nome?*'

'*Non lo conosco io.*'

With the door already being closed in her face, Clio tried again, urgently apologizing for being a nuisance, and trying to explain that someone called Luisa Caetani *had* lived there long ago. Could the *signorina* ever have heard the name mentioned, perhaps by her parents? A man's rough voice called out from a back room, and the girl's face scowled still more. She'd never heard the name, and didn't want to hear it either. With that the door *was* slammed, and Clio was left staring at its peeling paintwork, shaken by a display of rudeness that seemed to have something inexplicably malevolent about it.

Already unnerved, she crept down the stairs to the landing below and almost stopped breathing when a door there suddenly opened, and a witchlike old woman swathed in shawls hobbled out in front of her.

'*Aspetta, signorina . . . momentino, per favore.*' Her voice sounded rusty from lack of use, but it had once been more cultured than her neighbour's upstairs. Recovering now, Clio tried to smile at her, assuming that some help was needed. But it wasn't that at all; the newcomer wished to be of help to *her*. She explained that she'd heard the conversation on the landing above. She *had* known Luisa Caetani . . . it was long,

long ago, of course, when things were different, and the house had been more respectable than it was now. With someone to talk to, she would have gone on and on . . . the place was falling to pieces, her neighbours quarrelled all the time, how sad it was, growing old . . . but gently Clio brought her back to the subject of Luisa Caetani. Did she know whether her friend was still alive, did she perhaps know where she was?

Alive, it seemed; why not when she herself, older than Luisa, was still not quite dead? But *where*, she couldn't say, except that there'd been talk of a *rifugio*, a home for old people the *signorina* must understand, somewhere . . . yes, somewhere out by the Porta San Sebastiano. She stopped talking, suddenly doubtful if she should have said anything at all.

'I discovered that Luisa knew my grandmother, who came here at the end of the war. I just wanted to talk to her,' Clio explained. 'I'm very grateful for your help.' It was her turn to be hesitant now, not sure whether the offer of money would be welcome or not. In the end she took out some notes and put them in her companion's small, cold hand. 'They'll buy you some flowers to cheer up your room,' she suggested gently. 'Thank you again.' Then she kissed the old lady's cheek by way of farewell, and walked down the stairs, and out to the still-waiting taxi. A glance at her watch said that she'd been in the house no more than ten minutes. It seemed far longer than that, but for the moment she scarcely remembered that her search for Luisa Caetani had probably come to a dead end; she was wondering whether anyone would know or care if the old lady she'd just left failed to wake up one morning.

Ten

It was a relief to be back at the *palazzo* and to hear, as she opened the door, Lucia singing Musetta's cheerful aria from *La Bohème*. She was doing it rather well except that its highest note defeated her and she sensibly left it out.

When the piece was over Clio smiled and asked for her help. 'Lucia, tell me how I can find out about old people's homes – who would know such things? I don't have a name for the one I want and only a very vague address.'

She couldn't blame Lucia for looking doubtful, and there was even the possibility that her shawl-swathed old lady had made up the little information that she *had* got in order to seem helpful.

'There's a department that deals with such things – at the town hall, I think. But don't go there, *signorina*, unless you've got a day to spare queuing up to speak to someone who closes his window just as you get to it, and tells you to try again tomorrow!'

Clio knew that it was all too likely to happen. The amount of time Italians spent trying to prise information or essential documents out of public officials added up to weeks out of their lives in the course of a year. But she was anxious not to trouble Luigi again; from now on she wanted to manage on her own.

She put the problem aside and forced herself to settle down to the work she was supposed to be doing, but when lunchtime came she couldn't stay cooped up indoors. With a map to study in her pocket, and sandwiches bought on the way to give to the ever-hungry cats, she walked down to the Forum

– still empty of tourists despite a spell of unusually fine February weather.

With her friends fed, she pulled out the map and spread it over the stump of a marble column. Porta San Sebastiano, the old lady had said; well, it looked the sort of district away from the city centre where old people's homes might be located and, more tellingly, for someone living there it would be a short walk to the Porta San Paolo and the Protestant Cemetery.

She was still considering this when a shadow fell across the map and she looked up to see that she was being watched from a couple of feet away – not Matteo di Palma this time but – oh God – his gaunt-faced wife, Isabella. It was turning out to be a very wearing day.

'*Not* my husband, *signorina* – I hope you weren't expecting *him* again.' Isabella's voice, like her expression, warned Clio that they were close to a precipice. The woman was wound tight with nervous tension; one false step and they'd be over the edge.

'I was expecting no one at all,' she said as calmly as she could. 'I usually have the ruins all to myself, though it's true that your husband happened to walk through one lunchtime while I was here.'

She made herself look at Isabella, clinging to the hope that her own longing to reassure a desperately unhappy fellow human being could be seen and understood. There was no way of knowing what it would be safe to talk about, so she returned to the only other meeting they'd had.

'I'm afraid I upset your family at Signora di Palma's dinner party. Costello took me to task afterwards for talking about Mussolini. I promise you that I didn't know how distressing it would be.'

Isabella's shrug dismissed Il Duce. 'I don't concern myself with politics. People tie labels on themselves that are quite meaningless; they're still all looking out for their own good, and no one else's.'

It seemed an easier subject that any other, so Clio went on with it. 'As I understand it, that wasn't your father-in-law's vision, at least; he saw things in terms of societies, not individuals; and he truly believed in equality and justice for all.'

Isabella's smile was even more worrying that her taut frown had been. 'Are you going to find something hopeful to say about Gino Forli as well? I think that might even defeat *you*!' But the smile faded again. 'Do you know that Lorenza leaves her children in the care of servants? She and Gino are too busy to look after them. They have to fawn over the shoddy, powerful people *they* think matter – people Mario di Palma would have told them to shun like the plague. Why does God give children to the wrong parents – can you tell me that?'

The question was heart-breaking, and unanswerable. 'No,' Clio said sadly, 'any more than I can explain why too many other tragedies stalk the world as well.'

'I don't believe in God now,' Isabella said, with anguish in her deep voice. 'I used to . . . loved to go to Mass. But not any longer – why should I when He kept letting my babies die.'

Clio took hold of her companion's hand, the only comfort she could offer; it was easiest to blame God after all, even for the pain human beings inflicted on each other. Finally she decided to risk a question of her own. 'You and Matteo could adopt a child – why don't you?'

'He wanted to, but I refused.' She stared at the girl beside her with huge, angry eyes. 'Can't you understand – I needed *our* child, not some wretched waif that not even its own mother would cherish.'

'Or was *able* to cherish perhaps,' Clio gently pointed out. 'You've had the agony of losing babies; can't you try to imagine what it feels like to have to *give* your child to someone else?'

Isabella answered this by snatching her hand away, but after a moment or two she spoke in a calmer tone of voice. 'I wanted to find you here so that I could be angry with you . . . go on hating you, because you're English, and young, and not yet beaten by life; but I don't hate you after all. Luigi said I wouldn't be able to.'

Clio's strained face finally broke into a smile. 'You don't

have to do what he tells you, even if he *is* accustomed to laying down the law! But he's a very nice man in spite of that.'

Isabella's nod seemed to agree; then abruptly, she asked an unexpected question. 'Do you always come here at lunchtime?'

'If it's fine; if not, I take myself off to Miss Babington's English Tearooms in the Piazza di Spagna. I'm not homesick; I go there because it's a nice friendly sort of place.'

Then she got to her feet, holding out her hand to say goodbye.

'I *must* go now – I haven't achieved much today, and Costello will tell me so when he comes in.'

Isabella stood up too. 'I'll walk with you – I've nothing else to do . . . hours to fill until Matteo decides he can bear to come home.'

Clio reminded herself that the woman was sunk deep in loneliness and melancholia; she needed help, from Matteo in the first place, but also from the rest of her family. Failing them, she must try herself. 'I scarcely know your husband, Isabella, but I'm certain of one thing: he devotes himself to sick children because he believes that's what you *want* him to do. It's the only comfort he can give you for the babies you lost. If that doesn't make sense to you, all I can say is that it does to me.'

She wasn't sure what she expected – either to have Isabella scream at her, or simply stalk away; instead they walked in silence towards the exit gate by Septimus Severus's Arch. Then, at last, Isabella spoke, almost inaudibly. 'Thank you . . . thank you, Clio, perhaps you are right.'

They parted company at the gate, but she suddenly turned round. 'May I come again if it's fine? I'll bring some food for the cats.'

'We'll all look forward to it,' Clio said solemnly, and saw her smile before she walked away.

Back at the *palazzo*, she found Costello already there, and looking at his watch as she walked in.

'I know I'm late,' she said at once, 'and before you remind me that I'm here to work, I must own up to wasting some more of your time this morning.'

'Luigi found something out for you, I suppose, and you went there hot-foot.'

'He got a name and address from the undertakers; all *I* got was the door slammed in my face by a very surly woman, so I slunk away. But an elderly lady on the floor below said she remembered the name, and thought Luisa Caetani might still be alive in an old people's home somewhere near the Porta San Sebastiano.' The expression on Costello's face made her hurry on. 'I know it isn't much, but it's better than nothing.'

'And now you intend to spend tomorrow morning looking for it?'

'I'm afraid that wouldn't be fair to you,' she said solemnly, 'but I've had a much better idea.'

'Luigi is to hand the problem to his clerks?'

'That wouldn't be fair to him; but I need to short-circuit the system at the town hall, which Lucia rightly says can take for ever.' Clio smiled at the man watching her. 'In *your* very prestigious name I'm going to ask someone at the American Embassy to assist our research and contact the right department for me. At least, I am if you don't object.'

He managed, with a very great effort, to keep his mouth straight and answer as earnestly as she had spoken. 'It's thoughtful of you to mention it, but you mustn't hesitate for a moment – of course, use *anything* of mine that might come in handy.'

She wasn't sure for a moment whether it was Costello being unusually polite or Costello being lethally sarcastic; the latter, probably, because he went on to suggest in the same tone of voice that, if it wasn't upsetting her own plans too much, perhaps they could now get on with some work. On the point of walking along the hall to her office, she stopped suddenly and turned round to look at him.

'It's been a day of interesting encounters! I bumped into Isabella at lunchtime in the Forum – well, I think the truth is that she came looking for me.'

'And she accused you of putting a spell on Matteo, no doubt.

I know about English understatement, but is interesting really the word?'

Clio shook her head. 'We began badly, but finished up on good terms. I only mention it because she spoke of Lorenza and Gino and the dubious people that they associate with. Mirella must surely know *something* about the Massini family, but is she likely to know that her son-in-law still has a foot in the Fascist camp?'

'I think she knows that he has more than that,' Costello said grimly. 'Gino Forli and his relatives need to be watched; but she adores Lorenza, and she enjoys the aristocratic connection; she'll turn a blind eye as far as she can to whatever is going on.'

'Life here is getting very complicated,' Clio suggested. 'Perhaps you wish you were back on familiar territory in New York.'

'Not particularly, and if you think that's where I live, you're wrong,' he pointed out. 'I rent an attic in Greenwich Village to stay in when I have to. My home is on the Connecticut coast – Stonington Point, surrounded by water on three sides. No traffic, just the sound of the sea; no droppers-in, my guests only come by invitation.'

It sounded beautiful but lonely, needing someone as self-sufficient as he was himself to be happy there. Where, she wondered, did elegant, sophisticated Francesca fit into such a scenario? It was tempting to ask, but she'd tried his limited patience enough for one day. Then she finally remembered something else worth mentioning.

'My father was here for a night, before flying on to Sicily. He said that he'd met you several times; perhaps you don't remember, or it didn't occur to you that we're related.'

'Since you resemble him, it *did* occur to me. But my impression was that you and he have no contact. A brilliant cameraman he undoubtedly is, but he seems to me to be a lousy father.'

'Not to his new family,' Clio said fairly, 'and even he and I got on unusually well over dinner. One never knows when life is going to spring another surprise, does one?'

'How very true! Now will you stop talking and get some work done?'

But he made the suggestion mildly, and she walked away registering still one more surprise – it had become easy to say to him whatever was in her mind, because in some strange way she'd become certain of him as a friend. At last she put the idea aside and concentrated instead on the harrowing post-war history of terrorist bombings in Italy, for which, on very little evidence, communists had always been blamed. Immersed in summarizing an especially long-drawn-out trial of one of them, she was unaware of Costello, until he spoke from the doorway.

'I thought we might get a little more help from the Embassy if I rang myself – I happen to know someone there. He promised to call back in the morning, having found an official in the right department at the town hall to kick into something approaching life.'

Clio stared at him, forgetting that it would have been more tactful not to look surprised.

'Thank you! That's very kind – of course they'll have paid more attention to you than they would to me,' she almost stammered.

He shook his head. 'Wrong again – it wasn't my name; it was the charming way I asked!' Then his voice changed again. 'By the way, I've decided to ask Mirella to call the family together – not just yet, but before we finally decide what to do about the book.'

'*All* the family – Gino Forli as well?' she rather nervously asked.

'Forli especially; he's concerned in it, wouldn't you say? I'd like you to be there too.' She hadn't even got an objection framed before he went on. 'You're involved and you know as much as I do about what happened; that's my excuse. The truth is that I'd be grateful if you'd consider sharing in a difficult discussion.'

From Paul Costello she thought it amounted to a plea for help. 'Then I will, of course, though your family might resent my being there,' she felt obliged to point out.

102

'I'm afraid they'll have more to resent than that.' Then he shrugged the problem aside. 'Now, for God's sake stop working and go home – you've had a long enough day.'

She took this to mean that he would now like his apartment to himself, and made haste to clear up and leave. Then, in the hall downstairs, she met Francesca Cortona coming in, and knew that her guess had been correct. Francesca was dressed for an evening out, and as always her taste was flawless.

'Only just leaving, *signorina*? I shall tell Paolo that he works you too hard. You look tired and no wonder – it's not earthshakingly exciting, is it, plodding through dismal official records!'

It could have been kindly meant, like the smile that went with it, but Clio suspected that she was meant to understand more than had been said. Francesca would have preferred her not to be there at all, but since she *was* under their feet she must be made to seem as dreary as the work she was doing.

'You'd be surprised by official records,' she said gravely. 'Reading about the trial of someone accused – wrongly as it happened – of killing eighty people with a bomb in Bologna is quite earth-shaking enough for me.' Then she said good-night, and let herself out into the piazza.

She stopped for a moment to watch the water falling into the old stone 'boat' that was Bernini's *Bocaccia*; at night dramatically lit, it was lovely to look at. Every fountain she passed in her walks about the city was different and beautiful – she'd remember them as the chief pleasure Rome had to offer her when she was back in London. Then she walked on towards the Via Margutta, aware that she felt tired and very lonely. It had been a day of unsettling encounters, but she knew they weren't at the heart of her present trouble. Nor even, was it the oppressive feeling that they were approaching a point of no return, when whatever was done could no longer be undone, no matter what the consequences were.

She knew what *was* the matter: her grandmother's first stay in Rome had suddenly become so real to her that she seemed to have *become* Antonia, riven by the loneliness and rejection and despair that had gone with her back to England. She stopped for a moment, overwhelmed by the terrible sensation of having stepped into someone else's life, but the cold touch of glass against her forehead revived her and she straightened up from the shop window she found she'd been leaning against.

She walked on again, coming to terms with the painful truth. It had begun with Francesca Cortona's pitying smile, and the knowledge that the Italian woman was going upstairs to Costello's apartment, probably to make him laugh over the peculiarity of the *Inglese* just met down in the hall. She didn't begrudge them laughter – God knew the world needed all it could get – but oh how she envied them their companionship and shared love. There was nothing more she herself could hope for from Paul Costello beyond the respect and friendship that she did nowadays sense; but when that seemed not to be enough she would have to think of Antonia, and try to remember that she had blessings to count.

Eleven

It was a relief to find only Lucia in the *palazzo* the following morning. There was no note from Costello saying why he'd gone out, so it was reasonable to assume that he'd spent the night in Francesca's apartment after their evening out. Clio tested herself with this thought, anxious to prove that the nightmare sensation of her walk back to the *pensione* had been born of tiredness and stress. Things were normal again now; she could safely admit that she enjoyed working for Paul Costello; she might also go as far as to say that she wouldn't forget him, or any part of this extraordinary visit to Rome. But that's all it would be in the end – an episode in her life whose events and heightened emotions had knocked her off balance for a moment or two.

She was congratulating herself on this sensible summing-up when Lucia answered a ring at the door-bell, and then showed into the office a fair-haired, pleasantly blunt-featured man who introduced himself as William Thompson – Costello's friend from the American Embassy. Offered coffee, he was happy to accept. Nothing urgent seemed to call him back to his office in the Via Veneto, and it seemed to Clio that the diplomatic life must be a pleasantly leisured affair.

She dealt rather sketchily with his curiosity about their research interest in *rifugios*, and asked instead how he and Costello came to know each other – they'd been fellow freshmen at Yale, it turned out; and from then on it only needed another question or two to keep the conversation flowing.

'Of course we knew even then that Paul would strike out

on his own,' the cultural attaché said with a hint of wistfulness in his voice. 'The rest of us were content to do our family thing.'

'If yours is representing your country abroad, it doesn't seem a bad tradition to follow,' Clio pointed out.

'That's very true,' William agreed earnestly, 'and Rome is one of the postings everybody wants, but . . .'

'. . . but it's full of Italians – naturally! – who don't always see things in the American way; on top of which they *will* expect us to start every meal with a plate of pasta.'

'Exactly!' William was grinning now, happy to have discovered in this delightful girl someone who understood the situation perfectly. Trust Paul to have found himself a winner; she even had the trick of keeping her nice mouth straight while her eyes were smiling.

'You're right, Clio – may I call you that? It's a very unusual name and, if memory serves, wasn't she the Muse of History?'

'Yes, and she's probably the reason I got this job, because Costello made the same connection!'

With William Thompson's mind clearly no longer on the subject that had brought him there, she was wondering how to ask him for the information he'd found when footsteps sounded on the marble floor of the hall. A moment later Costello stood in the doorway of her room.

'Hi, Will! Nice of you to call, but I hope you've been useful. We . . . I . . . were looking for information, not a social call from charming Embassy layabouts.'

His friend looked at Clio. 'I think I hear the tough New York cop speaking, don't you? The rude, incisive hero of a dozen best-sellers!'

She shook her head. 'I'm afraid I don't know; I haven't read any of them.'

Costello struggled not to laugh at the expression of wonderment on William's face. 'My assistant thinks it's good for me to be put in my place occasionally; she doesn't mean to hurt my feelings,' he explained carefully.

To someone accustomed to what he reckoned were normal

working relationships, it was hard to see how this one functioned at all; yet his conviction was that it *did* work, and probably rather well. And since Paul Costello was no ordinary employer, it seemed fair to assume that his assistant was a far from ordinary girl. He put the puzzle aside and laid a sheet of paper on Clio's desk.

'I hope I've been useful enough – there are three possible places within a mile radius of the Porta San Sebastiano; the names, addresses and telephone numbers are all there.'

'Prompt, thorough, and free of charge,' Costello said with a smile. 'What more can we ask of our foreign service? Thanks, Will. Now, if I bribe you with the offer of a drink, perhaps you'll come next door and let my handmaiden get on with some work.'

Nice as he was, she was happy to see William Thompson led away. She picked up the telephone at once and rang the first number on the list. Luisa Caetani, a rather bored-sounding voice insisted, was not an inmate there. She got much the same response from her next enquiry. The third time a more pleasant-sounding woman regretted that Signorina Caetani wasn't there – of course not, Clio thought sadly; like Antonia, she's long since dead. But just as she was remembering the bowl of narcissi on the grave – surely proof that someone was still alive who'd known Antonia – the woman spoke again. Luisa *had* been there, but had been moved to another home, not far away. Now, where was it? Yes – the Via della Piramide. Clio thanked her warmly and rang off. Luigi had driven her past the pyramid obelisk on their way to the Protestant Cemetery, so it meant that Luisa must be living within walking distance of it now.

There was one last call to make, and this time she got the answer she needed – she'd found the woman who'd arranged Antonia's burial. Still deep in thought, it required an effort to smile when William Thompson returned to say goodbye. But his inclination to still linger wasn't lost on Costello who briskly saw his friend off the premises. Then he went back to Clio's room, and guessed from her face what she was about to say.

'Thanks to Luigi, and to your very nice Embassy friend, I've *found* Luisa Caetani.'

He merely nodded, still concerned with the idea that it might have been safer for her to leave the past alone. Clio decided that he was merely bored with the subject of her grandmother, and spoke of William Thompson instead.

'It must be nice for you both, to meet up again here. He's a very pleasant, helpful man.'

Costello now looked concerned. 'So he is; but I'm afraid he's rather taken with you.'

'Is that bad?' she enquired cautiously.

'I think so. William needs a wife – for all sorts of reasons, of course, only one of them being that the right sort of help-mate is almost a necessity in furthering a diplomatic career. His family is Boston at its best and worst – old money, old standards, old prejudices. It's not surprising that he's still a bachelor. A goer among today's movers and shakers he definitely is not.'

'I'm not sure what that means, supposing that it means anything at all.'

'Put simply, my friend William isn't up to snuff where women are concerned. Take you, for instance. But for me dropping a helpful hint he'd have gone away thinking that he'd finally met a charming, intelligent girl who'd make him the sort of wife his ambassador and family would approve of.'

'May I ask what sort of hint?'

Costello smiled sweetly. 'I merely suggested – no more than that, I swear – that you aren't nearly as docile as you look.' He even wagged a finger at her. 'I'm thinking of you as well; you and William wouldn't suit at all.'

Not sure whether the conversation hadn't just been made up in order to provoke her, she missed her chance to answer because he spoke again in a different tone of voice. 'You intend calling at the old people's home, I suppose. Will you make certain before you go that it's what you really want to do? We now know it wasn't the elusive Filippo who made the funeral arrangements, so it's more than likely that he isn't the person who visits your grandmother's grave. If there was no happy ending to her adventure, do you really want to know what happened?'

He spoke now with such gentleness – anxiety even – that she was distracted for a moment from the matter in hand. It sometimes seemed as if even the little she thought she knew about Paul Costello wasn't correct. How much easier it would be if he always remained the overbearing, unlikeable man she'd met at the Savoy.

'Yes, I do need to know,' she finally answered, 'and I want to thank whoever *is* visiting Antonia's grave.' Then she smiled, almost shyly. 'Thank you, though, for the warning.'

The subject wasn't referred to again until, on the way out that evening, she asked if she could call at the *rifugio* before coming to the *palazzo* in the morning. 'I'll make up for the lost time,' she promised.

'Not by skipping lunch you won't. You look as if you skip too many meals as it is.'

Compared with the lusciously shaped Francesca, she supposed that her own slimness was bound to be noticeable. The fact that it was in the genes, not the diet, didn't seem worth mentioning, so she said nothing at all except a quiet goodnight.

The following morning she left the *pensione* earlier than usual, and walked until she found a flower shop just opening up. Then, with an armful of scented freezias, mauve, pink, bronze, and cream, she asked a cabbie to take her to the Via della Piramide. It was a slow journey, but she scarcely noticed the heavy traffic – chaotic-seeming but still more or less controlled in some contradictory way known only to Roman drivers. At last they pulled up outside a house set back from the road. Its faded pink stucco was peeling, but the windows shone, and it was pleasantly screened from the noise of the traffic by a line of young pine trees.

She rang the bell and a young girl stopped mopping the hall floor long enough to come and let her in. Then, with the usual assessing stare at the newcomer's corduroy jacket and tweed skirt – not Italian obviously – she promised to fetch the *soprintendente*. This turned out to be the woman Clio had spoken to on the telephone, who seemed suspicious at first of a visitor from England asking to see one of her inmates. Signorina Caetani was frail, she pointed out, and might be upset at being confronted by a stranger.

'I just want to give her these flowers and thank her for her kindness to my grandmother,' Clio pleaded. 'It will only take a few minutes, *Signora*, and I'll leave at once if she seems upset.'

The *soprintendente* relented enough to show her into a small side room. '*Aspetta, signorina*,' she said and bustled away.

Five minutes passed, then ten, and Clio told herself that, even now, she wasn't going to see Antonia's friend. Luisa Caetani might still manage the short walk to the cemetery, but obviously it was the only effort she now wanted to make. It had been a mistake not to warn her, but if asked beforehand she'd probably have said no anyway.

Clio stood up, oppressed by the unnatural quietness of the house and the image in her mind of old, sad people sitting alone in their separate rooms. She was about to find the maid again to say that she'd decided to leave when the door opened and a small, bent woman hobbled in.

'Signorina Caetani?' Clio asked uncertainly, abandoning even at first glance the idea that this crippled lady ever left the house at all. But a nod agreed that at least it was who she was. Clio led her to a chair, and then introduced herself as Antonia's granddaughter. Luisa *was* frail – severely arthritic, it seemed – but her eyes were intelligent, and unfriendly.

'Antonia's granddaughter, you say? Someone from the family should have come long ago,' she pointed out sharply. 'For so many years no one ever seemed to care about her.'

'We didn't know where to start looking,' Clio tried to explain. 'She left England to go to America, we thought. I found her grave in the Protestant Cemetery here entirely by accident, and then the hospital and the undertakers led me to you. If it upsets you to talk about what happened long ago I'll just say thank you for what you did then, and for the flowers I saw on the grave the other day, and leave you in peace.'

The hostility in Luisa's wrinkled face was giving way to sadness now. 'I can't get there now, but my daughter still takes the flowers for me.' Her thin, misshapen fingers twisted in her lap. 'I didn't like not going – I loved my English friend.'

'She was here before the war ended,' Clio said gently. 'Did you know her then?'

'No – only when she came back afterwards . . . looking for someone she'd known . . . a man, of course.'

'Did she . . . did she ever mention his name? I know it's a long time ago . . . probably too long for you to remember.'

'I'd have remembered, but she never did.' There was silence in the small room, and Clio thought that it was time to leave. Luisa's face said that she looked back on memories that were best left undisturbed. But suddenly she began to speak again, the words pouring out now, as if held bottled up for far too long.

'The war was just over but things were very bad – nothing worked, there was very little food, and we never really knew who was in charge. My parents had been killed in an air-raid; I was eighteen, hungry, and without money, but there were a lot of soldiers about so I sold myself to them – what else was there to do? Then I got pregnant and couldn't work any more.'

Luisa stared at Clio with eyes that now brimmed with tears. 'I was begging in the street when Antonia stopped and spoke to me. Other people didn't – they either gave beggars a few coins or else they ignored us and walked past; they didn't recognize that we were human. Only Antonia did that.'

'Then what happened?' Clio prompted her gently.

'She took me to her room, gave me food, and let me stay with her. I was still there when my daughter, Roberta, was born. We had very little, but we were happy. Antonia *made* us happy . . . made us laugh! But underneath I knew that *she* was sad. Then came a winter that was very cold and wet – imagine snow in Rome! – but she kept going out because we

Sally Stewart

needed money and I wasn't well enough to work. She got ill, and I tried . . . tried so hard to look after her . . . but she died.'

Clio held tight to Luisa's hands. 'Antonia had a job of some kind – that's why she had to go out?'

A faint, sad smile touched the face she stared at. 'Well, you could call it that – she was a *prostituta*, like me. No one would employ her because she didn't have the right papers. Just once I asked her why she didn't go back to England but she said she loved Rome, and in any case she'd behaved too badly to go home.'

'She left a husband and a small son there – my father. Even they didn't count enough – she needed the man she'd loved here. I suppose she never found him again.'

Luisa's reaction to this was very definite. 'Oh yes, she found him, but he sent her away – he was married himself by then. I think he pretended he didn't know her.'

There was another long silence before Clio asked her last question. 'How did you manage after Antonia died?'

'She left me a little money – imagine that! When she was dying she told me where to find it – she'd sold some jewellery she'd brought with her. It kept me and Roberta until I was well enough to get work as a housekeeper. But there was something she didn't sell.' Luisa fumbled in her pocket and brought out a man's gold signet ring, heavily engraved with a family coat-of-arms. 'I think the man had given it to her a long time ago. I just kept it, because I didn't know what else to do; now I can give it to you.'

Clio put the ring in her purse, and smiled tremulously at the woman she'd been afraid she might never find. 'I'm working in Rome for a few weeks, and now I must go back to my job. But I'd like to come again and meet your daughter. Will you let me do that?'

Luisa didn't answer the question immediately. 'You reminded me of Antonia just then when you smiled, even though you don't look like her.'

'I know – *she* was very beautiful!'

'She was . . . but not just to look at though . . . beautiful in herself was what my Antonia was.' Then Luisa remembered what she'd been asked. 'Roberta comes to see me on Saturday mornings – could you visit us then?'

Clio promised she would, kissed Luisa's lined cheek and said goodbye. Then, after telling the *soprintendente*, who was hovering outside the door, that she'd be coming back, she let herself out of the house. The morning would be gone before she got back to the *palazzo* but, even so, she couldn't go straight there. She walked to the Protestant Cemetery and stayed for a while by her grandmother's grave. How ridiculous it had been to think the night before that she could remotely have imagined what Antonia endured in Rome. But probably thanks to her, Luisa and her small daughter had been salvaged from the wreck of her own happiness. She'd even, Luisa remembered, made them laugh, and they had loved her in return; that was something else to remember.

At last, cramped from kneeling and beginning to shiver with cold, Clio left the quiet, peaceful place, and signalled to an empty taxi out in the road.

Twelve

M irella di Palma wasn't in the habit of consulting either of her sons – *she* was the hub of the family, its matriarch, and the natural order of things was that her children should take advice from her. But this was different; she'd had to summon Luigi – the clever one and a lawyer like his father – to help her decide what to do.

'*You* know about the book Paolo plans to write. He says that before he leaves Rome we must all meet to discuss whether or not he should go on with it. I take this to mean that he thinks we shan't like it.'

'I'm afraid it means a little more than that,' Luigi pointed out. 'I don't know exactly what he's uncovering, but since he went to Milan he's been concerned about *our* reactions to his and Clio Lambert's research.'

Mirella looked puzzled. 'What do our reactions have to do with it? I don't understand.'

'Nor do I at the moment, but Matteo is convinced that the problem concerns Gino.'

As he'd known she would, his mother took exception to this. '*Caro*, you know as well as I do that your brother is obsessed about his brother-in-law. Gino can no more help the fact that his family were Fascists than you can be blamed because your father believed in Communism.'

'It's more than that, Mamma,' Luigi said again. 'Gino's grandfather *was* Mussolini's known friend and confidant. Gino was brought up to believe only good of the Fascist revival of Italy; anything in it that might seem to the rest of us to be brutal or even evil had to be ignored.'

Mirella could see no way of denying this. 'All right, Prince Massini *was* what you say, and no doubt he died a disappointed, disillusioned man. But Gino *chose* to marry the daughter of a Communist patriot who spoke out against Fascism until the day he died. Gino knew the family he was marrying into. Mother of God, why can't we forget the past? Why must Paolo rake it all up again?'

Luigi gently brought her back to the matter in hand. 'You said he wants us to meet. I think we should, Mamma. For too long now we've pretended that we're a normal, united happy family; let's face the truth at last.'

He thought she might take refuge in anger or tears; being Mirella, she did neither. Instead she managed a painful smile. 'Tell me, please, whose family is normal! Nowadays we all have secrets to hide. Paulo must have his meeting, but I won't have Lorenza and Gino upset – *they*'re nearer to us than he is. And there's another thing: he wants to bring the English girl to our discussion, because he says she's involved in the book; the truth is, of course, that he wants her on his side.'

Luigi smiled and shook his head. 'If I know Clio Lambert, she'll just be herself – not on anybody's side.'

'I didn't realize that you *do* know her,' Mirella said disapprovingly. 'Why not find an Italian girl to admire?'

'I admire several,' he agreed, perfectly well aware that his failure to marry any of them was an ongoing irritation to his mother. Again he dragged her back to the subject of the meeting. 'When the time comes, would you like me to call the family together?'

She was tempted to leave it to him, but changed her mind; they would see it as the first sign that she was getting too old to control them. 'No, I'll attend to it myself, but I shan't invite them to dinner – it won't be a social occasion.'

He didn't argue, thinking that a long-drawn-out meal would make the evening in store even worse than it was already going to be. His cousin was used to the American way of doing things, but Italians preferred to sidle round problems, not meet them head-on. God knew how the discussion would end, but

Sally Stewart

it would be a miracle if Clio didn't see the di Palmas embroiled before it was over in a full-blooded Latin melodrama.

He walked back to his own apartment, still thinking of her. He wanted to know how her search was getting on; if he was honest with himself, he just wanted to see her. But he was shy, and unable to assume that she liked him to the extent that he very definitely liked *her*. His chief hope was that she'd need his help again – there was no difficulty involved when it came to being useful to her.

Clio was, in fact, uncertain what to say to anyone about her meeting with Luisa. If he'd been there, Costello would have asked her outright what had happened, but when she got back to the *palazzo* his note said that he'd gone to return Pietro Nenni's diary. She was able to return to the *pensione* that evening without seeing him, her mind still full of Antonia's story.

In the *pensione* dining room Monsignor Fiocca was back in his usual place that evening after a visit to a sick friend in Florence. She went to join him, realizing that he was the very person she needed to talk to first.

'Father, may I tell you some family history?' she asked when their meal was finished and the maid had brought coffee to the table. 'I need your help, of course!'

His gentle smile said that it was what he was there for, so she recounted Antonia's brief adventure, ending with her own visit to Luisa Caetani.

Monsignor Fiocca wasn't shocked, nor had she expected him to be. Instead, as usual, he went straight to the heart of the matter. 'You're troubled most of all, I think, about what to tell your family – the brother who obviously loved your grandmother dearly, and the sisters who've led a life so different from hers that they will find it hard to understand what happened to her. Should they be told the truth, or only as much of it as you think they can bear?'

'My problem in a nutshell,' Clio agreed sadly. 'You've listened to confessions for so many years that you know all

there is to know about the human heart; and nothing shocks
you. But Uncle Edward and my great-aunts aren't part of
today's world. They live in a secluded cathedral close, and
have no idea what some people must do in order to survive
at all. I suppose I want them to remember Antonia as she was,
not as a broken, unhappy creature forced to stand at street
corners selling sex.'

The old priest nodded, not offended by this plain speaking.
'We've talked a lot, you and I, about telling what is true,
instead of what is false or a distortion of the truth. As far as
your grandmother's story is concerned, why not let her brother
and sisters know part of it – that she came back to the place
where she'd been happy, that she took care of others and made
them happy, and that she fell sick in a particularly harsh
winter? That would be a sadness for them, but it would not
break their hearts.'

'That's what I hoped you'd say,' Clio admitted. 'Uncle
Edward will want to know that she *was* loved, and taken
care of at the end; the rest can be forgotten now.' But back
in her own room she remembered something that hadn't
been mentioned in her conversation downstairs. It was still
in her purse, and she took it out to stare at it again – a wide
circle of gold, with a square central panel engraved with the
figure of a rearing wolf – 'rampant' in heraldic terminology.
Beyond the fact that the family it represented had a taste
for fierce-looking emblems that spoke of their own arrogance, it told her nothing; 'Filippo' – her grandfather, she
had to keep reminding herself – remained as elusive as
ever. But now she scarcely cared. If he'd dismissed Antonia
as if she'd been a servant with ideas above her station he'd
treat her granddaughter in exactly the same way even if he
was still alive. She put the ring away, and sat down to write
to Edward Woodward; what needed to be told required
careful thought, not words carelessly used in a telephone
conversation.

There were two other people who knew about her search
for Luisa – Costello and Luigi di Palma – but she would

continue to follow her old friend's advice: tell them the truth, but not quite all of it. Exactly *how* Antonia had kept herself and Luisa and the child alive was something none of them needed to know; keeping that secret was the one small service she could do for her grandmother.

Clio was spared the call she might have had from Paul Costello, who'd hurried back to the *palazzo* in the hope of catching her before she left. He was on the point of picking up the telephone when Francesca unexpectedly arrived – elegant, seductive, and familiar as usual, and yet not quite as usual; he knew her intimately enough to sense that something had prompted a meeting they hadn't in fact arranged.

'A pleasure I didn't expect,' he said, smiling at her. 'I thought you were going to be otherwise engaged.'

Her shoulders lifted in a little shrug. 'I really couldn't face another dire evening with a bevy of visiting fashion editors; I decided to let them entertain each other after I'd welcomed them – very sweetly! – to Rome.'

'As bad as that? Sit down and recover while I pour you a strong drink.'

He spoke with the kind of amused tenderness she was used to from him, but this evening it required an effort. He was irritated, he realized, because all the way back to Rome it had seemed important to hear how Clio's meeting with Luisa Caetani had gone; at this moment it was *her* he wanted to talk to, not Francesca, and the realization made him feel slightly ashamed.

'I'll take you out to dinner,' he suggested to make up for it, 'as long as you don't expect me to do more than watch you eat. I was offered an enormous lunch by Pietro Nenni's wife – Lucia's mother, in other words.'

'I *had* made that connection,' Francesca said, sounding rather bored, 'but I can't understand why you had to go at all. Lucia could have taken the book back for you – in fact I can't see that it was needed here in the first place.'

118

Costello shook his head. 'It's an authentic document – what historians call a piece of primary research; of course Nenni should have been persuaded to let us see it.'

Francesca gave another weary shrug. 'If you say so, *caro*, who am I to disagree?'

He stared at her for a moment, remembering all the reasons why he shouldn't allow himself to be sharp with her. 'All right – you rather disapprove of what I'm doing. You think it's not worth the trouble I'm probably causing, because what happened fifty years ago has no relevance today. I can't agree with you, Francesca.'

She drank some of the whisky he'd poured for her, and smiled at him over the top of the glass. 'I didn't think you would.'

He didn't answer, and she went on herself in a voice so casual that he realized they'd reached the real reason for her unexpected visit.

'I spoke to Mirella this evening. She rang just as I was about to go out, so I couldn't talk to her for long, but I gathered that you want the family called together. It's worrying her rather – *amore*, is it really necessary?'

'I think so,' Costello answered. 'Otherwise I wouldn't have suggested it.' He sounded pleasant but firm, and at any other time she would have smiled and turned the conversation to something more amusing. But her main objection had still to be aired.

'Mirella also said that you want your English assistant to attend the meeting. She doesn't quite understand why and nor, I must say, do I.'

'*Cara* Francesca, my assistant has a name – Clio Lambert! I explained to my aunt that Clio knows more than I do about the matters we need to discuss; and she's intimately involved in producing the book I hope to write. It seems obvious to me that she ought to be there.'

Francesca managed a rather taut smile. 'We could say that I'm intimately involved with *you*, but you haven't suggested that I should be there!'

119

He realized with astonishment that the idea had never occurred to him, but he knew that it wouldn't do to say so. Beneath her air of brittle amusement he detected wounded pride and she was not someone he wanted to hurt in any way. He leaned forward and took hold of her hands,

'Sweetheart, it's going to be a difficult discussion about something you think I'd do better to abandon. The only way we shall be able get through it at all is to keep it as businesslike and impersonal as possible. I can't believe that you'd find it anything but an embarrassing waste of time. Mirella will tell you afterwards what happens, and so shall I; you'll be ideally placed to take a calm, impartial view! *Now* am I allowed to take you out to dinner?'

She shook her head. Her resentment over Clio Lambert was fading now, but because she was acutely aware of *him*, she knew that when she arrived he'd had to make an effort to look welcoming. The first feather-touch of fear felt cold on her skin. She'd never known that before, never dreamed of a moment coming when she no longer felt sure of him.

'No food, *amore*,' she said, smiling at him. 'I'd much rather you took me to bed and made love to me!'

He managed to return her smile. 'I'm sure the programme can be arranged.' And so it was, but not for the first time that evening he was aware of the effort that had to be made. Afterwards, content and reassured, she fell asleep; he lay beside her, tired and unhappy. For the past several years she'd been part of his life, recognized as such by his family and friends. At the beginning of their relationship, if she'd wanted marriage he'd have made her his wife. But they prided themselves on being sensible and sophisticated; matrimony had been a disaster for both of them – no need to risk it again. He knew though, that their coupling was intended to be permanent; Francesca took it for granted, and so had he; and so it must remain in future.

He stumbled from the warmth of the bed, pulled on a dressing-gown and sat looking out of the window; it was the brief hour of peace before the early-morning traffic began to appear. He could even hear the sound of the fountain in the middle of the square.

It was Francesca's voice that broke the silence. '*Amore*, is something wrong? Why are you sitting there?' She was sitting up in bed when he turned round, and he saw the shadow of anxiety in her face.

He smiled at her, and shook his head. 'Nothing's wrong . . . nothing at all, except that I think you're right! I'd have done better to let history take care of itself and leave the Muse alone.'

Not sure what that meant, she paid no attention to it. 'Dearest, I hate women who say "I told you so"! But it's sweet of you to agree with me. Let's go back to New York as soon as we can; I'm rather tired of Rome, aren't you?'

The following morning Clio rang Luigi's office and was told that he'd gone down to Naples again. No, there was no message, she told his helpful clerk – she would write him a note instead. She'd just finished scribbling it when Costello walked in from his own room. In the clear morning light she thought his face looked drawn, and he seemed disinclined to talk at all.

'I hope you liked Lucia's parents,' she ventured nevertheless.

He nodded after trying to remember, she thought, who they were. 'I did; Nenni was wary to begin with, but he loosened up and took me to see several survivors from the war – tough old men and their even tougher wives; we had a good time together.' Costello then inspected Clio's face but for once it told him nothing. 'Would you now like to know how the weather was or what Maria gave me for lunch, or am I going to be told how *you* got on yesterday?'

'I was working round to it,' she said. 'Luisa's *rifugio* is pleasant as far as such places go. She was unfriendly at first, until I explained that the family hadn't ignored Antonia from choice; from then on it was a very poignant trip back into the past for her. She's a small woman crippled by arthritis – it's her daughter, Roberta, who now takes flowers to Antonia's grave.'

'How much did she remember of the past?'

'Everything, I think; but she couldn't remember what she never knew – who "Filippo" was. Antonia didn't tell her that, only that she found him – by then he was married and not inclined to recall that he'd ever known her.'

'Poor Antonia,' Costello said quietly. 'What happened next?'

Clio's voice was sombre now. 'Conditions were still very bad here then but she . . . she got work of some kind, and met Luisa, who'd been orphaned in the war, begging in the street – pregnant and unable to work herself. Antonia took her in, and they shared what little they had from then on. Luisa's daughter was born and the three of them stayed together until Antonia fell sick in a particularly harsh winter and died. It happened fifty years ago but Luisa still weeps when she has to say that.'

'So looking after her and the child was what kept your grandmother from going home . . .?'

'I think so, although she *said* that she loved Rome and had behaved too badly to her family.'

Costello had one final question to ask. 'Does the "Filippo" trail come to an end now, or do you still want to find *him*?'

'It's come to a dead end, but now I think my father's right; I don't even want to know who Filippo was. I should hate him if I ever met him, supposing he's still alive. But there's too much hatred in the world already; and I'd rather leave the past behind now.'

'It's a tragic little story,' Costello said gently. 'I'm sorry Antonia didn't get her happy ending.'

'Me too, but at least I understand now what a lovely, brave person she was. Uncle Edward always *said* that, but all I knew of her then was that she'd abandoned a kind husband and a small child. Now I know her better.'

'Will they come to Rome – Edward and his sisters?'

'I'm sure so,' Clio said definitely. 'Nothing will keep them away.'

But when she next heard from Wells, it was to be given the astonishing news by Edward Woodward that for once in her life Hester was unwell. He would come alone for a very brief visit, and then hurry back to Vicars' Close.

Thirteen

A couple of days went by, with Costello often away from the *palazzo* – a state of affairs that Clio now welcomed. Then William Thompson rang, to ask whether his information had been of any use, but also to invite her out to dinner.

When they were settled at a restaurant table – he didn't choose Trastevere, and she was grateful for that – she was tempted to ask whether he *had* been warned how unsuitable she'd be for Boston or for embassy soireés. But she decided that she didn't know him well enough to be sure that he'd appreciate Costello's brand of humour.

William took the business of ordering their meal seriously, but when it was completed she told him that, thanks to him, she'd been able to find the person she was looking for. Then she went on to offer the apology she knew was due.

'I have to admit that Costello approached you on my behalf, William. I should have asked my own embassy people for help, but *his* name seemed likely to have more clout with you than I could muster! Forgive me, please.'

He looked amused by the confession rather than offended that he'd been made use of by his friend. 'We're here to help – whoever! May I know why there was someone you needed to find? It sounds like an interesting story.'

'Quite by accident I found my grandmother's grave here in the Protestant Cemetery. I knew she'd been here with the Army when Rome was liberated; afterwards she chose to disappear, but obviously ended her life here. Her grave is still cared for and I wanted to thank whoever was responsible.' Clio gave a faint smile. 'Not the complete story, but I don't know that myself yet.'

'But you have a connection with Rome even if you weren't aware of it,' William said seriously. 'Perhaps it wasn't a co-incidence that Paul's work brought you here.'

'That's what I think,' she agreed, pleased with an imaginative streak in him that she hadn't expected. But she hoped he wouldn't labour the point, and he didn't. Instead he spoke of what she was doing.

'You know, I can't quite square your research work with the sort of books Paul has written in the past. That's not to say I don't lap them up – I do, along with millions of other Costello fans. But I doubt if he'd claim that they contain any serious, properly documented history.'

'I'm sure he wouldn't, but this is something entirely different. He cares about it because it involves his family, but he also knows that the truth of what happened here has been systematically distorted or covered up by people with an interest in rewriting history. Unlikely as it may seem, he's a man with a mission!'

Looking at her eloquent face, William acknowledged to himself once again that his friend was no mean picker of women. 'My guess is that you like him, even though he claims you give him a hard time.'

Her smile reappeared at the memory of that first interview at the Savoy – it seemed a long time ago now. 'We didn't hit it off at all to begin with. I only got the job because the other candidates looked worse than I did!'

After a moment or two William grew serious again. 'He's been on the receiving end of too much attention. Success came suddenly when he was a young man; and that's hard to handle. Women like him a lot as well, and tend to throw themselves at him now that he's single again. I expect it's why he's holed up at his Connecticut place most of the time – he's grown not to like New York.'

'He told me about his wife.' Clio said quietly. 'Her death is something he still seems to blame himself for.'

William nodded – but didn't say he was surprised that she knew; Costello didn't freely hand that information out. 'He was in a bad way until he met Francesca Cortona. She may look much too glamorous for the rôle of ministering angel, but there's no doubt that's what she was. They've been very close ever since – not married, but a couple nevertheless.'

'Yes . . . you're right; that's exactly what they are,' she agreed, and then smiled at the waiter who was putting their first course on the table. 'What about you?' she asked when the waiter had wished them '*buon appetito*', and gone away. 'How much longer are you here, and what happens next?'

'Another year in Rome, then a different posting – in Paris or London, probably, provided I've done nothing to upset the Ambassador in the meantime, *or* his wife – very important, *that*! It depends most of all, of course, on the people in Washington.'

'You don't get to see very much of your home,' Clio pointed out. 'The novels of Henry James come to mind when I think of Boston, but I expect you'll tell me that isn't fair.'

'It isn't *un*fair,' William conceded with a smile. 'My parents are true Bostonians still, and they can't quite understand why I'm happy to live anywhere else. I expect I'll retire to it in twenty years from now, but that will be soon enough. Where might you be by then – in London?'

'No – more likely in a small place you won't even have heard of – Wells, in the county of Somerset. It's where my family have always lived, apart from my parents who prefer to be abroad. I shall become another Great-Aunt Hester, kind to stray cats, but regularly giving the dustman and the window-cleaner hell for not doing their work properly!'

'It won't happen that way. Some man will offer you a different future, if he hasn't done it already.'

Clio shook her head. 'No, I have it in mind to become an eccentric old spinster lady,' and she spoke so firmly that he realized he was being warned to leave the subject alone.

They spoke easily of other things, and it wasn't until they strolled back towards the *pensione* that William risked mentioning the future again. 'I assume you won't be here much longer, Clio. May I call you in London . . . so as not to lose touch?'

She agreed readily enough and rummaged in her purse for a card with her address and telephone number on it. As she pulled it out there was something else in her hand that it had caught on, and William glimpsed in the light of the street lamp the heavy gold band of a man's signet ring. She disentangled it and dropped the ring back in her purse again. Then she smiled faintly at him. 'A bit of the unfinished story I told you about.'

'Will you be able to finish it?' he asked, suspecting that it was her own story, which she didn't intend to share with him.

'No, not now.' Again it was brief, and sounded final.

They walked in silence after that until they reached the entrance to the *pensione.* She thanked him for an enjoyable evening, and didn't feel like protesting when he risked kissing her goodnight – a sweet, gentle kiss that seemed to match the man himself.

'I hope it's London next, not Paris,' she said with a smile, then set off up the staircase before he could get enough breath back to answer her.

At lunchtime the following day, on her way back from Rome's main library, she was caught in a downpour of rain, and dived into Miss Babington's Tearooms for shelter. Looking at her from a table in the corner was Matteo's wife.

'I thought this *might* be a day when you'd be here,' Isabella admitted, not mentioning that she'd come before in the hope of coinciding with Paolo's English assistant. 'It's a nice place – I like it!'

Smiling at her across the table, Clio agreed that it was.

Isabella now had a small confession to make. 'I didn't tell Matteo that we met in the Forum, but I *shall* say that we bumped into each other today.'

Clio answered lightly, as she thought she was required to. 'I hope he doesn't mind! Costello warned me when I first arrived that your husband, and Luigi too, weren't disposed to like the English; and it was obvious that Lorenza and Gino Forli don't think much of us either!'

'Luigi's ideas about the English have undergone a rather sudden change,' Isabella pointed out with a smile. 'Fortunately he doesn't share Gino's obsession with football!'

Her shy attempt at humour was the most encouraging sign Clio had seen so far that Isabella wasn't sunk too deep in melancholy to be restored to normal life. But she couldn't be allowed to think that her brother-in-law had been anything but helpful to a chance-met visitor that Costello had dumped in his lap.

'Luigi was kind enough to help me trace someone here who knew my grandmother when she lived in Rome after the war,' Clio said, with the feeling that she'd now explained this many times before. 'He said a lawyer had a better chance of getting information that I had.'

'Did you find the person you were looking for?' Isabella wanted to know.

'Yes, I did – I was able to meet her in an old people's home. I shall go and see her again before I leave Rome.'

Isabella's face was suddenly sad again. 'I want you to stay here. Wouldn't you like to marry Luigi and live in Rome?'

Clio smiled but shook her head. 'Rome's marvellous, and your brother-in-law is kindness itself; the fact remains that I belong in England – in London where I normally work, and in the west of England in a small beautiful cathedral city called Wells where my family have always lived. Anyway, you know very well that Romans don't hold with foreigners coming to settle in their city!'

'Not as a general rule,' Isabella agreed ruefully, 'but we *do* make exceptions!' She paused for a moment, then went on in a different tone of voice. 'You know about this meeting we all have to attend? Yes, of course you do; Mirella said that you were to come as well. I wish Paolo didn't think it was necessary; why ask *our* permission to publish his book if he believes it should be written?'

'He's afraid of hurting all of you,' Clio explained slowly. 'You look surprised when I say that because you see him as a large, arrogant American accustomed to always getting his own way. It's how I saw him myself to begin with. But he cares about other people's feelings, even though he tries to hide the fact.'

Isabella stared at her curiously. 'I think you like him . . . don't you?' It was the question William Thompson had asked, and it made Clio nervous. Did her face, her voice, change when she spoke about him? Were they *all* imagining that a bookish English freak had committed the usual idiocy of falling in love with a man who didn't even notice she was around unless he wanted a fact verified or a date checked? It was time to make matters clear.

'We work together for the moment; soon I shall have done all I can to help, and then I shall go back to London. It will be another job finished as far as I am concerned; for Costello it's only the beginning. He still has to write the book.' She hadn't answered the question she'd been asked, but by now Isabella would have lost interest in it anyway. In fact she'd now been reminded of something else.

'Matteo doesn't say very much, but I know he hates the idea of the family meeting. If it should get very heated, will you remember that it's the Italian way to make a lot of noise? We shall probably give the impression that we're about to murder each other, but the storm will blow over – it always does.'

Clio promised not to expect a phlegmatic English discussion, then, pointing out that the rain had stopped, suggested that it was time to leave. She said goodbye, but walked out wondering whether just for once Isabella hadn't been unduly optimistic. This might be the one storm that wouldn't blow over. If the di Palma family was about to be so riven that not even Mirella's authority could hold it together, then nothing would ever be quite the same again.

Back in the *palazzo* she found Costello in the office, examining her meticulously written-up notes. He looked up when she walked in. There was no greeting – well, she didn't expect that any more – but what he did say took her by surprise.

'If this damn book ever gets written, it'll be largely thanks to you. You're the research assistant every plodding author should pray for.' She thought he made it sound like an accusation, just in case she should imagine she'd been paid a compliment.

'John Wyndham's expectations of his staff are high,' she managed to say. 'We do our best for him.'

'I suppose you walked back from the library in the rain?'

'Yes, but I took refuge with Miss Babington and found Isabella there. I enjoyed talking to her.'

Costello stared at her. 'Are you *that* lonely here? It's my fault if so. I've not done much to look after you.' He didn't say why not – that something had changed in his relationship with Francesca. In New York they sometimes weren't together for weeks on end; but here in her home city she seemed to take it for granted that his evenings and nights were to be shared with her. It was as if he *had* married her, without noticing the fact.

Clio refused to have him think she couldn't manage on her own, or even that she had to. 'My social life is quite busy enough, thank you. Dinner with William Thompson last night was very pleasant; lunch today with Isabella; and Uncle Edward is arriving on Saturday morning – just for one night. He wants to hurry home again.'

'Then I'd better get you to the airport to meet him,' Costello said.

She was pleased to be able to shake her head. 'I needn't trouble you, but thank you for the offer.'

'William to the rescue again?' He knew the word would irritate her, but he was irritated himself; pushy people, diplomats.

She smiled very sweetly. 'No, Luigi! He rang this morning to suggest a visit to Tivoli on Saturday. I told him why I'd got to refuse, and he kindly offered to help me collect Uncle Edward instead.'

Costello was silent for a moment; if she expected some snide comment about his cousin, again he then surprised her. 'He's a nice man – I told you that once before.'

'And I agreed with you,' she said, but it seemed time to change the subject. 'What have you discovered about something called "P2"?'

'Not a lot, because it's been carefully kept under wraps. But I know it was a sinister, masonic organization in which a lot of very influential people were involved.'

Clio nodded. 'They were high-ranking service and secret service personnel, politicians and powerful businessmen who tried to incriminate known left-wingers in acts of terrorism, and ultimately planned a coup that would take over the country. The leaders were eventually tried but on appeal, of course, they all went free. It was a *very* secret society, but there's information to be found if you dig deep enough for it. At the library this morning I turned up some names that I'm afraid will trouble you. You know already about Prince Stefano Massini, who was one of the ring-leaders of the Decima Mas group implicated in the Piazzale Loreto massacre. He had two sons: Fausto – now the present Prince – whose daughter Carla married a rich Milanese businessman called Giancarlo Forli.'

'And became Gino's mother,' Costello put in.

'Yes, and there was a brother as well – called Filippo as it happened but of no concern to Antonia's story, because the Massinis were always in Milan, not Rome. Both men, Fausto and Filippo, were deeply involved in the P2 scandal and only escaped trial because of their influential friends.'

Clio stared at Costello's impassive face for a moment before going on. 'The di Palma family almost certainly knows nothing about "P2". Are you going to tell them . . . are you really going to be able to go on with something that will tear them apart?'

'They must listen to everything I know,' he finally answered. 'Then I shall let *them* decide what is to be done with the truth; but that may not be enough to preserve my own connection with the family. If you're a betting woman, I'll offer you odds they decide unanimously to scrub my name off the family tree! Even Matteo and Luigi will toe Mirella's line rather than see her hurt.'

He sounded wryly amused, but she knew him well enough by now to understand that he wasn't half-Italian for nothing; belief in the importance of the family had been bred in him, and it would matter very much if the di Palmas rejected him for the sake of protecting Lorenza's husband.

'There's one other possibility you might like to consider,' she suggested slowly. 'Instead of turning yourself into a historian, why not remain the story-teller you are? All the facts could be there, all the lies disentangled but woven round a fictitious family that doesn't exist. The result would be a big historical novel that could tell the truth about modern Italy without damaging your family.'

There was so long a silence in the room that she finally held up her hands in a little gesture of defeat. 'All right, it's a rotten idea; forget I mentioned it.'

Costello had buried his face in his hands for a moment, but now he looked across at her with dawning amusement in his face. 'I don't know whether it's that, or the brainchild of an inspired lunatic. I shall have to think about it and let you know!'

But he smiled as he said it, and there was something in the smile that she could store up for future comfort. Back in London when she remembered these weeks of shared work, she could now be certain that he'd think of them too with the same kind of contentment. Against all probability they *had* collaborated well together and enjoyed each other's company. It would be something to take home with her – not a lot, compared to the richness Francesca had; but something.

She thought the conversation was ended but he suddenly reverted to the subject of her great-uncle's visit.

'I expect you'd rather spend Saturday evening alone with Edward . . . or would you let me take you both to dinner?' The question was so simply asked that she changed her mind about refusing.

'I think he'd like to meet you again . . . and maybe sample some of Marco's *porchetta*!'

Costello nodded. 'Trastevere it shall be then; I'll pick you both up at the *pensione*.'

She suddenly smiled at him. 'To salve your conscience quite unnecessarily about not taking care of me?'

'That's right,' he agreed. 'It's the only reason I can think of.'

Fourteen

In the arrivals lounge at Fiumicino airport Clio and Luigi drank coffee while they waited for the flight from London to arrive. When he asked how she'd finally found Luisa Caetani it was time to explain that Costello's friend, William Thompson, had been helpful. Luigi smiled, but the smile was rueful.

'You were right to use some powerful diplomatic leverage, but I'm sorry you didn't let me try. I enjoy a battle with our overpaid, underworked bureaucrats!'

Clio firmly shook her head. 'You'd already done enough; I couldn't trouble you again, and it didn't seem as if Mr Thompson's working day was particularly stressful!'

Luigi was fair even to the unknown American Clio unfortunately seemed to like. 'It's the reassuring impression diplomats are trained to give, just as doctors are supposed never to seem in a hurry in hospitals – or so Matteo says!'

She seized the chance to talk about something else. 'You've just reminded me to mention that I've met Isabella a couple of times since your mother's dinner party. I was very wary of her then but I know her better now and like her.' Clio hesitated for a moment, then went on. 'She thinks the family discussion that Costello wants will probably get heated, but then she reckons you'll all go on afterwards as if it hadn't happened. Do you believe that?'

Luigi didn't answer immediately; the question seemed to need thinking about. 'I don't know what my cousin is going to say, although I can make some guesses. If my guesses are right we certainly shan't be able to pretend that nothing has changed.'

'That's Costello's own fear,' she admitted. 'He's prepared for the rest of you to hate him for rocking the boat – does that English expression mean anything to you?' Luigi nodded, smiling faintly at the anxious question, so she finished what she wanted him to know. 'He isn't doing it lightly, but I expect you know him well enough to realize that.'

She hoped he'd say that he did, but at that moment she spotted the tall, thin figure of Edward Woodward towering over the rest of the passengers coming off his flight. He saw her wave and came towards her; she went to meet him, and then brought him back to be introduced to Luigi.

On the drive back into Rome she explained that they'd be passing close by the cemetery. If he wasn't in need of a rest most of all, they could visit Antonia's grave on the way in, rather than make the journey again later.

'I'd *like* to go there now . . . I should indeed prefer that if Signor di Palma agrees,' he answered, courteous as always.

Luigi smiled at him in the driving mirror. 'Signor di Palma is entirely at your service – Clio knows that, I hope.'

She patted her great-uncle's thin hand. 'We're being beautifully looked after, are we not? Luigi was even kind enough to come and meet me when I first arrived, and he brought me here the day I found Grandmother's grave; so he knows a little of the story.'

She saw Edward nod, and felt sure that he understood: Luigi knew all that he needed to know about Antonia.

Arrived at the cemetery gate, he said that he would stay by the car until they were ready to leave – but there was to be no question of them feeling that they must hurry away; he was happy to wait.

'A charming man, my dear,' Edward said as they walked along the path. 'Are all Mr Costello's relatives as pleasant as that?'

'He has a nice brother and sister-in-law; the others don't make quite the same impression. But they all seem to think that the British made mistakes here when the war ended. I'm bound to say that they have cause to – we *did* allow Fascists to creep back into positions of influence again in order to block Communists getting into power.'

'Perhaps, but we had good reason to distrust the régime in Moscow,' Edward pointed out quietly. 'It was hoped we'd chosen the lesser of two evils.'

Clio halted suddenly, then steered him off the path on to wet grass. He could see now himself what he'd come to find – Antonia's lonely grave, graced by her friend's usual offering of fresh flowers.

'I told you that Luisa and her daughter take care of it,' Clio said in a husky voice. 'They still love the memory of her.'

Edward fumbled in one pocket of his overcoat and brought out a package wrapped in foil; then from the other he produced a small plastic trowel.

'Hester's brainwave,' he admitted unsteadily. 'She said the airport metal detector would spot a steel one.' The foil contained a rooted shoot of rosemary, carefully swathed in damp cotton-wool. He offered Clio a shame-faced smile. 'Against the rules, I know, but I wanted her to have a little bit of Vicars' Close here, just for remembrance.'

They dug the damp ground beside the grave and planted the rosemary shoot. Then at Edward's suggestion, they softly spoke the lovely words of the Nunc Dimittis together. 'I think she does rest here in peace,' he said afterwards. 'It's a quiet, lovely place and I'm so glad we *know* at last where she is.'

Clio took his arm and led him back along the path to Luigi. He halted before he'd gone very far and looked back. 'I hate to leave her here alone, but we have to, don't we?'

'I think so – this is where she was happy,' Clio said gently.

He nodded and didn't say anything more until he reached the car and thanked Luigi for waiting so patiently. At the door of the *pensione* they said goodbye to him when Clio's invitation to share a pot of afternoon tea with them had been refused on the grounds that the traveller now needed the rest he'd turned down earlier.

'I shall be here tomorrow to take you back to the airport

unless there's something I can do to help before then,' Luigi insisted.

'Dear friend, nothing at all,' she said unsteadily. 'You've been kindness itself as it is.' He touched her cheek with gentle fingers, shook hands with Edward and walked back to the car. They watched him drive away; then Clio smiled at the old man standing by her side. 'Dearest, I warned the *padrona* that *we* should be needing tea; so now come and meet Signora Rollo. She understands a little English, but she'll be enchanted if you can remember even a few words of Italian.'

Alone again when the tea had been brought and the *padrona* had made her new guest welcome, Clio asked for news of her great-aunt.

'She doesn't admit to anything at all except feeling a little tired,' Edward explained sadly. 'So unlike my dear Hester; she's been the family lynch-pin for all our adult lives. There *is* a problem with her heart, Tom Goodhew says, but he doesn't recommend inflicting major surgery on her at this late stage; better to let her live quietly as she is.'

'I suppose my other dear great-aunt tries to help too much, and fusses her,' Clio suggested with a rueful smile.

'If so, Hester doesn't complain; she knows that Hetty would choose to be unwell instead of her if she could.' Edward sipped the tea that had been poured for him before he went on. 'They both long to see *you*, of course, but they know that your work here isn't finished yet. Remembering Mr Costello's visit to Vicars' Close, they expect me to report that you are exhausted, homesick and unhappy, but it doesn't seem to me that you are any of those things. Is he easier to work for than we feared?'

'We sometimes disagree,' she answered carefully, 'even cross swords on occasion; but it doesn't matter because ill-feeling isn't left behind. By the way, he has offered to take us out to dinner this evening. You've time for a little nap, but if you'd rather stay in and eat here I'll ring and tell him so.'

Edward shook his head. 'No, don't do that – I should like to meet him again, and, nice though it is, I expect you see more than enough of this *pensione*.' Then he looked down at his venerable tweed suit. 'Hetty packed a clean shirt for me, but that's all I can do about changing for dinner.'

'You can go just as you are,' she said, smiling at him. 'Costello will take us to Trastevere across the river – it's old Rome, still fairly genuine, and not at all sophisticated.'

'Then no one will even notice me,' he suggested contentedly.

She doubted that – he was, even in his shabby tweeds, a distinguished-looking old man; the *trattoria*'s usual clientèle would notice him all right. But instead of saying so she ushered him upstairs to his room, with instructions to rest until Costello came to collect them.

It was an unwelcome surprise to find that Costello didn't arrive alone; beside him, talking graciously to Signora Rollo, was Francesca Cortona. Perhaps following instructions, she was inconspicuously dressed for once, but her genuine glamour – a word that properly used meant magical charm – couldn't be disguised. Clio saw Edward blink at the sight of her, then smile – his tribute to beauty when he encountered it.

Francesca smiled at Clio as well, content to have established the fact that where Paul Costello went she was entitled to go too.

'I told Edward it would be a simple evening,' she muttered to him while Francesca was getting on friendly terms with the male guest. 'He liked the idea of the *trattoria* I promised him.'

'It's still where we're going.' But the expression on Clio's face made him apologize. 'I'm sorry – a foursome that includes someone Edward doesn't know isn't what you expected. But Francesca thought she could help by rounding off the party.' It was a generous interpretation of her motive, but he couldn't explain that.

'Kind of her, I'm sure,' Clio commented in a voice from which all expression had been carefully removed. 'I dare say Edward will survive the bombardment of charm and go home to tell the girls that he had a very Roman evening.'

She wasn't looking at Costello, so missed the twitch of his

mouth. Instead, she was aware that her pleasure in the outing to Trastevere had seeped away like water losing itself in sand. How soon could she plead tiredness on her great-uncle's part and bring the evening to an end? But, with the general perversity of things, Edward gave every sign of enjoying himself as they took their places at the table Marco had waiting for them.

Having won her tussle with Costello by what she knew to be unfair means, Francesca was now well-nigh perfect in the rôle of unofficial but indispensable hostess – charming to her elderly guest, and even smilingly pleasant to the English assistant who regrettably had never realized that she was required to make herself invisible. Costello was a careful host, but it seemed to Clio that what the party had gained from Francesca's presence – and there was no doubt that she did add a mixture of Roman elegance and New Yorker pzazz – it had lost from his purely automatic attentiveness; his heart wasn't in it, as it had been when he first suggested the outing.

Clio watched Edward, silver head cocked on one side in the courteous way it always was when he listened to what someone else was saying. He *was* being entertained, and it was a better finish to the day than that the two of them should sadly contemplate the way Antonia's love affair with Rome had ended. She looked away to find Costello watching *her*, with an expression on his face that she couldn't interpret.

'Francesca was right,' she suddenly murmured. 'It *is* a help to have her here. I'm sorry I didn't realize that when you both arrived.'

Costello was still looking at her. 'Handsomely said; but then if Francesca is always right, all *your* ways are ways of pleasantness.'

She was silenced by that; for a very strange moment her heart seemed to stop beating, until she managed to remember that he enjoyed disconcerting her, and wasn't to be taken seriously.

'Don't tell me I've finally succeeded in getting the last word,' he remarked over her downbent head, and she knew that it had only been Costello amusing himself again. But when she looked up at him he was faintly smiling, and now she wasn't sure what to believe. It was a relief when Francesca decided that she'd been left to entertain Edward long enough, and drew Costello back into their conversation.

She was even more thankful when he suggested that it had been a long day for someone who'd begun travelling from Wells early in the morning. The voyager charmingly agreed, and they began the lengthy process of saying goodnight to Marco and his friendly staff. Back in the Via Margutta again a little while later, Clio left it to Edward to thank their hosts, and only spoke when Costello asked about the return trip to the airport in the morning.

'Luigi insists on taking us,' she was able to say. 'No wonder Uncle Edward thinks we are being showered with kindness.'

'Then I shall see you on Monday as usual, Miss Lambert. *Buona notte*,' he said with a sudden return to formality. He held out his hand to Edward but not to her, and she was glad of that; then they watched him hand Francesca back into the taxi, and Clio closed her mind to the thought of them driving back together to the apartment in the Palazzo Soria. All that must concern *her* was the elderly man beside her, now rather wearily climbing the stairs.

She kissed him goodnight at the door of his room, and then asked a final question.

'Which would you prefer tomorrow – we could go to the early service at the Anglican church, or ask Luigi to come in time to call at the cemetery again on our way to the airport?'

'I think we should check on our planting, don't you?' Edward suggested. 'Almighty God will understand, I'm sure.'

'I think so, too,' she agreed, smiling at him. 'Now, sleep well; I'll see you in the morning – Sunday breakfast in the dining room is at half past eight, and you can meet my dear friend, Monsignor Fiocca.'

Over coffee and rolls the next day the two old men took an instant liking to each other, as she'd known they would, and they were still deep in conversation when Luigi arrived. From then on it seemed no time at all before they were back at Fiumicino and the moment had come to say goodbye.

'It's been brief but very memorable,' Edward murmured unsteadily, '. . . in fact it's the crowning happiness of my life to have been able to say goodbye properly to Antonia.'

Clio nodded, blinking away the tears that she knew would upset him. 'I'll be home soon,' she promised in a voice that broke a little. 'Tell Hester and Hetty that, please – I'll come straight to Vicars' Close.'

Then his flight was called, and after a final hug they watched him walk away, the quintessential, diffident English gentleman that he was.

Clio mopped her eyes and tried to smile at Luigi. 'He's special,' she said, almost apologetically. 'That's why I'm a little upset to see him go.'

'He's very special,' Luigi agreed gently. 'But now, dear Clio, let me drive you back to Rome.'

Fifteen

Already it was the first day of March – six weeks since she'd arrived on a day of pouring rain to find a polite stranger waiting for her at the airport. Leaning out of her bedroom window, Clio registered a change in the fresh morning air; not yet quite spring but, as the Song of Solomon promised, the winter was past and the rains were over and gone. She counted up the weeks again, scarcely believing that she hadn't been in Rome for half a lifetime; that was what it felt like. It needed an effort now to remember that she'd set out thinking how interesting it would be to delve into the very period her unknown grandmother had lived through – enough to set against her lack of liking for the man she was going to work for.

'Interesting' didn't quite describe the discoveries of the past six weeks. She believed that she knew Antonia intimately now . . . and therefore felt sure that the man she'd seen in the photograph was her grandfather; Antonia hadn't been a prostitute from inclination, only from desperate necessity. Peter Lambert had been wrong about that, and one day she would tell him so.

But she'd become entangled as well in a family not her own; it mattered to her now what happened to the di Palmas; it mattered to her very much indeed that Paul Costello should be able to complete the task he'd set himself and, in doing it, somehow work out his own salvation. Twelve years was long enough to have blamed himself for the death of a girl who'd chosen to kill herself.

The only change she didn't choose to examine very closely

was her attitude towards Costello himself. Beyond admitting that he was a man it would be hard to forget, she proposed to think of him only as someone coupled with Francesca Cortona; their connection was now so close and clearly permanent that she couldn't separate them in her mind. But that had nothing to do with her insistent feeling that it was time to go home. There was little left for her to do, and whatever else he wanted he was capable of searching out himself; on the other hand, she was growing more and more certain that she was needed in Vicars' Close.

She closed her bedroom window at last, with the decision suddenly clear in her mind that she must ask for the date of her departure to be fixed, and half an hour later at the *palazzo* it didn't surprise her when Costello raised the subject himself as soon as she walked in – she'd noticed before that their trains of thought sometimes arrived coincidentally at the same station.

As usual, he began abruptly – no tactful lead-in bothered with. 'You said some while ago that you weren't ready to leave Rome. I get the impression that you are now. Am I right?'

She nodded, pierced by a stab of pain because it was clear that he wanted her not to disagree. If it was bearable to *choose* to go, it was much harder to feel that she was an encumbrance he wanted to be rid of.

'I'm getting anxious about Aunt Hester,' she managed to answer calmly, 'and in any case I think that what I can usefully do for you now is coming to an end. I was going to suggest a leaving date – a week from today, perhaps, if that sounds convenient?' She feared that she sounded like a nervous housemaid giving notice, unnaturally stiff because she suddenly wanted to weep. But Costello nodded – anxious, she thought, to accept what she suggested.

'A week from today gives me time to arrange the family showdown. You haven't forgotten, I hope, that I asked you to be there?'

'No, I hadn't forgotten,' Clio said politely. 'In fact I should prefer my visit to end with a bang rather than a whimper.' She was rather pleased with that – if he could disconcert her by quoting from the Book of Proverbs she'd offer him T. S. Eliot in return.

But something had changed between them, because the expression on his face said that her attempt at a joke had foundered. Their useful collaboration seemed to have come to an end and she abandoned the idea of asking whether he'd thought any more about her other suggestion – a historic novel in place of a work of history. She was on the point of retreating into the office when he spoke again.

'You've gone as far as you can with your grandmother's story – that no longer keeps you here; but something else could – I imagine you must know that Luigi has fallen in love with you.'

He'd done it before, she remembered; made something that should have sounded complimentary into an accusation. This time she met it head on.

'You mean that, having encouraged him in some unspecified but unfair way, I'm ready to leave him flat and go back happily to London. Well, I've been grateful for his kindness, but that's the only encouragement I've given him. I think it's true that he has what the French call a "*tendre*" for me at the moment, but I don't believe it will be long before he manages to remember that he's never liked the English anyway.'

She waited for Costello to answer, but he said nothing at all; and with the feeling that she'd protested much too much she walked away to her own room.

After she'd gone he sat for a while staring out of the window at the piazza, thronged with morning traffic as usual – no, not quite as usual; the first tourists were beginning to appear on the Spanish Steps on the other side of the square. Soon there'd be legions of them and the flower-sellers, coming out of hibernation too, would be setting up their stalls. But he wouldn't be there to watch them; the apartment would have a new tenant and he himself, thank God, would be back at Stonington. Then, as if the thought had released him from some kind of paralysis, he picked up the telephone and dialled Mirella di Palma's number.

Two evenings later he set out with Clio for his aunt's beautiful apartment. It was a silent taxi ride until they were almost outside the door.

'Cheer up,' he said suddenly. 'I won't let them eat you.'

'I doubt if it's me they'll want to eat,' she pointed out. 'What will happen if they all agree for once and ask you not to go on with the book?'

'I shall write it anyway,' he answered after a pause, 'but not publish it. The manuscript can be lodged at the Smithsonian for the benefit of future scholars. Your idea of a novel was brilliant, but I don't think I'm the man to write it; I'll go back to doing what I *can* manage. Does that sound unadventurous?'

'It sounds reasonable,' she managed to say.

'Then that's all right. Let's go in and get it over with, shall we?'

They found the others already there, Lorenza and Gino sitting near Mirella; Isabella and Matteo with Luigi were on the other side of the fireplace. Two empty chairs were left facing it, too clearly suggesting a courtroom dock, Clio couldn't help thinking. There was a polite murmur of greeting, but no cordiality in the air; even Luigi seemed to be withdrawn into some private communion with himself, which might simply, she thought, have been a fervent longing not to be there at all. But then he smiled at her and she felt better. He might reckon that he couldn't openly support Costello – after all this *was* a family affair – but at least he wasn't hostile.

Mirella took charge. They were there at Paolo's request. All she asked was that they should remember their ties of blood and kinship – excluding Signorina Lambert of course – and behave accordingly. Then she gestured to her nephew, and Costello got to his feet. He had the unhurried movements common to large men, and sauntered over to stand in front of the fireplace.

There was a moment or two in which Clio could inspect the rest of them: Mirella, still elegant but sharp-featured in old age; Lorenza groomed to the last eyelash and expensively dressed – probably by Versace; Gino by her side, dapper and handsome in an epicene way that Clio found distasteful. The trio opposite them were less glamorous but more real: Isabella's gaunt face looked pale and strained, Matteo's simply tired as usual. Luigi, hiding behind his horn-rimmed glasses, had been trained to give nothing away. What did they make of the man who stood looking at them, Clio wondered, and could he possibly be as calm as he seemed? If *she* could feel the tension in the air, so surely could he. But when he began to speak, his voice was quiet and impersonal; he might have been a university don taking an evening seminar.

'You know how this began: like you, probably, I was raised on the legends of wartime Italy – the heroism, the atrocities, the privations, and the sheer damn muddle of it all. Primarily, of course, I heard about my uncle's murder by the Germans, and the exploits of his fellow Partisans. The legends – embellished a bit perhaps – were grounded in facts; but as time went by the facts themselves became discredited. No longer patriots at all, the Partisans were now being depicted as militant Communists whose only allegiance was to Moscow. And the people who peddled these lies were the very same ones who'd been in power *before* the war began. That's why I decided to find the truth and make it heard. Straightforward so far, but it gets more complicated.'

He stopped speaking for a moment, and ran a hand through his hair. Now, Clio knew, it got not only complicated but dangerous, and she understood how fierce was the strain that he was managing to conceal.

'When I first met Clio in London, she warned me that the truth would be not only hard to find, but also painful – nothing in Italy was quite what it seemed, she said. I was too arrogant to listen, but I know better now; instead of black and white there are only infinite shades of grey. Partisans committed atrocities just as their German and Italian opponents did; and some of them were very last-minute patriots indeed, only jumping on the Resistance band-wagon when the Allied armies were on the mainland. But even though my Partisan heroes weren't always heroic at all, I still reckoned that their history – as truthful as I could make it – should be written and published.'

He hesitated now for so long that Matteo finally had to prompt him. 'But something has made you change your mind – some of the truth you found is *too* painful?'

Costello nodded. 'I learned in Milan about a secret organization called the Decima Mas – these were fanatical Fascists who carried out savage reprisals against the Partisans.'

'There were atrocities on *both* sides, you said,' Gino Forli now snapped. Then with an effort, he achieved a faintly patronizing smile. 'My dear Paolo, there was a bitterly fought war going on – men *were* fanatical, on one side or the other. Forgive me if I say that an American citizen is not well-placed to understand such things.'

'Of course you can say whatever you like, but I'm not quite at the end of my discoveries,' Costello told him. 'The man who betrayed Giorgio and his friends to the Germans, a leading light in the Decima Mas, was Prince Stefano Massini – your maternal great-grandfather, I believe.'

The silence in the room was so profound that Clio wondered if everyone had stopped breathing; there was no protest, no outcry, but equally not the faintest hope of any of them forgetting what had just been said.

It was Luigi who finally found his voice. 'So now we understand why we are here: are we, as a family, to urge Paulo to publish his research, or to implore him to burn it?'

'No, Luigi, that is *not* the question,' Lorenza suddenly cried out. 'Are we to *believe* in his so-called "discoveries" – why don't we ask that instead?' Then she turned on Costello. 'You don't belong here; you've no right to listen to slander about Gino's family and offer it as the truth.'

He shook his head. 'I'm afraid it's not slander, Lorenza – but the first-hand evidence of people who were there.'

Now it was Gino's turn. Ignoring Costello altogether, he spoke only to the others. 'It's no secret that my family were Fascists, as were millions of our countrymen. Like them, Prince Stefano believed that Il Duce worked miracles – under his leadership a poor, backward country had become proud and powerful again.' Then Gino stood up and went to stand in front of his mother-in-law. 'Mamma, Italy and Germany were allies, and aiding their enemies in time of war *was* treason. Forgive me for putting it so harshly, but that is why your young brother died, even if it's part of the truth that Paolo won't admit to in his book.'

Mirella put out her hand in what might have been a gesture of forgiveness and Gino kissed it very gracefully.

It was a pretty scene, Clio acknowledged to herself, but historical accuracy – which was what she was there for – unfortunately insisted that she spoil it. 'Could it really have been treason when the King had declared war on Germany at least six months before Giorgio Costello was shot?' she asked. 'By then, the Germans were not allies, but an occupying force.'

The question echoed in the room, quiet but insistent, until Matteo answered it. 'You're right, of course; by then treason didn't come into it. The Germans and their Fascist friends were simply trying to terrorize the population into not supporting the Partisans.'

It was so unanswerably true that Gino didn't even go on denying it. 'Vittorio Emmanuele was a coward,' he said instead – with a certain amount of truth, Clio acknowledged to herself. 'He betrayed Il Duce, and went into virtual hiding down in Brindisi, sheltered by the Americans and the British. Why should any true-born Italian have listened to what he said?'

Costello decided that it was time to call the meeting to order.

'We aren't here to argue about the dubious reputation of Italy's last king,' he reminded them. 'And I haven't quite finished my story. Perhaps you haven't heard of it, but there also was an infamous post-war organization known as "P2". Its members, all influential, all high-fliers, certainly *did* plot treason – nothing less than the overthrow of the Republic, which by then Italy was. Again our research led us to the name of Massini – your uncles, Fausto and Filippo,' he said directly to Gino. 'They escaped trial but they shouldn't have done.'

Gino was on his feet again now, livid and almost screaming. 'That's a *lie*. Filippo even left Milan and went down to Rome as a Partisan. My God, what more does a young man have to do to prove that he's a patriot? He stayed there after the war, helping to restore some kind of order, when he could have been living in comfort in Milan.'

Costello shook his head. 'Filippo infiltrated the Partisans as a spy, so that he could name them as Communists after the war.'

It got worse and worse, Clio thought; her heart wept for the numb despair on Mirella's face, and even Gino Forli she could feel sorry for, faced as he was by the implacable avenging presence Costello had become. She wanted to know what Luigi was thinking, but instead of looking in her direction he was studying his hands as though he hadn't seen them before.

At last Gino spoke again to his tormentor, with more self-control than she would have expected.

'If we can't let the past remain the past but must dig it up to apportion blame, then I will say this – it's easy enough to claim that the Fascists were at the bottom of everything you dislike, but why not remember that the countries that you and Miss Lambert represent were in control here? *Your* authorities disbanded the Insurrection Committees because they feared the Communists so much. Is that something you can conveniently deny?'

For the second time that evening Clio knew that she must say something, and she made a little gesture to Costello, asking him to let her speak.

'We can't deny what is historical fact,' she answered Gino quietly. 'It's true that our people – the British more than the Americans – saw Communism as a threat; though with good reason when Russian armies had already taken control of half of Europe. They chose to allow back into power people who gradually restored Italy to remarkable prosperity, but at the cost of what has dogged this country for the past fifty years – corruption in high places, the desperate weakening of the judiciary, collaboration with the Mafia and Cosa Nostra – the list could go on and on. Blame us for all of that if you want to, but you've had time enough since then to put your own house in order.'

Finally she stood up, speaking now directly to Costello. 'It's time for me to withdraw from what's supposed to be a family discussion.' She saw him about to object, and went firmly on. 'You *must* stay here, but I think I should leave, and I can easily find a taxi in Piazza Navona.' She walked over to Mirella di Palma and held out her hand. 'I'm sorry you've had to endure this evening.' Then, before anything else could be said, she left the room, and Mirella's manservant hovering outside the door let her out of the apartment.

Sixteen

She expected a sleepless night and got one. Like an aching tooth that couldn't be left alone even though touching it made things worse, her mind replayed the scene in Mirella's drawing room. She could hear again every word that had been said, and still feel against her skin the coldness in the room when Costello had spoken about his 'discoveries'. She pitied them all, even Gino Forli – perhaps him especially; he was being asked to bear the burden of crimes he may not even have known about.

There'd been something else to keep her awake; her mind refused to think about it, but she knew that the memory of what Gino had said lay in wait for the moment when she could no longer bear to ignore it.

At last her bedside clock signalled that she could dress and go downstairs to toy with the breakfast she couldn't eat. It was too early for anyone else to be in the dining room, and she was grateful for that. Monsignor Fiocca would have seen at once the trouble she was in. She let herself out into a street that was still only just waking up, knowing that she couldn't appear at the *palazzo* for at least another hour. Instead, she walked towards the river, crossed the Ponte Sant'Angelo, and headed for the tremendous, colonnaded piazza of St Peter's. The Irish journalist, Patrick O'Connor, had claimed it as his favourite summer-morning spot, she remembered. It was scarcely even spring yet, but she could see what he'd meant, and empty of people and tourist buses as it now was, she could hear the sound the fountains made. The basilica itself, immense and ornate, wasn't the kind of church that appealed to her, but she went inside and knelt down to pray. Then, to the chiming of a chorus of different church bells, she walked back to the *palazzo*.

Costello was there, waiting for her. 'You look in need of coffee,' he said after a quick glance at her. 'Follow me, please.' In the kitchen, she sat down at the table, suddenly aware that she'd walked a long way. Something needed to be said, but she waited until he'd brought mugs of coffee and sat down himself.

'I'm sorry if it looked as if I was deserting you last night, but it seemed the moment to leave.'

He nodded, then confirmed the nod. 'It was – you were right to go then.' But he halted for so long that she had to prompt him.

'Are you going to tell me what happened? The suspense is terrible, I have to say.'

'So it was last night,' he said in a sombre voice, 'although I think I knew all along what their choice was going to be. In the end two of them wanted the book written and published, four of them voted against.'

'Four?' Clio queried sharply. 'Mirella, Gino and Lorenza, of course, but who else?'

'Luigi finally agreed with them.' Costello saw the expression on her face, and shook his head. 'Don't blame him. He's a lawyer after all, much more realistic than his brother. Apart from that he can't bear to see Mirella and his sister hurt – and they *would* be if the Massini name was dragged in the mud.'

'So what will happen now?'

'What always happens here – nothing!' Costello said with wry bitterness. 'Matteo will continue to dream of a fairer, more honest society than the one he lives in. Gino will go on flirting with today's powerful people – new-style Fascists in fact, although Italy is theoretically a democracy. And Luigi will work doggedly at his job – a man who knows what is wrong but sees no hope of changing it.'

'What will *you* do?' Clio asked.

'I'll give all our material to the archives of the Smithsonian; at least it won't get lost there, and sometime someone will make good use of it. Don't imagine that the work we've done has been wasted.'

But she saw the sadness in his face and thought she understood what he was feeling. 'You mustn't despair of this beautiful but maddening country,' she suggested. 'People regularly write it off – they've been doing that down the centuries; but it always survives because its ordinary people are good and indestructible.'

Costello smiled then. 'My indispensable helpmate – right as usual!'

That silenced her for a moment, then she suddenly spoke again. 'Gino said something last night that I keep remembering.'

'I think I know what it is – his great-uncle went down to Rome, ostensibly to join the Partisans.' Costello stared at her across the table. 'I discovered that for myself, but I was afraid you'd read too much into it if I told you, and by then you'd said that you no longer wanted to know who your grandfather was.' His hands reached out to grasp hers where they rested on the table. 'My dear girl, you know better than I do that Filippo is a favourite name here; Antonia's lover doesn't have to have been Massini.'

Clio released herself, then regretted it – her hands felt lonely now. 'Edward knew, because she told him, that some princely family was involved. Gino wears a signet ring – do you happen to know how it's engraved? Does it have a crest belonging to the Forlis?'

Costello shook his head. 'They're rich Milanese merchants – Carla married into the family for its wealth, not its antecedents. But Gino likes to flaunt his aristocratic connections, so he uses his mother's family crest. I haven't examined it very closely, but it's quite striking – a rearing animal of some kind.'

Clio opened her purse and took out the ring Luisa Caetani had given her. 'Anything like this?'

Costello stared at it for a moment. 'Exactly like that! Did Luisa get it from your grandmother?'

'Antonia brought it back with her to Rome. She sold the rest of her jewellery when things got very hard, but not this. Luisa gave it to me when I went to see her; she'd kept it all these years, not knowing what to do with it.'

'So Filippo Massini *was* your grandfather,' Costello said slowly, '– still is; he's an old man now, but he's alive.' He hesitated a moment before going on. 'Do you intend the others to know about this – or Gino at least?'

'No; it has nothing to do with them, and last night was painful enough.'

'So – is it over now that *you* know . . . a line drawn under the past?'

'Not quite – I shall go to Milan before I fly home.' Clio saw the objection Costello was about to make and answered it. 'I know more of Antonia's story than you do. I haven't told Edward and never shall, but I'd like to tell you now. Filippo Massini gave her a child which he disowned, so she went to England. But she blamed his family, not him, and always believed that they were meant to be together. That's why she abandoned everything at home and came back to find him. He was married himself by then, and in order to get rid of her pretended that he didn't know her. Her dream was finally over but she was too ashamed to return to Mark Lambert. Then she found Luisa begging in the street – another reject, like herself.'

'At least she was able to work and keep her friend alive – there's comfort for you in that.'

'Not very much! Because she had no papers no one would employ her. She became what Luisa had been before she fell ill – a prostitute. That's how she caught pneumonia, walking the streets in a cold, wet winter.'

'Dear God,' Costello said quietly. 'No wonder you want to find Massini. But will you remember, please, that he sent Antonia away? He'll do the same with you almost certainly, and he'll do it with the insolence that comes from a long lifetime of wealth and privilege.'

Clio's face broke into an unexpected smile. 'There's nothing

he can do to hurt me, and I'm not going to ask him for anything
– I just want to give my grandfather back his ring!'

She saw Costello's strange look, as if he was seeing her for
the first time and, as usual when she most wanted to, she
couldn't penetrate that long, intent stare. 'Do you disapprove
very much?' she asked diffidently. '. . . Reckon I'm being too
cruel and vengeful?'

It was so far from what he *was* thinking that it took him a
moment to find an answer. 'No, *I*'d say it's the proper ending
to Antonia's story. But you aren't going to Milan alone – I'm
taking you.'

She was touched almost to tears by that, and couldn't say
that her fixed intention was to go by herself. Still wondering
how to reply, she heard the telephone ringing in her office,
and made it an excuse to leave the kitchen without explaining
that she refused to embroil him in a journey that she had to
make alone.

The caller, as she half expected, was Luigi, urgently asking
to see her. She *must*, please, allow him to take her to lunch.
The brief conversation over, she told Costello about it, hoping
that it would distract him from the subject of her visit to Milan.

'*You*'ll get an apologetic explanation from my cousin, and
I'll get hell from Francesca,' he said morosely. 'She was set
against the book from the outset, and she's very attached to
Mirella and Lorenza. By now she'll have heard *their* version
of what happened last night, and I shall be accused of achieving
nothing except upsetting them.'

'Then perhaps it's just as well that you're not going on with
it,' Clio suggested quietly. 'It would have been rather a funda-
mental thing to disagree about.' His nod confirmed it, but he
seemed to have lost interest in the conversation, and she
returned to her own room, to finish tying up whatever needed
attention before she returned to London.

Her arrangement with Luigi had been to meet him at a
nearby restaurant, to avoid the embarrassment of having to
meet Costello again so soon. She walked there wishing that
she could have avoided seeing him herself, but regret vanished

at the sight of his unhappy face as he stood up to greet her.

'I'm very glad to see you,' she managed to say at once, 'but only if you don't feel you must apologize for anything – Costello explained what happened.'

'It didn't "happen", Clio,' he pointed out when they were seated at the table. 'I *chose* to vote against Matteo and Isabella, despite knowing that what they wanted was right.'

'Well, if so, you had your own good reasons.' His expression didn't relax, and he seemed so unaware of the waiter hovering beside them that she ordered *spaghetti alla carbonara* for them both. 'Luigi, listen to me, please. You know as well as I do that Costello's book wouldn't have changed the way this country is run, but at least there will be a store of accurate archival material for future scholars – that's something gained, *non è vero?*'

'*Si – è vero,*' he conceded with a faint smile.

'There's this to remember as well,' she went on. 'Not everything that Gino claimed last night was wrong. Mussolini did things that *were* good for Italy, and if he hadn't sided with the Germans, the chances are that Italy would have been overrun by them anyway. Also true?'

'True enough,' Luigi agreed.

'Well then, throw in the fact that not all Communist Partisans were saints, and not all Fascists were double-dyed villains, and you're left with what Costello began by saying – that nothing here is quite what it seems. And, last but not least, you rightly can't bear the idea of punishing Gino and your family for Massini sins that he had no part in.'

'It's all true,' Luigi admitted, 'even though I think you're saying it to make me feel better.' He poured the wine the waiter had brought them but sat nursing his glass instead of drinking from it. 'Your work here is finished, I assume?'

Clio nodded. 'I've a couple of personal things to do; then I shall go home.'

'Would you stay if I asked you to – if I asked you to marry me?'

She had the odd feeling that he'd surprised *himself* as well as her with the abrupt question. Still thinking about a tactful reply, she was too late to stop him speaking again – with the painful shyness of a man not given to laying out his feelings for anyone else to see.

'I shan't do this very well because I have no experience, Clio – I always expected to remain a bachelor, you see. But I didn't bargain for *you* to come along and make me understand what I was missing. I can't imagine why you should abandon your life in London to share mine here; but I love you very much, and would give all I have to make you happy.'

'For a man with no experience you manage very well,' she said unsteadily. 'Dear Luigi, I *must* go home; Edward and my frail elderly aunts need help, and they gave *me* love and security when I needed looking after. But there's something else as well; unlike you, I haven't changed my mind about wanting to stay single.'

'Something happened in the past . . . am I right?'

'Yes. It was long time ago, but I decided then that I'd never depend for happiness solely on someone else in future.'

He gave a little nod, as if not surprised by what she'd just said. It could have been his own guiding principle, she thought, rashly abandoned for the moment because she was soon leaving Rome. The time might come when he'd be grateful to find himself still a bachelor.

'We shall stay in touch at least, Clio?' he asked next. '. . . You will come to Rome, and maybe I shall visit London – is it agreed?'

There was so much feeling in the question that she was afraid of having misjudged him; he *was* suffering, and there was nothing she could do to help him. 'You may have to visit Somerset,' she pointed out shakily. 'It's probably where I'll be.'

The waiter interrupted them again, and when he'd gone Luigi returned to what she'd said earlier. 'The personal things you still have to do – can I be of help?'

'Only by telling me about fast trains to Milan – I need to make a brief visit there.'

He looked curious, but he was too polite to question an unexpected journey. 'There's a frequent service from the Stazione Termini – the *dirittissimo* will get you there in not much more than three hours. And if you need to stay a night, try the Hotel Manin, in the street of the same name; it's comfortable and reasonably quiet.'

'All I needed to know,' she said with a smile. Then, as casually as if the subject had only just occurred to her, she asked another question. 'I suppose Gino's relatives live in semi-feudal style outside the city?'

'The Massini estates are much further north,' Luigi confirmed, 'run now by Fausto's eldest son. But *he* still lives in the family *palazzo* in the Via Morone; his brother and Gino's mother are there too, occupying a floor each in true Italian fashion.'

'It sounds very sensible,' Clio said with a faint shrug. Then she abandoned the subject of the Massinis and Milan, and talked instead of general things until it was time to leave the restaurant.

Luigi wanted to excort her back to the *palazzo*, but she said that she had shopping to do. 'I shall see you again – you won't go home without saying goodbye?' he wanted to know.

'Of course not, and I'll want to see Isabella and Matteo as well. The rest of your family will just be glad to see me go!' She smiled to show that it didn't matter very much, and quickly kissed his cheek. Then, in a moment, she was swallowed up in the crowd of lunchtime passers-by and he sadly headed for his office.

It was mid-afternoon when his half-hearted attempt to grapple with a document even more abstruse than usual was interrupted by a telephone call from his cousin.

'Luigi, sorry to disturb you. It's not about last night – that discussion is over and done with; I'm ringing about Clio. I know she was to have lunch with you, but she hasn't got back since; the witless girl who answered the *pensione* telephone seemed to think she'd come in, and then left again quite quickly. Did she say what she was up to?'

'We parted company at the restaurant,' Luigi reported. 'Clio merely said that she had some shopping to do, that's all.' He hesitated for a moment, then went on. 'Something was odd – she asked me about getting to Milan by train . . . just a brief visit that she wanted to make. Could she have been meaning to go straightaway? I recommended the Hotel Manin if she needed a room, and then we spoke of other things. Are you . . . are you anxious about her for some reason?'

'Not in the least,' Costello said untruthfully. 'I just think she's got a bloody nerve, romping off to Milan without telling me! Thanks, Luigi; I'll let you know when she turns up.' Then he banged down the telephone, and picked it up again a moment later to give a message to Francesca via her maid who answered the call. He was called out of Rome unexpectedly, but would ring Signorina Cortona as soon as he returned. Then he packed an overnight bag, locked up the apartment and walked to the garage that hired him a car when he needed one. He was going to drive all the way to Milan, he told himself, for the pleasure of firing Clio Lambert before she thought of something else she urgently needed to do.

Seventeen

Clio checked out of a hotel the following morning that, just as Luigi had promised, *was* quiet and comfortable. She'd arrived tired out the previous evening, but the dinner she forced herself to eat revived her, and afterwards she'd gone to bed and slept the night through.

Now, with the concierge's instructions committed to memory, she set out to walk to the Via Morone. Anxious not to arrive too early, she loitered in front of lavishly dressed shop windows. Milan had a different air about it from the capital she'd just left. Romans didn't feel the need to strive very hard; it was enough to be who they were. But the Milanese seemed prepared to strive very hard indeed; this was a northern city – aggressively busy and aggressively rich.

She knew what she had to make for – the famously Gothic cathedral, with its airborne forest of white marble pinnacles and saint-crowned spires. She skirted the Piazza della Scala, noticing that she could have heard a performance of *Il Trovatore* in the opera house that evening, and thought regretfully of Lucia. It would have been money well spent to give her the pleasure of a night at La Scala. By now she'd be wondering why the *signorina* hadn't arrived at the *palazzo*. But Costello would know, because Signora Rollo had been asked to tell him where she was.

The Via Morone street-sign put an end to any thought of Rome. All she had to do now was find the Palazzo Massini, and persuade a manservant – probably elderly and cantankerous – to let her through the front door. It was the massive pile she expected – heavy, rusticated stonework and iron grilles protecting the windows on the ground floor; grand but not beautiful. She thought it must give its inmates the impression of living in an imposing prison.

There *was* a hall porter, who stirred himself long enough to point to a list of names ornately displayed on the wall. The Massini she'd come to find was on the second floor. Presumably on the one below – the *piano nobile* in Italian terminology – lived the Prince himself, Filippo's brother, Fausto.

She climbed the marble staircase very slowly, to give her heartbeats a chance to calm down. It wasn't the moment to discover that she wanted very much *not* to be there at all. Costello had probably been right – she should have let the past rest in whatever peace it had found after fifty years. But equally it wasn't the moment to turn tail and run; she had to see it through now to the bitter end.

On the second-floor landing she chose what seemed to be the main door and rang the bell. A servant opened the door and stared at her, and she explained that she wished to see his *padrone*.

'He expects no one,' said the man, getting ready to close the door. 'Perhaps an appointment next time you call, *signorina*,' he suggested insolently.

'His granddaughter doesn't need an appointment. Open the door, please, and tell him I'm here.' Her voice was crisp with anger now, and an instruction was something he was too accustomed to being given to ignore. She walked into a wide hall, splendidly furnished and cared for, but with an air of deadness about it. There were no flowers on the elaborately carved table, no cushions on the chairs ranged along the walls, and no sign that anyone actually lived there.

She had to wait five minutes or so before the servant returned, now looking pleased.

'The *Signore* has no strange granddaughter. He says that you are to leave, *subito*.'

Clio walked to one of the chairs and sat down. She took the Massini signet ring from her purse, put it into a small silver tray on the table beside her, and held it out. 'I'm afraid you'll have to try again,' she suggested with a sweet smile. 'Tell the *Signore*, please, that I've brought it from England, and shan't leave until I've seen him.'

A longer wait now, but at last the servant returned. 'Come with me, *signorina*,' he said, this time with more curiosity in his voice than insolence. He was pleasantly aware of a mystery involving his employer, and he had an Italian's relish for a family intrigue.

She was led into a room that nothing, she thought, not even a fire glowing on both great stone hearths, could have made welcoming. There were long windows at each end, ornately curtained, but the daylight seemed to lose heart and peter out, leaving the huge room full of shadows. The man seated in a wing-chair didn't get up as she walked towards him, but she made allowances for that; he was old and might, for all she knew, be very infirm. His voice, though, was sharp enough when he spoke.

'I don't know who you are, or why you've forced your way into my home. Please explain, if you can, and then leave.'

Clio selected a chair within speaking distance that also allowed her to see him clearly. She was in no hurry to begin, feeling sure that having got this far she wouldn't be hustled out before he'd heard what she'd come to say. Such light as there was in the room fell on his face and silver hair. Old and lined – he must now be an octogenarian – it was hard to equate him with the smiling young man in Antonia's photograph; but in some odd way she could see in him the old man her father would one day become. The resemblance lay in their bone-structure, and the arrogant carriage of their heads.

'My reason for coming here requires you to listen to a story that began fifty years ago. My grandmother was with our Army in Rome, but at the end of 1944 she was dismissed and sent home, pregnant. Her lover declined to admit that he was responsible. She married in Somerset and her son was born there – my father.'

'I'm afraid the story is of no concern to me, *signorina*; leave now, if you please.'

'The story gets more interesting,' she suggested gently. 'My grandmother continued to love the man who'd given her the child – *this* man.' She got up and added Antonia's photograph to the ring on the tray beside him. 'You'll see his name written on the back – Filippo! She left her husband and went back to Rome to find him, hoping that in the interval her lover would have grown up enough to ignore his family's commands. She expected too much; he pretended that he couldn't even remember her. But, in sending her away he forgot that she might still have his ring. She died in Rome two years later of neglect and abuse; I found her grave by accident in the Protestant Cemetery in Rome – she was just twenty-eight.'

'The story is sad,' Filippo Massini said after a long pause, 'but it belongs to your family, not mine. Filippo is a common enough name, and the ring – admittedly with the Massini crest on it – could have been lost or stolen. You merely assume that *I* gave it to your grandmother, but we are Milanese people, not Romans.'

Clio nodded. 'That's true; but you joined the Partisans in *Rome*, not Milan. The records show that clearly, and you stayed down there for years after the war ended.' She held up her hands in a little gesture of despair. 'If you refuse even now to admit that you knew Antonia Woodward – that was her name then – I can't make you. But I don't need modern DNA tests to prove that you sired my father – at your age he will look just like you.'

Now the silence seemed to go for ever, but what she'd come to say had been said; it was his turn to speak.

'Why have you come?' he asked at last. 'What is it you want?'

She pointed to the ring. 'I came to bring that – I don't want it, I don't want anything of yours; I *would* like you to admit the truth, but that seems too much to ask. So now I might as well leave, as you suggested.'

She stood up to go, but he suddenly shouted, 'Sit *down* . . . no, I'm sorry . . . *please* sit down. I live alone now and forget my manners. You're a child still compared with me – what can you know about this country . . . about the futile, wasted years of war, and the muddle of it all afterwards?'

The contemptuous question sparked anger in her again. 'I know quite a lot, by listening to what other people have remembered, or by studying what they've written about it. I know that the Massinis were, perhaps still are, Fascists; that Prince Stefano was involved with the infamous Decima Mas; and that you and your brother were implicated in the no less discreditable "P2".'

To her surprise he suddenly smiled, almost with approval. 'So . . . you *have* learnt a little, at least, but I'm afraid you use words too loosely. My father and his friends simply punished men who were dangerous insurgents; my brother and I were proud to help forestall a Communist takeover of this country. We saw nothing to be ashamed of in that.'

'We shan't agree,' Clio said quietly. 'Remember that I was raised in a more liberal society – we may vote governments out of power sometimes; we don't hijack them or assassinate our opponents.'

'A society gone soft,' Massini suggested with a sneer. 'Under Il Duce we fought to recover the empire we deserved; you British gave yours away. You should have joined the Germans, not fought them; together you could have ruled half the world.'

'We shan't agree about that either,' she pointed out. She was about to announce that she was leaving when he suddenly stood up himself with the aid of the silver-knobbed stick by his chair. On his feet, he was a tall man, now skeletally thin and frail.

'I do remember Antonia – even after all these years – and you don't remind me of her at all. She was fair, and always happy when I first knew her. I was twenty-five, aflame with the excitement of the dangerous work I was doing in Rome and pitchforked into love at the sight of her. But my father ruled out any thought of marriage – I was already half-promised to the daughter of wealthy friends in Milan. Antonia went home, and I was thankful – she would be safe there, and so would the child.'

He stopped talking for a moment and wiped a trembling hand across his eyes. 'I was already married when she returned to Rome – what could I do but send her away? She should have gone back to England.' A bitter smile touched his mouth for a moment. 'Will it make you happier to know that my marriage was a failure? My wife presented me with two daughters, and then left; we lived separate lives until she died two years ago. I had no son, therefore no one to carry on my name.'

'You *have* a son,' Clio reminded him, 'but his name is Lambert, not Massini. He prefers to live in America, with my stepmother and his new family.'

'I'm sorry I denied you to Tomaso when you arrived,' Filippo Massini said unexpectedly. 'I think I always knew that one day I'd be confronted with the past, but when the moment came my courage failed me. I apologize.'

'Mine almost failed me *outside* the door,' Clio admitted, because he looked old and lonely, and she had inflicted the interview on him without warning.

'You spoke of your grandmother's grave,' he remembered. 'Is it taken care of?'

'Yes, by someone she befriended and helped to survive.'

Massini stared at Clio, as if registering properly for the first time the blood link between them. He could see it now, of course, in her tall slenderness and delicately cut features; she wasn't like Antonia, but she *was* a Massini, a granddaughter he'd been tempted to reject without ever meeting her.

'What are you going to do now?' he asked.

'Catch a train back to Rome, and return to London in a day or two. The research work I came to do is finished now.' She was tempted for a moment to explain about Costello's book; but it wasn't her story to tell, and in any case the man in front of her looked exhausted already.

She stood up and stared at him in her turn. 'I'm glad I came,' she said gently. 'The past *can* be buried now, and Antonia can rest in peace; that's all I wanted.'

He gestured to a writing table against the wall. 'Leave me

your address, please; I should like to know how to get in touch with you.'

She wrote it down for him, then almost smiled. 'I *am* going now – don't trouble Tomaso; I can find my own way out.' And before he could protest she walked out of the room and closed the door behind her.

It didn't occur to her to look for a taxi-rank out in the street; she just walked back the way she'd come. She was sufficiently aware of where she was to retrace her steps, but otherwise was still reliving her interview at the *palazzo*. The streets were busy, and she paid no attention to the people around her; but one of them suddenly spoke beside her as she waited for traffic lights to change. It was the voice of Paul Costello.

'This English passion for walking will be the death of me. Thank God the Galleria's just across the road – somewhere we can sit down at last.'

He got that far because for the moment she was speechless, and having to fight a strong inclination to burst into tears. She stared at him with eyes that looked over-large and haunted, and he understood the ordeal that the morning had been for her. He took her by the hand and led her into Milan's beautiful, covered arcade, and stopped at the first café they came to.

Still without speaking she subsided into a chair and ducked her head for a moment, willing herself not to faint. Costello calmly ordered coffee and croissants, and finally she was able to look up and try to smile.

'You're like the demon king in pantomime – always popping up when I least expect you.'

He shook his head. 'I did mention that you weren't to come alone, but you don't listen to a word I say.' Then he smiled at her with enormous kindness. 'You're as pale as a ghost. Drink your coffee, and eat something. Then I'll hear what happened this morning – if you want to talk about it, that is.'

She did as she was told, discovering suddenly that she *was* hungry as well as very tired. It seemed no more strange than the rest of her life in the past few weeks had consistently become that he should be there with her now, instead of several hundred miles away. She didn't even propose to ask why or how; it was enough to know that for the moment she need worry about nothing at all; the sky could fall, but it wouldn't matter – Costello would take care of it.

'I was nearly turned away before I got inside the door,' she began, 'and things weren't much better when I *did* finally come face to face with my grandfather. I went, of course, in the expectation of hating him, so it was *very* confusing to find myself pitying him deeply instead. He's old and lonely but still faithful to the memory of Benito Mussolini and the Fascist cause.' She smiled faintly at Costello's expression. 'Wrongheaded if you like, but also admirable in its loyal way! He tried to suggest that he hadn't fathered Antonia's child, but when I said that his son resembled him he rather suddenly caved in.'

'I know why that is from Gino Forli,' Costello said quietly. 'It's one of life's more bitter ironies that his unsuccessful marriage only produced two daughters who take after a wife he didn't love. It will eat like acid into his soul to think that Antonia *had* produced a son who was his.'

'Yes, I'm afraid so,' Clio was forced to agree. 'I'm not sorry I came, but it's over at last. I can go home and tell Edward we've done with the past.' She smiled across the table at her companion. 'Thank you for being here – now I'm myself again. Assuming you also came by train, there's one leaving for Rome at midday; we can catch it if we hurry.'

'I came by car, and I suggest that we both go back that way.' Aware that she was about to refuse, he went straight on. 'We'll do what we haven't allowed ourselves to do so far, just enjoy Italy – no work, no long-buried secrets to uncover, no pain! A brief stop in Parma, then a longish drive to dinner and a night in Siena; a little research into pleasure for a change. Don't you think we've earned it?'

Clio wavered and was lost. It was wrong to reject kindness, and that was what had inspired his offer. He was quite capable of remembering himself that Francesca would be without him in Rome; but she had a host of friends there, and in any case they'd soon be flying back to America together.

'Earned or not, I accept your kind suggestion, provided dinner is simple. I didn't even bring a change of sweater.'

'You know me – a humble *trattoria* is where I feel at home. Now, all we have to do is find where I parked the car last night, then we'll say goodbye to Milan. It's not a city I like; and even Francesca's dubious claim that it's the fashion centre of the world doesn't alter my opinion.'

'Not so dubious,' Clio said wistfully, eyeing a mouth-watering display of shoes in a nearby window. 'Otherwise I agree with you – let's leave Milan behind.' It wouldn't be so easy to abandon her memory of an old, embittered man waiting to die alone, but that was the price she had to pay for coming to find him.

Eighteen

The long morning drive left her with images of a flat, tended landscape dotted with old towns – Pavia, Piacenza just south of a loop in the Po River, and then Parma itself. There were tantalizing glimpses of its cathedral, campanile and baptistery, the central group of any ancient Italian city, and signs everywhere of the famous hams and cheese that made it the country's gastronomic capital; but Costello firmly ruled out sightseeing – Siena was still a long way south. Clio didn't mind what they did. She recognized, as she thought he did himself, that they'd stolen a day from time. Every minute was to be counted – a shining bead on a necklace she would never be given to wear again.

Siena, when they arrived in the evening, *was* familiar; she could even direct Costello to a *pensione* overlooking the beautiful, central piazza where the Palio would be run later in the year. When she came downstairs after a quick shower he'd been quicker still himself, and even out already to select the restaurant that he liked the look of most.

But it seemed to her that he looked tired now, and distant. She'd been wrong to imagine that he was content to be there. He was probably as sick of her family affairs as he was of his own, and only wanting to take Francesca Cortona back to New York or Stonington as soon as possible.

They walked almost in silence to the restaurant he'd chosen, but once the complicated business of ordering dinner had been settled she decided to make him talk.

'I don't understand how you came to be in Milan – I asked Signora Rollo to telephone you this morning to say where I was.'

Costello put down the wine-list he was studying. 'When you didn't come back from lunch yesterday I rang Luigi. He was kind enough to mention that you'd asked about getting to Milan; he even gave me the name of the hotel he'd recommended. All I had to do after that was drive there.'

She was debating whether or not to say that she wished he hadn't bothered, when he spoke again.

'I suppose Luigi asked you to stay in Italy and marry him?'

Clio nodded, but again it was Costello who spoke. 'You were quite right to turn him down.'

'Why be so certain that I did?' Her eyes challenged him across the table, suddenly bright with anger.

He could have said that he wasn't certain at all . . . that she could have done far worse than take a good man who would cherish her for the rest of his life . . . or even that her refusal was simply what he most wanted to hear. But, instead, he gave his little shrug. 'You'd have told Luigi about Filippo Massini and *he*'d have gone with you to Milan.'

'He's sad, but not *too* sad, I hope,' Clio acknowledged, 'because a part of him still hankers for a bachelor life. He *is* upset by the idea of having let you down, but I expect you know that already.'

It was Costello's turn to nod. 'I hope I've reassured him. It's more important that he and Matteo shouldn't fall out; if that were to happen I should really feel that I'd done much more harm than good.'

'Matteo won't let it happen,' Clio insisted. 'He's too wise and kind.' She hesitated for a moment over what she was going to say next. 'Will that family showdown make any difference to Gino Forli, do you suppose?'

'None at all – aristocrats, among whom he includes himself, aren't like the rest of us; they don't have to mend their ways. It's why they lose their heads occasionally!'

She smiled at that, but grew serious again. 'It's a strange feeling to realize that his mother and my father are cousins. The Massini arrogance is in all of *them*, but not in me, I hope; it's an unpleasant family trait.'

170

'No, I've told you before that your besetting sin is to mislead people.'

She thought that sounded even worse, but the waiter arrived at that moment with the *scaloppini di vitello* that they'd ordered, and it was easy to ignore what he'd said. There was little chance of being in Siena and not talking about the Palio – the murderously dangerous horse-race that took place twice each summer between every *contrada* in the city. They'd both seen it, and in the course of arguing about its mixture of fantastic beauty and downright chicanery, ease returned. Costello had recovered from whatever irritation or regret he'd been feeling and become himself again, perceptive, funny, and intolerant and deeply humane, both at the same time.

Awkwardness only returned, suddenly, when he finally announced that it was time to walk back to the *pensione*. Out in the piazza it was a fine, mild night, and moonlight laid a wash of silver over the city's medieval loveliness.

'Romantic enough for you?' he enquired as they walked along. 'I'm sure we ought to be lingering in all these shadowy corners made for lovers but, God help me, it must be the first sign of middle-age that I can't help remembering our very early start tomorrow!'

The careless, amused apology – if that was what it was – gave her a stab of pain that transfixed her for a moment. Then she was able to move again, and pride came mercifully to her rescue. 'I shall truthfully point out that it's not our romantic youth but inclination that is lacking,' she managed to suggest with a good enough imitation of his own tone. 'We agreed right at the beginning that we didn't match!'

'So we did,' he answered after a pause. 'And I've just remembered something else as well – I set out for Milan with the intention of firing the most troublesome, argumentative assistant I'm ever likely to have.'

She couldn't, now, hear a trace of amusement in his voice, and knew that she must believe what he'd just said. 'Then it's a good thing I'm going home as soon as I've seen Luisa Caetani again tomorrow – that makes it scarcely worth the bother of giving me notice.' With the *pensione* just ahead of them, and escape from any more hurt in sight, she managed to smile at him. 'What time is "very early" tomorrow? The sooner we get back to Rome the better as far as I'm concerned.'

'Then we'll leave at eight,' he said deliberately, ending the conversation until she said a brief goodnight in the *pensione*'s hallway.

The following morning, anxious to settle her own bill, she was thwarted to be told that he'd already done it. She thanked him stiffly when he walked down the stairs a moment later, then headed for the door too quickly to see the glimmer of amusement in his face. He was serious again when he caught up with her, and the rest of the journey was accomplished by two polite but uncommunicative travellers who happened to be sharing the same car, but had nothing else in common at all. She whipped herself with the magnitude of her own stupidity – the idea that he'd see the journey back to Rome as anything but a tiresome, exhausting necessity now seemed almost heroic in its error. But what *he* was thinking, she had no clue to at all; he merely concentrated on the road and the traffic they had to share it with, and drove at a speed that was only just on the right side of safety.

They drew up in the Via Margutta as dusk was falling, and she thought she could feel in her own bones Costello's own mixture of tiredness and relief. He'd be longing to get rid of her and pick up his own interrupted life again, but before getting out of the car she must first *try* to sound grateful for what he'd done.

'I've been an awful, time-consuming nuisance,' she said quietly. 'Thank you, though, for taking all that trouble to keep an eye on me. I think you'll find that I've left everything in order in the office. I'll go and see Luisa and her daughter tomorrow, and probably take a flight home on Sunday. So we might as well say goodbye now. It's been a . . . very interesting two months, taken all in all.'

'What happens after that?' Costello asked. 'You go back to John Wyndham's staff in London?'

'Yes, unless things at home are worse than I think they are.' Her mouth sketched a smile. 'What about you – back to the brave New World by the next available flight, with the dust of old, muddled, maddening Europe wiped thankfully off your feet?'

'Something like that,' he agreed. Then his hand came down sharply on the steering-wheel. '*Nothing* like that, as it happens.'

There was no reason not to get out of the car, no need for her to stay, nor for him to explain what he'd just said. But she waited, aware that it was what he wanted her to do.

'I told you about my wife's suicide,' he went on abruptly. 'I didn't say that I pretty much went to pieces after that – felt far too sorry for myself, drank a great deal, and did no work. I was quite successfully launched on the road to ruin when my friend John Wyndham came over to New York and saw the mess I was in. He introduced me to Francesca and she took me in hand. Until recently she's been against marrying again, after a failed first attempt, and so, God knows, have I, but I think Francesca has changed.' Costello suddenly twisted round to stare at Clio. 'Do you understand? She and I have been together a long time. We shall marry if that's what she now wants.'

'Why not, when you obviously mean so much to each other?' Clio agreed in a calm voice. She was pierced by a sudden fear that he thought she might have expected something else. More of an effort was needed, and she dredged up a smile that would have convinced doubting Thomas himself. 'Every other man Francesca knows will probably hate you for it, but that mustn't stop you. I'm very glad she's changed her mind. Now, I must dash . . . I've just remembered that Isabella di Palma is someone else I must say goodbye to before I leave. Remember me to Lucia, please, and say that I enjoyed her singing.' She quickly unlatched the car door and stepped out on to the pavement, then bolted up the staircase with a cheerful wave. After a moment she heard him start the engine and drive away; now she could safely weep, lie down and die of sadness maybe, or just get on with a life that had seemed perfectly adequate until John Wyndham sent her to the Savoy Hotel two months ago.

Showered and changed out of clothes that she seemed to have been wearing for days, it was possible to go down to the dining room as usual. Since she'd decided on life, not death, a first positive step was to eat something whether she felt hungry or not. There was no sign of her old friend at his corner table and she was grateful for that; even *his* gentle company was more than she wanted at the moment.

To ward off anyone else's attempt to be sociable, she sat through dinner industriously compiling a list of things to be done the next day: first, obviously, she must book her flight home on Sunday and then ring Edward at Vicars' Close; she had to visit Antonia's grave and call again on Luisa to meet her daughter; say goodbye to some at least of the di Palma family; and probably write a note to William Thompson – it seemed unlikely that a Saturday would find him toiling at the embassy. Throw in the packing that had to be done, and a farewell visit to Marcus Aurelius and his old horse on the Campidoglio, and there'd be no time at all in which to remember that she'd said a final goodbye to Paul Costello.

Her mind, so sensibly clear about everything else, shied away from facing this one fact; it would have to be dealt with, but not just yet. She intended to let it lie in some unvisited corner of her box of memories; then, when she'd got quite used to it being there, she'd confront it again and remember these two strange months in Rome.

By mid-morning she'd ticked off the most urgent items on her list; now she could set out for the Protestant Cemetery and the Via della Piramide, stopping on the way to buy flowers for her grandmother's grave and a present for Luisa. She said goodbye to Antonia, and then walked on to the *rifugio*, to find that Luisa's daughter had already arrived. Unlike her mother, whose lined face still showed traces of the prettiness she'd once had, Roberta was plain and stoutly built, but her smile was warm, and she blushed with pleasure when Clio thanked her for the flowers she took to the cemetery.

'I don't quite remember her, *signorina*,' she confessed. 'I was too young. But it's a small thing to tend her grave for my mother.'

Then Clio spoke directly to Luisa. 'I found the man Antonia loved – he's old and frail and lives in Milan. The ring you gave me is now back with him where it belongs, so her story is complete at last.'

'What was the man like? Someone to hate, I'm sure,' Luisa suggested.

Clio hesitated over how to answer. 'It's true that I wanted to,' she admitted, 'but I find it hard to hate an old man who lives on loneliness and bitter regret.' It was as much as she wanted to say about Filippo Massini, and she produced her gift for Luisa instead, suddenly afraid that the choice had been all wrong. But the cardigan's delicate pink wool and gilt buttons had first to be stroked, and then Luisa held its softness against her face, murmuring, '*Che bella . . . che bellisima!*'

With her eyes suddenly full of tears, she listened to Clio explaining that her work in Rome was finished; now she must return to London. 'But we shall keep in touch,' Clio promised. 'Here is my address, and whenever I can, I'll come back to see you.'

'Yes, please . . . please,' insisted Luisa unsteadily. 'We'd like that, wouldn't we, Roberta?' Clio hugged them both, and said goodbye, and left the house, thinking that without the help of the old lady in Trastevere she would never have traced Luisa and her daughter at all. She'd once explained to Costello her conviction that *her* life's pattern had been linked with Antonia's, and she was more sure of it than ever now. It didn't rule out the freedom to make choices that dictated whether patterns were completed or not; she simply found it comforting to believe that everything that happened was purposeful, and not just the result of some chaotic universal muddle.

It was lunchtime already; her last day in Rome was wearing away too quickly. She stopped for coffee and a sandwich in a café in the Via Veneto, having delivered her note to William Thompson at the embassy. Only the di Palmas were left now, and she decided in the end to go back and ring them from the *pensione*. It was Isabella who answered her call; Matteo and Luigi were out together, visiting an old friend of Mario di Palma's. Clio *must* come and wait for them to return.

Rather wearily now, she set out again for the address Isabella had given her, aware that she was at a low ebb for a conversation with Matteo's intense wife. But she was struck at once by a change in Isabella, and if the alteration was heart-lifting, the explanation was simple.

'I've got a job,' Isabella said proudly. 'Well, Matteo got it for me, of course; but he's sure that I can do it.'

'Of course you can, but what *is* it?' Clio asked, smiling at her.

'I'm to help look after small children, babies even, who are waiting for adoption.' She saw doubt for a moment in her visitor's face, but firmly shook her head. 'It's all right – I shan't be mad enough to imagine that they belong to me; I shall just feel useful, helping to take care of them.'

'Lovely, then,' said Clio. 'It's a piece of good news to take home with me tomorrow.'

Isabella's expression grew suddenly sad. 'You're going because of us, aren't you – that's why your work with Paolo has finished suddenly. I did so want you to stay.'

'It was soon going to come to an end anyway,' Clio pointed out. 'All your family's decision did was speed things up a little. Costello understands why Luigi voted as he did; I hope you and Matteo do too.' She saw Isabella hesitate about how to answer, and went on herself. 'Don't disappoint me, please! You said it yourself: Italian storms are violent, but they blow over quickly. This one *must* or Costello will feel that all he did was damage you as a family.'

The urgency in her voice made Isabella stare closely at her. 'Does that concern you – that he should be happy?'

Clio achieved what she hoped was a careless shrug. 'Of course, but Francesca will make sure that he is. I think I was given a hint that they finally intend to marry – there'll be great rejoicing among the Costellos in New York!'

Reassured, Isabella was about to bring the conversation round to her brother-in-law when he and Matteo walked in.

'Clio's here to say goodbye – leaving tomorrow,' she announced, 'but I'm not sure that we can do without her.'

'I think she'll be glad to go,' Matteo suggested, registering the tiredness in a face that had surely grown thinner since her arrival. 'Two months are quite long enough to cope with Paolo *and* live in a Roman *pensione!*'

'I've enjoyed almost all of it,' she said honestly, 'but Matteo's right – my own home, my own people, *are* beckoning.' To avoid any awkward discussion about the suddenness of her departure, she even stretched the truth a little. 'I should have had to leave anyway – my elderly relatives have asked me to grow tired of Rome! They need help in Somerset.'

'Tomorrow *is* sudden,' Luigi pointed out with a lawyer's usual pounce on something that was being played down too deliberately; but the pleading in her glance made him abandon it. 'You have a flight booked, Clio? I may drive you to the airport?'

'Yes and no,' she answered, smiling at him. 'I have a reservation, but I also have a taxi booked. Dear Luigi, I couldn't expect you to make that tedious drive again, and Sunday mornings are precious to a hard-driven working man.' Her smile begged him to understand and not be hurt, and he *did* understand that, for some private reason of her own, she wanted to go alone.

'Goodbyes at railway stations and airports *are* painful,' he agreed gently.

Isabella then mercifully intervened, asking Clio to stay and share their supper, but this she also refused.

'I've packing still to do, and my elderly friend, Monsignor Fiocca, will be looking for me in the dining room at the *pensione*. So I'll say goodbye here, and thank you for making my visit so memorable.'

She quickly kissed them in turn, asked Isabella to keep in touch, and then made a dash for the door.

Luigi followed her out and caught up with her on the staircase. 'May I not even see you back to Via Margutta?'

'No need, but thank you again for everything.' She kissed his cheek and ran down the stairs, and this time he let her go.

There was still supper with Monsignor Fiocca to get through, but now she felt ready to talk about her visit to Milan and, apart from mentioning her grandfather's name, told the old priest the rest of the story.

'So now you can leave Antonia here in peace,' he suggested gently. 'That circle is complete. What about the other one – Mr Costello's search for the truth?'

'Fairly complete but not acceptable to some of the people involved. They're his own family – *he* can't go on with it at the cost of damaging them; perhaps someone else will when the time is right.'

The monsignor nodded his silver head, not at all surprised. 'Anyhow, you're thankful to be going home? Yes, I can see that you are.' He didn't ask to know the reason for her sadness; she thought he probably guessed it already. Instead, he put his old, veined hand on her head for a brief moment. 'Then I shall ask God to bless you and take care of you, my child. He knows how much pleasure I've had from our dinners together.'

She left a little kiss on the hand he held out to her, and then stumbled rather blindly from the room – it had been a very emotional day all round.

She left in a taxi the following morning before the rest of the *pensione* was awake. They drove through streets quiet for once except for the chiming of church bells, and empty but for the lonely figure of priest or seminarist hurrying to hear the first Mass of the day. It was Rome at its most beautiful, with spring only just around the corner. She stored up the familiar images in her mind – pictures to remember when she was back in Wells. There hadn't been time, after all, to say goodbye to Marcus Aurelius, and if she felt like weeping it was because of that – not because Costello hadn't bothered to come, at least to wish her *'buon viaggio'*. A brief note or telephone call would have done, but there'd been nothing at all. The rest was silence, as someone had once said.

Nineteen

Instead of going straight to Wells she rang Edward Woodward from her flat in London. She thought he sounded very comforted by the knowledge that she was back but, as usual, he had to be pressed to reveal the true state of things at Vicars' Close.

'Hester is going downhill, but quite peacefully, my dear. Hetty is . . . is upset, of course, but we're managing,' he finished up with heroic calm.

'Tell me what Dr Goodhew *says*, please,' she insisted. 'I must know, Uncle Edward, so that I can decide what to do. Is Aunt Hester dying?'

'Yes, she is,' he confessed, defeated by the blunt question. 'A few more weeks and we shall say goodbye to her.'

Clio was silent for a moment, visualizing the little household in Vicars' Close, and knowing the extent to which it had depended on Hester Woodward.

'I'm sorry,' she murmured, '. . . I'm so sorry.' Edward, at the other end of the line, could now say nothing at all, and Clio had to go on. 'I'm going to change my plan, dearest; *not* come down straightaway. It will be better to get everything settled up here – it might take a day or two – and then I'll be down to stay – by Wednesday at the latest.'

'To stay . . . you mean, really stay? Dear child, how can you?' Edward scarcely dared to ask. 'Your work in London, your home there . . .' His voice failed altogether, and she firmly finished the sentence for him.

'. . . Can all be put on hold! Now, give the girls my love, and I'll see you very soon.'

But she put down the telephone knowing that what she'd just said wasn't true. While Edward or either of her great-aunts were still alive, she would take care of them, and that was too long to leave anything on hold. This was where the pattern of her life took a different shape altogether – but it didn't even need thinking about; she saw it as inevitable.

The following morning she gave up the rental of her flat, then went to hand in her resignation to John Wyndham.

'Don't be silly,' he said when she explained why she had to go. 'Take leave of absence – extended for as long as you need.'

'You're very kind, but it wouldn't be fair,' she had to insist. 'I could be away for years.'

'You're a misfit, Clio,' he suddenly roared, because he knew that he wouldn't be able to make her change her mind. 'No young woman in this day and age turns her back on an excellent career to nurse a flock of elderly relatives mired in rural England! No one but *you*, that is.'

'You don't *know* of any other, that's all,' she insisted quietly.

John Wyndham flung a sudden question at her. 'Has this anything to do with Paul Costello? I wouldn't be surprised if you'd had a monumental row, but that would be no dishonour – he's quite as intractable as you are!'

'We disagreed sometimes, but I enjoyed working with him. If I was intractable, he didn't hold it against me as far as I know. Giving up on the book wasn't anything to do with us.'

'I know – I've heard from him about that bloody family of his.'

'They aren't all bloody,' she had to point out. 'One or two of them are people you'd enjoy knowing.'

Wyndham stared at her for a moment, thinking that she looked tired and sad. *Something* had happened in Rome but it was clear that he wasn't going to be told about it.

'Go to Somerset, Clio,' he said finally, 'but keep in touch. This isn't the end of our working friendship; at least you can do some translation work for me down there.'

She thanked him, rather tearfully, and went back to Holland Park to start packing up her belongings in the flat. When her doorbell rang that evening she supposed that her landlady had something to discuss, because no one had used the front-door buzzer downstairs. But it was a large man who stood there . . . the last person in the world she wanted to see, even if he was the only one she would ever need.

The one question she could frame was totally unimportant. 'How did you get in?'

'I met someone else on the doorstep. Aren't you going to invite me inside?'

She knew that she had a choice. If she said no, he would go away without an argument. But his face looked too strained and unhappy for that, and she held the door open. He followed her into her attic sitting room, and glanced round. 'Nice! Simple but interesting.'

'Mostly my landlady's doing, not mine. I'm sorry to be giving it up.' It seemed that they could only talk in very short sentences. Then she sat down because her knees were trembling, and Costello took time to select the largest armchair he could find before he spoke again.

'I went from the airport to see John Wyndham this afternoon. He said you'd given up your job as well. Why, for God's sake – he says you're the best editor he's ever had.'

'I'm going back to Wells to live – that's why,' she answered. 'Aunt Hester is dying, and Edward and Hetty won't be able to manage without her.' She shook her head at the expression on his face. 'It isn't family duty carried to a mad extreme – I love them dearly, and I couldn't *not* take care of them. They took care of me when I needed them to.'

'All right – I accept that; but you have a brain, Clio, and you're accustomed to putting it to good use. What can you find to do in Vicars' Close?'

'Nothing for the moment. When . . . when things settle down I think I'll try my hand at teaching – French and Italian, probably. There are plenty of good schools nearby to choose from.' She managed a cheerful smile. 'That's my future dealt with. I suppose you're on your way back to New York. Is Francesca with you?

182

'She's going direct from Rome. I looked in on John to explain about the aborted masterpiece I was going to write, but my real need was to see you. I didn't mean you to leave without me seeing you again, but we'd been out of Rome and got held up because Francesca was unwell. When I finally reached the airport yesterday morning I found that for once your flight had been called on time.' He didn't say that he'd doubted the reason for Francesca's sudden sickness, or that she'd made it a test of his love that he should stay with her, not abandon her to their friends and go back to Rome without her.

'We'd already said goodbye,' Clio managed to point out, 'on the journey back from Milan. But thank you for trying to speed me on my way!' Now he could surely leave, she thought, having said what he'd come to say; there was too much tension in the room. She felt afraid to move in case she broke the frail shell of her own self-control; she had no way of knowing about his.

'This is all *wrong*, Clio,' Costello said suddenly, with what sounded merely like anger. 'You should be coming with me to Stonington. The novel you suggested should be written, but I can't do it without your help.'

Now she understood – his urgent need of her was to help him write a book. Anger ripped through her – anger at herself for her own stupidity in imagining, however faintly, that it could be anything else.

'I'm going to Vicars' Close,' she finally insisted in a voice she didn't recognize as hers. 'You'll have Francesca to help you; you don't need me.'

He didn't answer for a moment; what she'd just said was all wrong, but he couldn't admit why it was, or do anything about it in any case.

'That's true,' he finally agreed. 'I shall have Francesca, I was forgetting that.' He got up, and stood for a moment looking at her with a smile she couldn't understand. 'We haven't exactly "heard the chimes at midnight", you and I, but at least we've worked well together, wouldn't you say?'

It was impossible to deny it and she didn't try. 'I think we have. Write the book, please – I'm sure you can, and should.'

'Miss Lambert's final instructions. I shall miss them in future.' Then with nothing more to say he walked out of the room. She didn't move, only listened to his footsteps on the stairs, and then the slam of the front door. Then at last, with a long, shuddering release of the breath she'd been holding, she got up stiffly and walked into the room next door – after a while she managed to remember that she'd been packing when he arrived . . . a long time ago, it seemed now.

She'd forgotten how small Wells was. To eyes grown used to the baroque extravagance of Rome, the heart of the little city seemed too compact, too smugly sure of its own medieval beauty. She could understand now why Antonia had felt stifled by it. Set down by the taxi-driver at the gate in Vicars' Close she had a sudden longing to turn round and implore him to take her away. Like a retreating tide, life was ebbing away from the people who lived here and, if she stayed, her own youth and energy would fade with it. But it was too late, of course – Edward and Hetty already had the door open, and escape was out of the question.

Inside the house she found Hester lying on a day-bed in her room. Skeletally thin now, she was nevertheless still herself. As few concessions as possible were being made to a death she didn't in the least fear. She'd feared nothing, Clio realized, except the possibility of outliving the people who needed her, which would leave her nothing to do; but now that fear had been removed.

'I turn my back on you for a couple of months and *this* happens,' Clio said, trying to smile.

'Nothing to do with you at all,' Hester insisted, with a faint trace of her old sharpness. 'I knew something was wearing out long before you went away. Tom Goodhew knew as well, but he's a good friend, and didn't bother me with pointless efforts to make me last a little longer.' She was quiet for moment, recovering enough strength to go on.

'I can stay now,' Clio said gently. 'Everything's been sorted out in London.'

'Good; Edward and Hetty will need you.' She had no time or energy to waste on insincere concern; whether it was unfair or not, she had to hear her great-niece say that she wouldn't leave them to muddle along by themselves. Her eyes closed and Clio thought she'd slipped away into a doze, but suddenly she was awake again.

'I think you know what happened to Antonia. If it was something bad, don't tell the others; it would only upset them.'

'I won't . . . she *did* have a cruel time in Rome, but at least the friend who took care of her loved her and is still tending her grave.'

'Good,' Hester said again, and then smiled at the girl kneeling beside her. 'Don't be sad about her – at least she lived every moment of her short life; Hetty and I after eighty unadventurous years still know less than Antonia did.'

Exhausted by the effort of talking, Hester drifted off into sleep, and Clio went downstairs. Hetty, looking tired and even more chaotically dressed than usual, burst into tears.

'It's all wrong,' she said between sobs. 'Dearest, your career . . . your life in London . . . we both think, don't we, Edward, that we can manage on our own?'

Clio smiled at them, but shook her head. 'Go on like that, and I shall think you're trying to get rid of me! I've *had* a life in London; I don't need to go on having it – now I'll try something else instead.'

Comforted, Hetty dried her tears. It sounded so reasonable when dear Clio explained it like that; and who, after all, *could* want to live in London . . . such a noisy, violent place she believed it to be.

'I shall go and make tea . . . Hester always says . . .' her voice wobbled, but she swallowed and went on, 'that four thirty is the proper time to drink tea; so that is what we must do.'

When she walked out of the room, Clio looked at her great-uncle. 'Poor love, how will she bear being without the twin sister who's told her what to do for more than eighty years?'

'At the moment, tending Hester keeps her going; after that, I simply don't know. But Hetty was right just now, my dear; we *should* somehow manage on our own, not rely on you.'

'The subject is closed,' he was told firmly. But he looked so sad that Clio had to explain a little more. 'I'm not giving up on any special happiness by being here; the truth is that I'd already lost that before I left Rome. No, even that isn't true . . . I never had it to lose because it belonged to someone else. So now, please just let me stay and be useful!'

Edward examined her face, known and loved since her childhood. She'd never as far as he knew been anything but entirely honest, even as a small girl struggling with the knowledge that she'd been abandoned by two equally selfish parents. He knew that she spoke the truth now.

'You sometimes talk about Peter Lambert,' he said abruptly, 'but you don't mention your mother; aren't you in touch with her at all?'

'I called on her once in Geneva,' Clio answered with a reminiscent smile. 'She managed to remember my name, and tried very hard to sound interested in what I did, but I was an awkward left-over from a past life. Her world now is a prosperous Swiss husband totally different from my father, and a young family of well-behaved and *very* Swiss children! We shall go on exchanging Christmas cards and leave it at that.'

'Virginia was a lovely but foolish young woman,' Edward said with unusual severity. 'I'm afraid it sounds as if she's foolish still.'

What he wanted to do was rail against the stupidity of *anyone* who could know his great-niece and not love her – who was this man in Rome who'd allowed her to slip through his fingers – Luigi di Palma? No, *he* hadn't seemed stupid; it must have been someone else, who wasn't perhaps a fool, but merely inextricably attached already. And then he remembered the beautiful woman who'd entertained him so charmingly alongside the American, Paul Costello; at last he thought

186

he understood why Clio no longer minded about staying in London; it wasn't where her lost happiness was.

While Edward worked this out, she watched him with a certain wry amusement. 'I'll tell you what happened in Rome,' she promised, knowing that he would never ask. 'But not just yet. Now I'm going to unpack and get used to being in Wells again. The views need scaling down a bit!'

His anxious face broke into a smile at last. 'Francis Bacon said that "small matters win great commendation" – try to think of Wells as a small matter, Clio!'

She agreed that she would, and went upstairs to unpack. The moment of panic at the front gate had been simply that; frightening for the heartbeat or two that it had lasted. With the help of Edward, and his friend Francis Bacon, and provided she banished all thought of Paul Costello, she'd be able to manage very well.

Twenty

H ester died three weeks later as stoically as she had lived. In her will she asked to be laid near Mark Lambert, and this was done. Although forceful, she hadn't been a noisy woman; nevertheless the house seemed unnaturally quiet without her. Hetty bore the ordeal of the funeral with unexpected calm, but it seemed to Clio as time dragged by afterwards that it was because she'd taken almost permanent refuge in her own imaginary world. She heard what was said to her, smiled sweetly, and even answered more or less rationally, but below this surface level of communication she wasn't with them at all.

'Should we try to do something about it . . . supposing that there's anything we *can* do?' Clio asked one evening when Hetty had retired to bed. 'The easier we make it for her, the more completely she'll slip away into unreality.'

Edward shook his head. 'I think we mustn't even try. Reality would mean accepting that Hester is no longer here and she can't manage that. In her imaginary world she is able to arrange things exactly as she wants them.'

'Clever Aunt Hetty! You make it sound as if she's behaving with more sense than the rest of us,' Clio said with a wry smile.

'In her own odd way she always has,' Edward pointed out surprisingly. Then he put the question of his sister aside. 'I have the feeling that part of *you* is still in Rome – not imagining, but reliving something. I could be a listening ear but only if it would help to talk about it.'

Clio nodded, appreciating how gently he asked for information. 'There's a bit more of the story to tell. With the help of friends I managed to trace my grandfather. He's Filippo Massini, the brother of the present prince. I went to see him in Milan to return a ring that Antonia had passed on to Luisa Caetani before she died. He's arrogant and embittered, but so lonely that I could only feel sorry for him. Without Katherine and his new family I think my father would become just like him in old age, so I have to think more kindly of *her* now!'

Edward smiled at the rueful afterthought, then grew serious again. 'We're not supposed to say so nowadays, but surely he deserves to be unhappy? We only emasculate our religion by ruling out the idea of punishment for sin.'

'I think so too.' Clio hesitated but decided to go on. 'There turned out to be a curious link between Antonia's story and the one Paul Costello set out to write. His cousin, Lorenza, is married to a man called Gino Forli. It happens that Gino's mother is Filippo's niece.' She smiled faintly at Edward. 'If you dealt in clichés, which you don't, you'd now observe that it's a small world!'

But he was following his own train of thought. 'Purely by chance you went to Rome to work for Mr Costello. From that all these other discoveries have stemmed. *That* is what is so extraordinary. But why did he stop writing his book?'

'It was the family's decision not to wash its dirty linen in public. The Massinis were leading Fascists, implicated in unpleasant things, but *not* punished for their sins, I'm afraid.'

'I suppose you'll lose touch with them all now,' Edward finally ventured, '. . . Costello, and the people you met in Rome?'

'Costello certainly – he's back in America,' she answered in a voice that didn't waver. 'But apart from Lorenza he has two very nice cousins – Luigi, whom you met, and his brother Matteo. They, and Matteo's wife, Isabella, became friends I don't think I shall lose track of.'

But she doubted that even as she said it. One of the most engaging things about Italians was their pleasure in accepting the latest novelty with flattering speed; but they were just as quick to grow bored with it and move on to the next new experience. If she was honest with herself, she had no real expectation of hearing from the di Palmas again.

She blamed the lowering thought, and the depression that now gripped her, on a more miserable spring than usual. It was hard not to compare cold, sodden Somerset with Rome, now probably basking in the blue and gold days of a summer that arrived earlier there.

She struggled in the aftermath of Hester's funeral to restore the house to its normal state of grace and order, and thought resolutely about what else had to be done – she must find a training course that would enable her to become a teacher, and she had finally to dispose of the house Mark Lambert had left her. What she couldn't allow herself to do, during daylight hours at least, was think about Costello, now presumably back on his sea-washed promontory at Stonington. But the night-time was a different matter; then no amount of conscious will-power helped. 'With the first dream that comes with the first sleep, I run . . . I run and am gathered to your heart.' She knew now, if she hadn't understood before, what Alice Meynell had meant when she wrote those lines. Women had to find comfort where they could – in an imaginary world if they were Hetty, in dreams if they'd been fool enough to love a man entirely committed to someone else.

But Easter, later than usual, came at last, bringing its own sublime note of hope. She doubted if anyone in the packed Cathedral on Easter morning could hear the triumphant shout, 'Christ is risen . . . He is risen indeed', and not feel their hearts lift. Even Hetty, standing beside her, seemed to be really listening and sharing in the celebration. Afterwards it was as if that Easter promise of renewal transformed everything else. Spring *became* spring at last; the countryside almost overnight stepped into its new dress of vivid green, and gardens and hedgerows were awash with blossom. At last she would start to look forward again, with Rome and all its heartache locked away in the past.

But having come to that conclusion, the Fates decided to bring it to her mind again. She walked into the house one morning just as Edward was answering the telephone's ring. 'A William Thompson for you,' he said, holding out the receiver.

'You've forgotten me,' said a pleasant voice. 'I can hear you desperately trying to remember who William Thompson might be.'

'I remember very well,' Clio answered firmly. 'You aren't at all fond of pasta, and you're not ready yet to retire to Boston.'

'Two very salient points,' he conceded, 'but I wish my wit and laid-back charm had made an impression as well!' Then he went on more seriously. 'I swear I wasn't willing it to happen, but my opposite number in Grosvenor Square was called home by some family illness and that clinched my transfer ahead of time to take his place. So, *eccomi*, as the Italians say – very happy to be here, but hoping that you'll be able to get to London occasionally.'

'I don't see why not,' she agreed cautiously, aware that congenial company of her own age was something she lacked at the moment.

William wasn't to be put off by caution. 'There's a production of *Pelléas et Mélisande* at Covent Garden that everyone is raving about. Would that tempt you out of Somerset?'

'It probably would – it's an opera I've never seen performed. But there's a little problem, William – Wells isn't a late-night taxi-ride away from Central London. I'd have no way of getting home.'

'I realize that – I've looked at the map. But there are things called hotel rooms and I shall book you one.'

She was being told, she realized, that he wasn't expecting her to spend the night with him. William was what John Wyndham had called *her* – a misfit; a gent of the old school, and one of a fast-diminishing species at that.

'You're very kind – I'd love to come,' she admitted, 'but can you work the miracle of getting tickets?'

With them already sitting on his desk, he smugly explained that a cultural attaché had a little influence when it came to such matters. Then, with the details arranged, he rang off leaving her smiling at the treat in store.

Two days later she took the train to London, promising Hetty, who suddenly became very anxious about her going, that she'd be back within twenty-four hours. When the brief visit was over William escorted her back to Paddington, and looked shyly pleased when she told him he'd been a perfect host.

'At least that might mean you'll come again,' he suggested. 'I hope you will, Clio – I hope that very much.'

He sounded so serious that she felt obliged to retreat a little. 'William, I've had a lovely time, but I can't keep nipping up to the Great Wen. There are elderly people at home who depend on me and get upset when I'm not there.'

'The lady who gives the postman hell?' he remembered with a smile.

'No; her frail twin sister and brother are left, but Aunt Hester died a few weeks ago.'

'I'm sorry, Clio.' Then William's suddenly contrite face cleared up again. 'I could always come and see you; I'm very good with old people.'

She smiled at him, thinking that it was probably true; unlike someone else she remembered too vividly, he wouldn't frighten Hetty at all, and Hester was no longer there to remind her that they didn't care for Americans very much.

'Come if you like,' she said, 'but don't expect high excitement in Wells – the weekly market is about the most we can run to.'

William insisted that he would look forward to it and then kissed her goodbye. She wished with all her despairing heart that the touch of his mouth could raise some flicker of response in her; but he didn't seem disappointed or hurt, and she had to suppose that Boston bred its sons content with very little in the way of passion.

Back in Vicars' Close, she found a change that seemed to rule out any more trips to London. Hetty greeted her with a mixture of tears and laughter that was nearly hysterical, and would only agree to go to bed when Clio had patiently convinced her that she'd still be there when Hetty woke in the morning.

'My dear, I'm sorry,' Edward said miserably. 'Don't let that have spoiled your visit to London. I think you've become Antonia now in Hetty's mind, and she thinks that if you leave the house you won't come back. But you *can't* not have some life of your own; in time she'll get used to seeing you come and go.'

He said it with as much confidence as he could manage and Clio didn't contradict him, but she thought neither of them believed that it was true. Hetty was slowly drifting beyond the reach of reason. There was nothing to be done except say in her thank-you letter to William Thompson what the true state of things was at Vicars' Close. For the moment there could be no more visits to London, and even the gentlest stranger in the house would probably upset her great-aunt's fragile equilibrium.

Rather to her surprise William accepted the situation with so much understanding that she decided he must have within his own family at home someone not unlike Hetty. Even he would surely get bored before long with so tepid and long-distance a love affair, which meant that she needn't take it very seriously herself; but for the moment she was grateful for his regular telephone calls and for the thoughtfully chosen parcels of new books that arrived every so often. Suspecting that she was being unfair, she came to regard him as the best of friends, indispensably helping her through this strange, unreal period of her life.

Except that she was scarcely eating enough to keep a bird alive, there seemed no reason why Hetty shouldn't continue for a long time in her present state – always sweet-tempered and content, but also sweetly insistent that nothing about the ordered pattern of life at Vicars' Close should change.

Anxious about the future, Clio consulted the doctor who'd attended the Woodwards since the beginning of his days in general practice. 'I feel ashamed to even think this,' she said, 'but sometimes I can't help wondering whether Aunt Hetty isn't having me on! As things are she has the perfect recipe for always getting her own way.'

'You and Edward live under the thumb of a gentle tyrant,' Tom Goodhew said surprisingly. 'Hetty is very frail, but she *could* live for another ten years, Clio. You can't let her absorb you entirely.'

'So what am I to do?'

'Leave her with Edward sometimes . . . even leave her alone occasionally. I'm more worried about *you* than I am about her.' He said it lightly, but it was true – she looked tired and thin, and her eyes were shadowed with sadness even when she smiled at him. 'Listen to me, please,' he insisted, so seriously that she promised she would, without quite knowing how she was to do anything about it.

But with the neat timing life sometimes showed in arranging itself, she was given the chance almost immediately to follow Tom Goodhew's advice. A completely unexpected telephone call from Rome brought Isabella di Palma's voice bubbling with excitement along the line.

'Clio, I can't believe this yet, but I'm to come to London with Matteo. He's invited to read a paper there, and then in New York, but he refuses to go without me!'

'And like a good, helpful wife you've allowed yourself to be talked into it,' Clio said solemnly.

'Of course! I'm not sure how helpful I can be, but it's having Matteo *want* me with him that counts. Don't you think so, Clio?' There was barely time to agree before Isabella rushed on. 'I know you don't live in London but we *must* see you, please. Can you come? There's so much to talk about.'

But for her conversation with Tom Goodhew she would probably have felt that she must refuse. Now she heard herself agree, even though it would mean spending a night in London if she was to see Matteo as well as Isabella. With all the arrangements made, Clio put the telephone down and then, after a moment's thought, picked it up again and called William Thompson. Would he like to play host at her dinner party for the di Palmas? she asked. He agreed at once as she'd known he would; then it was time to tell Edward that she was following Tom Goodhew's instructions.

'Good,' he said simply. 'Forget about us for a little while, please.'

Hetty's reaction to the news left them uncertain whether it registered or not, because she smiled and nodded, just as she did whenever Clio suggested to her some little outing in the car. But they didn't mention the subject again, and Clio quietly left the house when her taxi came, deliberately not saying goodbye. She spent the train journey to London in a state of worry, but there was enough pleasure in seeing Isabella waiting for her in the lobby of the Hyde Park Hotel to drive the thought of Vicars' Close out of her mind.

'It's not fair,' she said, smiling at Matteo's wife. 'The rest of us grow older, you just get younger and more beautiful!' It wasn't an empty compliment; Isabella was scarcely recognizable for the haunted, unhappy woman of six months ago.

'It all started with you,' she said seriously, '. . . the day I went looking for you in the Forum, expecting to hate you because Matteo was bound to fall in love with you. But I knew at once that you wanted to help, not hurt me.'

'Tell me about the job,' Clio suggested, in the hope of avoiding a conversation that seemed to be too emotional.

'It's wonderful – you might think an orphanage would be a depressing place but it isn't at all; the babies are too young to know they've been abandoned, and they're loved and taken care of.' She met the question in Clio's face with a shake of her head. 'I still don't want an adopted child, and Matteo doesn't either; but I'm more useful anyway helping the Sisters, and I'm very content.' Her dark eyes examined Clio for a moment. 'I'm not sure I can say the same about you, *amica mia*; you looked happier in Rome, I think.'

'I'm not working at the moment,' Clio tried to explain, 'just keeping house for some dear but elderly relatives. Perhaps they're not quite so interesting as your babies!' Then she asked for news of Luigi.

'He's been in New York, visiting the Costellos. Mario di Palma wasn't a very typical Italian, but Enrico still is even after so many years in America, and he revels in his daughters' children; they're a very close family, noisy and extrovert, but Luigi enjoys being part of it.'

'More than Paul Costello does perhaps?' Clio suggested quietly.

Isabella nodded, looking sad. 'I think he gave up on family life when Teresa died. There's Francesca, of course, but I don't quite see *her* enjoying a crowd of rumbustious children. Luigi went out to Stonington to visit them. She was very glad to see him – bored out of her mind, he thought – but Paolo was working hard and not enchanted to have a visitor!' Isabella frowned over that. 'I'm afraid he's getting very selfish.'

'Writers are,' Clio pointed out gently. 'They probably have to be.'

Isabella gave a little sigh of regret, then smiled again. 'It's the besetting sin of people who are happily married – they want to see everyone else paired off as well. What about you, *cara*?'

'Definitely *not* paired off,' Clio heard herself say with heroic breeziness, 'but I've found a kind and charming friend to take us out to dinner this evening. He was at the American Embassy in Rome, but very conveniently he's been shifted to London.'

Half an hour later she left Isabella waiting for Matteo to return from meeting his fellow conference speakers, and went to change at her own more modest hotel. She walked to it, oblivious of the early-evening bustle of Sloane Street; her

mind's eye saw instead a lonely-looking house close enough
to the sea for the sound of it to be always present in every
room. Costello loved it and required company there, she
remembered, only by invitation; but its isolation might cost
him Francesca if he wasn't careful. She blundered into another
passer-by and had to apologize, and then walked more carefully back to her hotel.

Twenty-One

Long afterwards she still vividly remembered stepping out of the train on her homeward journey. Instead of the cabbie she expected to see on the platform, Tom Goodhew was waiting there, and without being told, she knew with a clutch of fear at her heart that he was waiting for her.

'It's not . . . not Edward – *please* don't say that,' she begged as he came towards her.

The doctor gripped her hands hard, but shook his head. 'My dear, Edward's all right, quite all right I promise you. But dear Hetty died last night – very peacefully in her sleep. We didn't want you to arrive at the house not knowing.'

White-faced, Clio ducked her head for a moment against his chest while her heart-beats returned to normal. Then she straightened up and stared at him. 'I know what you're going to say now. There's nothing I could have done if I'd been there! But I should have been, instead of . . . instead of . . .' Then her voice broke altogether and she gave up on the rest of what she'd been going to say.

Tom Goodhew released her hands, but with a firm grip on her arm steered her to the exit and his car parked outside. When they were settled inside, he turned to face her.

'Now, Clio love, let's get this straight,' he said in a voice that had never lost its gentle Somerset lift at the end of a sentence. 'Hetty could have died any time these past ten years; I certainly never expected her to outlive Hester. She hasn't been properly alive since her twin died, but that was something that not even your loving care could do anything about. She had the blessedly peaceful death we all wish for ourselves;

so don't regret it, please, or want her back in a world she didn't in the least fit into anymore.'

Clio smiled at him through the tears that were trickling down her face. 'I know you're right . . . it's just that it's been a terrible year for losing people. I *can't* spare any more.' Her voice wobbled, but recovered itself. 'Thank you for coming to fetch me. You're *sure* Edward's all right? It's been an even worse year for him.'

'He's only worried about you; but I told him you'd got more sense than to blame yourself for something you could have done nothing about.'

She didn't answer and they drove in silence for a little while. Then Tom Goodhew spoke again. 'It's an occupational hazard for doctors – they get the idea that they always know best! So take no notice if I'm interfering, but I think Edward will suggest leaving Vicars' Close; he'll say it's time he found a flat . . . sheltered accommodation . . . that kind of thing.'

'Because he reckons he'll become a burden? Well, he can forget *that* idea. Apart from two very charming but totally indifferent parents, Edward is all I've got.' Her voice was hoarse again, but she managed to smile when Tom Goodhew turned to look at her. 'We'll stay together, God willing, for a long time yet – in Vicars' Close because that's where he belongs.'

The doctor's hand patted hers for a moment while he waited for traffic lights to change. 'Just so long as you're sure, Clio.' They said nothing more, and five minutes later had drawn up outside the house.

She found Edward Woodward in the garden, sitting in what had been Hetty's favourite spot – the wooden seat that encircled the trunk of the apple tree. He stood up as she walked towards him, and held out his arms – not a normally demonstrative man, he knew they needed the comfort now of hugging each other.

'Kind of Tom to come and meet me,' she said unsteadily at last. 'He promised me you were all right. Are you?'

'All the better for seeing you,' Edward admitted. 'The house felt very lonely this morning. But, Clio – Hetty *was* smiling when I went in this morning, not looking as if she'd been frightened or in pain; I had the feeling that she'd already found Hester again, if that isn't being too fanciful.'

'Then we don't have to worry,' Clio said gently. 'They're both happy now.'

By the time the summer was drawing to a close they'd settled down again, Clio already embarked on the training course that would make her into a teacher, and Edward preparing a catalogue of rare colonial stamps, on which he was an acknowledged expert. It was a quiet life among elderly clerical neighbours – too quiet, he feared, for a young woman of thirty-one, but when he pointed this out to her one day Clio simply smiled.

'We should leave this house – it's a millstone round your neck, and so am I,' he insisted.

'That's what Tom Goodhew warned me you'd say, so we'll talk about it now and then not have to mention it again. We stay together *here*, please, for as many years as Heaven allows.'

He was framing an objection but she interrupted him. 'I work with young people all day long, and I've got Bath, Glastonbury and Bristol within easy reach. We're practically at the hub of things in Vicars' Close!'

'You work too hard,' Edward complained. 'Must you do so much translating for John Wyndham as well as everything else?'

'I enjoy it, and I *must* keep using the languages I'm going to teach.' She smiled at him with huge affection. 'Stop worrying about me, please – I'm perfectly content.'

'Content, but not happy. I can't help but know that, Clio.' He hesitated for a moment, then plucked up the courage to go on. 'William Thompson is a very nice man who must surely be hoping that you'll become his wife. He's kind enough to say that he enjoys the weekends he spends here, but I don't doubt that he'd much rather you joined him in London. I'm afraid you're superstitious about that now – at least it's what Tom Goodhew says.'

'But Tom also admits to thinking that he knows best – a doctor's occupational hazard, he says! William loves coming here – I don't even ask him; he invites himself!' It was her turn to hesitate. 'I'm not being unfair. William knows that he's my dear friend; the reason I don't marry him is *not* because it would mean leaving you, only because he's not the right man – unfortunately!'

'I wish he were, Clio – it's my only wish and prayer that you should be happy.'

'"Content" will do nicely,' she insisted, '. . . so now we've got *that* settled, tell me where we should plant the species crocus corms "young Jim" has brought; I've a fancy to scatter them in the lawn. What do you think?'

'He'll think it's untidy and he won't be able to start mowing as soon as he wants to next spring; but let's do it anyway,' said Edward.

She was busy with that very task the following morning when the post arrived. Edward brought mugs of coffee out to the garden table and, with them, a long airmail envelope addressed to Clio. Inside was an airline ticket and a letter from her father.

'Good heavens – I'd forgotten all about it,' she said, skimming through the note. 'Do you remember me telling you that he was off to Sicily when I saw him in Rome? He reckoned he might exhibit his photographs of classical sites. Well, it's all arranged in a very grand way, and I'm invited to attend the opening of the exhibition; in fact I'm commanded to appear because Katherine refuses to leave the children on the West Coast, and he needs a hostess, he says! It's fairly typical of my father.'

'But kind of him to send the air ticket. You *must* go, my dear, even if I have to do a little commanding as well; I shan't let you refuse.'

Edward rarely spoke in that tone of voice, and when he did

she didn't argue with him; she knew that he'd be deeply upset if she refused to go.

With Tom Goodhew and the neighbours primed to keep an eye on Edward, without him being aware of it, she set off a fortnight later for Heathrow and an extended weekend in New York. She'd been once before, and remembered it as a city of strange but rather frightening beauty – it wasn't user-friendly, she tried to explain to her father over dinner at their hotel that evening.

'I agree with you that the scale is inhuman, but it's an exciting place to visit.' He smiled at her more forgivingly than usual, because he was privately rather pleased that she had come. 'I expect that, given the choice, you'd choose a European city – Paris or Rome.'

'Well, yes – maybe!'

On the flight over she'd debated with herself whether or not to mention her visit to Milan. No conclusion had been reached, but now that he'd spoken of Rome she suddenly made up her mind. 'When I told you about Antonia's grave you said you didn't want to know who your real father was. I can tell you now, because I found him in Milan; but I won't go on if you truly don't want me to.'

Peter Lambert prized an oyster from its shell before answering. 'I make *some* allowance for natural curiosity, Clio! Unless it's someone I'd feel obliged to disown, tell me what you know.'

'His name is Filippo Massini, and he's the younger brother of the present Prince. I went to Milan to see him and found a lonely, embittered old man. The family were noted Fascists, involved in savage reprisals against the Partisans during the war, and mostly up to no good even after the war. *You*'ll have to decide whether you want to disown them or not.'

'I've understood always that my mother was in Rome – but you said you went to Milan?'

'Filippo *was* in Rome towards the end of the war. But when Antonia became pregnant the family reminded him that he was promised to the daughter of a rich Milanese businessman.

He'd married her by the time Antonia went back, only to be rejected a second time. The marriage was an unhappy failure and Filippo didn't get the son he longed for, but I told him about *you* – there's a resemblance, by the way.'

'Cruel, but I'm rather glad you did.' Peter Lambert laid down his fork and stared at Clio across the table. 'And I'm glad to know that I misjudged my mother; at least she was brave and persistent, even if she wasn't much good at picking a lover.'

'You had reason to misjudge her,' Clio said fairly. 'She did abandon you and grandfather Mark, but the truth is that she *was* a lovely person – I know that for sure now.'

He nodded and smiled with unexpected kindness at his daughter. 'The time-clock's all wrong coming from east to west; you must very soon go to bed. I'll have last-minute problems to see to in the morning – can you amuse yourself?'

'Easily, in the Metropolitan, and the Frick Museum. But I'll be ready for your grand opening!'

'Don't smile – it *will* be grand; I've seen to that. You're required to look good, but not so good that the guests admire you instead of my photographs!'

She promised to do her best, and said goodnight to him half an hour later, wondering whether she was now misjudging *him* and only imagined that he was trying out the name of Peter Massini in his mind to see whether it sounded more impressive than Peter Lambert.

They went to the gallery together the following evening, after his brief inspection decided that she did him credit.

'It's in the genes, of course, and with mine *and* Virginia's – at least she always had excellent taste – you could hardly go wrong. I shall leave you to charm the Italian Ambassador, by the way – he's very susceptible to female beauty.'

His Excellency turned out to be even more enchanted with a female happy to talk Italian with him, and they were getting on like a house on fire when an eddy in the crowded room showed her a late arrival talking to her father by the door. With the heart-stopping feeling that she'd stepped on a stair that wasn't there, she murmured some automatic response to what had just been said to her, and could have wept with relief when the Ambassador was intercepted by one of the great ladies of the New York social scene. Now she could recover herself, command her legs not to tremble, and her mouth to smile, since the gods had been kind enough to give her time to get used to the fact that he was there.

She was listening with rapt attention to an opinionated art critic when Costello managed to work his way to her side. He explained to her companion that she was needed by her father, and promptly steered her to a quieter space in an empty alcove.

'Thank you for the rescue,' she said unsteadily. 'He was a very boring man.'

'Well known for it,' said Paul Costello, 'but not by foreigners like you.'

He seemed in no hurry to find anything else to say, and stared at her instead – poised and lovely in a cream silk dress whose turquoise sash echoed the colour of the antique necklace she wore. In a room full of overdressed and over-bejewelled women she stood out, he thought, by virtue of her simplicity and grace. It seemed a very long time since he'd had the pleasure of looking at her.

'You arrived very late,' she managed to point out, 'and you've come without your beard.'

'I didn't just leave it behind,' he explained. 'I shaved it off. My nieces, of whom I have far too many, thought I might look younger without it; at my advanced age that *is* a considera-tion.'

Clio glanced round the room. 'There's such a crowd that I can't spot Francesca – I assume she's here?'

'Wrong assumption, I'm afraid – she's in Paris, as far as I know, celebrating her engagement to a very smooth French diplomat she met at some embassy party here. He's a widower in need of his next elegant wife; Francesca is ready to step

off the treadmill of the fashion world, but not to bury herself
– her words, not mine – at Stonington.'

She could detect nothing in his level voice except perhaps
a trace of self-derision. No offer of sympathy was required;
he was a man who liked company only by invitation, and
perhaps on the whole preferred to do without any at all.

'I saw Isabella and Matteo in London a month or two ago,'
Clio thought it safe to say. 'They'd heard from Luigi that you
were hard at work. Writing's a solitary business. You'll snub
me if I point out that Francesca was probably lonely at
Stonington, and bored with nothing to do.'

'I expect you're right,' and that was all he seemed prepared
to say on the subject of the woman who had shared his life
since Teresa Costello had died. Clio supposed that it was *his*
way of dealing with what had happened, and knew better than
to assume that he didn't bitterly regret the French diplomat's
gain.

'When I saw you in London you were about to go back to
Somerset to your clutch of elderly relatives,' he remarked next.
'I assume you're *not* bored and lonely.'

'It's scarcely a clutch any more. Aunt Hester died soon after
I got home; Aunt Hetty survived without her until a couple
of months ago. So it's just me and Edward now.'

'I'm sorry,' he said more gently. 'But you didn't answer
my question.' She still didn't, and with a sudden change of
tone he answered it himself. 'No, of course, you're not lonely
– I was forgetting my good friend William, now only as far
away as London. Isabella mentioned how useful he seemed
to be.'

'He's a dear friend, I'd rather say,' Clio pointed out, stung
by the jeer in his voice. 'Edward enjoys his visits as much as
I do.'

'Poor Will – I doubt if a "*ménage à trois*" is quite what he
has in mind. May I give you a word of warning? If I tried
Francesca's patience too far, perhaps you're making the same
mistake with him.'

Angry now, and glad to be because it made him easier to

deal with, she answered with her usual directness. 'I'm not misleading William – he knows my situation and accepts that I shan't leave Uncle Edward on his own.'

There was a moment's silence between them, isolating them from the buzz of voices and laughter all around. Then Costello spoke again.

'I'm doing what you suggested – writing a *novel* about Italy, but I've probably bitten off more than I can chew and some help would be appreciated. Would you like to reconsider coming to Stonington – bringing Edward with you?'

It was odd, she thought, in the small part of her mind that was still functioning rationally, to love beyond any hope of recovery a man so blind, so self-concerned, so plain damned stupid as this one.

'You still don't understand,' she managed not to shout it at him. 'We have to stay at Vicars' Close – Edward's whole life is there, in the only home he's ever known, with his garden, his books and stamps, and daily visits to the cathedral where he worships his God. Do you really think I could uproot him from all that now?'

Before Costello could answer, they were interrupted by Peter Lambert, smiling but intent on ending the conversation. 'I'm sure a *tête-à-tête* about your time in Rome is very enjoyable, but it's time my daughter did some hostess work. Why not join us for dinner after the party, Paul – we'd like that.'

'Thank you, but I'm afraid the answer's no, I must be on my way. In any case Clio and I have exhausted our stock of reminiscences.' Then he offered them a bow and polite smile and turned away.

She watched him leave, saw his tall, loose-limbed figure seem to part the crush of people as the waters of the Red Sea were parted for the Israelites, and reach the open doors. She hadn't ever expected to see him again, so there was no reason why it should be more unbearably painful to watch him go now; but it was . . . *much* more.

Aware of her frozen stillness, Peter Lambert touched her

206

arm. 'Sorry if I interrupted something just then, Clio. Are you all right?'

'Quite all right, thanks.' But he saw that her eyes were bright with unshed tears when she smiled at him.

Twenty-Two

B ack in Vicars' Close two days later, she gave Edward – still safely alive and well after her absence – a spirited account of the visit, including her own undoubted success with H.E. the Italian Ambassador, and her father's triumphant exhibition.

'The great and the good turned out for it in force, but so they should have done – his photographs *are* truly beautiful,' she finished up more seriously. 'You'll be able to judge for yourself because they're going to be published in a very sumptuous book, and if they don't make you want to fly off to Sicily, nothing will! Maybe we should think of going next spring?'

'Why not?' Edward agreed obligingly. He'd enjoyed the bright recital, almost felt he'd been there with her; but also felt, and wished he didn't, that in making a determined effort to entertain him she was trying to convince herself that something darker hadn't happened to ruin her visit.

'Did you mention Filippo Massini to your father?' he ventured. Peter Lambert's attitude towards his mother wasn't a secret. If he'd refused to change it, that would certainly have upset Clio.

But she nodded calmly. 'Yes. I told him, and I'm glad I did, because I think it altered his viewpoint – a little, at least.' A wry smile touched her mouth, making Edward realize that this wasn't what had troubled her. 'I'm afraid he's even a bit intrigued by the idea of being distantly related to a prince – good democratic American that he now is! *That* I didn't quite expect.'

'My dear, none of us is immune – I'm wondering how I can possibly mention it in passing to the Bishop myself!'

She grinned because he wanted her to, but he knew that her mind still lingered on something else. Then he dredged up out of his still very sharp memory a fact she would have preferred him to have lost.

'Didn't you once tell me that your father knew Paul Costello. Was he at the grand opening, too, by any chance?'

'Yes – he arrived rather late and left rather early; not an ideal guest.'

'And that charming Italian lady – was she with him? I suppose so; they seemed to be very much a couple, I thought.' Clio soon got herself under control again but not before he'd registered the desolation in her face.

'Francesca Cortona wasn't there; it seems that she and Costello aren't a couple any longer. She's about to marry someone else – a French diplomat. Don't blame *her*,' Clio added, seeing Edward's disappointment. 'Costello is immersed in writing out at Stonington; she was bored and lonely; and if he even noticed, he did nothing about it. He did nothing about his young wife either, years ago, and she committed suicide. He *was* kind enough to invite me to Stonington, but only to help him write his book. For a clever man he's very stupid!' Aware that the shake in her voice had given too much away, she tried to smile, but the despairing gesture of her hands suddenly confirmed the truth for Edward. He knew for certain now why she so often seemed to be listening for a voice she couldn't hear.

They were within a week of Christmas when he surprised her with a question about their preparations for the festival.

'Do we *need* preparations?' she asked in turn, not understanding what he meant. 'We'll do what we always do – invite Tom Goodhew to dinner, and anyone in the Close who might be lonely. We've preparations enough for that.'

'For someone to *stay* as well?' he insisted.

'Dearest, you've forgotten – William's going home to Boston for Christmas; he mentioned it when he was here last.'

'*Not* William,' Edward almost shouted, suddenly overcome by the fear of having done something she might not forgive. 'I wrote to Paul Costello and asked if he'd like to . . . spend Christmas here.' Speechless with shock, she could only stare at him, and he stumbled on. 'I thought we'd be lonely – without the girls . . . and then I thought *he* might be lonely too, without Francesca. Of course I didn't *write* that . . . it wouldn't have been tactful at all . . .' His voice finally petered out and he waited for Clio to say something instead.

'It wasn't the best idea you've ever had,' she eventually managed to suggest, trying to raise a careless smile as well. 'But it doesn't matter very much because he won't come. If he's in need of company, which I doubt, he has an enormous family to call on in New York.'

'He *is* coming – I heard from him this morning,' Edward said with quiet desperation. 'Forgive me, please, if I interfered far too much.'

She couldn't resist that plea, and went to wrap her arms about him, uncertain whether to laugh or weep. 'Who shall we invite to entertain him – dear, doddery Canon Jameson from next door, old Professor Cartwright from number 22, perhaps the retired dean and his wife?'

'Invite them all,' Edward said largely, '. . . let's have all the lonely people.' So Clio kissed him and agreed.

Thereafter she simply concentrated on the work to be done – got a guest-room ready, laid in sufficient stocks of food and wine, and decorated the old house beautifully with greenery. The details of Costello's arrival she left to Edward, who announced one morning that their guest would be driving himself from the airport in a hired car. They were to expect him sometime on Christmas Eve afternoon.

In fact the early winter darkness had fallen when he drew up at the door, and she heard his voice in the hall explaining to Edward that the journey out of London had been very slow. She lingered in the friendly warmth of the kitchen for a moment longer, telling herself that somehow she'd be able to manage his visit. It would be the only Christmas she would ever spend with him, and out of it might come some small joy that she could store up for the future.

He didn't smile when she went out to greet him, but she was prepared for that; the easy insincerities that most people felt required to offer were social coinage that he simply ignored. Instead, he looked round the firelit hall as if aware of its welcome. She felt ill-at-ease with him for the moment and left Edward to do the honours of the house. But dinner was a leisurely affair, with Costello so relaxed and gently mannered that her own tension gradually disappeared. It was even possible to believe that, whatever odd fancy had made him accept her great-uncle's invitation, he was content to be there.

Edward no longer attended the Christmas Eve midnight service in the Cathedral and, when Clio mentioned that she *would* be there, she expected their guest to make the excuse that he was tired from travelling. But he insisted that he'd like to go, so when the time drew near they crossed the Cathedral Green together, to join the throng of people arriving at the great west door.

The night was beautiful – frosty and appropriately starlit – and Paul Costello knew that this was one of the moments he would remember for the rest of his life; the star-scattered midnight sky, the great Gothic church filling with a quiet but expectant host of people, and Clio standing beside him, engaged in friendly conversation with a young girl in front of them who'd come alone.

Inside, with seats found at last in one of the side aisles, Clio knelt to pray and then sat down beside him. He turned to look at her gravely enchanted face under its cap of short dark hair, and without warning spoke the words that were in his mind.

'I love you very much. That's why I came – just to tell you what I've known for a long time.'

Then, all about them, the congregation rose at that moment as the choir began their long procession to the chancel, and 'Oh Come, All Ye Faithful' filled the air, commanding them to be joyful and triumphant on the way to Bethlehem. Once more the celebration of Christmas had begun.

Afterwards they walked back to the house in silence, both of them aware that, late as it was, something begun had still to be finished. No longer surprised at anything that might happen, Clio found that Edward seemed to have left his comfortable study ready for them – the fire made up and carefully guarded, whisky and tumblers on the drinks tray.

She gestured to Costello to help himself, and knelt down to stir the logs into a blaze.

'It's safe to put the poker down,' he said with a hint of unsteadiness in his voice. 'I'm not about to strong-arm you into staying to hear what else I have to stay.'

'I'm listening,' she said gravely.

'I want you to know the truth. Francesca didn't like being at Stonington, but she'd never stayed there all the time – I was always combined quite easily with the strange demands of being a fashion journalist. She only left for good because she knew that our relationship had come an end.'

Costello took a sip from his glass and looked at Clio's pale face, but she was apparently intent on watching the flames dancing in the hearth. 'I did my best to hide the fact because I owe her a great deal and wanted very much not to hurt her, but she understood the effort I was having to make. A man who had to flog himself through the motions of loving her wasn't what she knew she deserved. To the world at large, of course, it was she who left me, and that's as it should be.' He leaned over suddenly to touch Clio's hand. 'Are you dropping with tiredness or can I go on?'

'Not if the strong-arm tactics were only postponed – they won't get us anywhere.' She was tired, but not too tired to sound uncertain.

'Oh, I realize that! For all she smiles so sweetly and sounds so gentle, there's a thread of steel running through my love that I can't ever hope to break. I'm not sure I really want to – without it she wouldn't be who she is. Just know, please, that the invitation to come and work at Stonington was a poor excuse to get you there – I shall love you until I die. I accept that you won't leave Edward here alone but can't I persuade you to think of bringing him with you? I don't believe I could feel so strongly that we belong together if you didn't feel it as well. Or are you going to tell me I'm wrong?'

'Not wrong,' she admitted hoarsely, 'but there's still Edward – I *can't* uproot him, but nor can I abandon him; I owe him too much and love him too much.'

The door behind Costello was half-open, but a punctilious knock sounded before Edward, arrayed in his old Jaeger dressing-gown, appeared in the doorway and gave a little cough.

'Forgive me both of you – it wasn't my intention to over-hear what has just been said, but I'm glad I did,' he confessed quietly. Then he looked at Clio. 'Dear child, I need to confess to something that has been weighing on me rather, because I very much doubt that Paul will tell you himself. I didn't just invite him here for Christmas; I asked if he could find room for both of us at Stonington, because I knew that you wouldn't go without me.'

'You did *what*?' She stared at him with anguish in her face. 'I don't believe you – no, I don't mean that; but you've got it into your dear stubborn head that I'm not happy. Well, I won't go – we're staying here, where you belong. Costello understands that; why can't you?'

He steeled himself to ignore the pain in her voice and to sound convincing himself. 'Why won't *you* understand that if I stand in the way of your happiness I'd rather not go on living at all? Antonia's life was wasted; I can't allow yours to be wasted as well. I knew that if Paul came here he must love you very much, and I'm quite sure of what he means to you.' He offered her a sweet, youthful grin. 'The truth is that I'd be rather glad of a change from Vicars' Close myself! I'm as bored with our worthy neighbours as they probably are with me, and I've always liked the idea of living where I could see and hear the sea. That's all I wanted to say; now I can leave you in peace again.' Then he gravely wished them goodnight although the long-case clock had just chimed half past one, and walked out of the room.

It was Clio who finally broke the silence he left behind. 'I'm afraid my darling Edward forced your hand . . . very aggravating for the man who prefers to issue his own invitations! Suppose we just enjoy Christmas and then go our separate ways?'

He watched her firelit face for a moment, afraid that even now he might still lose her.

'I did invite you,' he reminded her gently, '. . . admittedly for the wrong reason, but I chose one that I thought might appeal to you. Edward's future isn't the only thing you're hung up on – there's the man who betrayed you in the past, as well as *my* lamentable failure to make women happy. I'd make *you* happy, my love, and take care of you until the day I die. And as for the dear man upstairs, believe what *he* said as well – all he wants is for us to accept the gift he's offered.'

Her face was so troubled that he got up and went to kneel beside her chair. 'If it's too much to ask – you and Edward giving up everything you're used to here – I'd give up Stonington and do my best to fit into Vicars' Close – provided small noisy children are allowed here. Ours *will* be noisy, don't you think?'

'Very likely,' she agreed, not sure whether to laugh or weep at the anxious question. 'It had better be Stonington after all.'

'You're happy, but you're also very sad,' Costello said, watching her downbent face. 'Why is that – does the price seem too high?'

She nodded, remembering his dead wife and unborn child, and Francesca – once so confident of being loved. Luigi would remain a bachelor and so, most probably, would dear William Thompson.

'There's never quite enough happiness to go round – someone always gets left out,' she said slowly. Then she smiled at him. 'If you can read my mind, I can read yours! You're about to say that we've all the *more* reason, not less, to make the most of what we've been given.' Then she got up and went to fetch a small box from Edward's desk. 'I left this here to show you – it arrived a few days ago.'

Costello stared at what she offered him – an exquisite cameo brooch engraved with the head of a young woman.

'Filippo Massini's note said that it had belonged to his mother,' Clio explained. 'For that reason he hoped I *would* accept it, whereas he expected me to refuse anything that came from his own family.'

'Shall you accept it?' Costello asked.

'Yes, and I'm going to ask my father to get in touch with *his* father. I don't know that he'll agree, but if he does it might heal the wound they both still have.' The silver chiming of the hour – two o'clock – broke the silence in the room, and Clio smiled at Costello. 'It's Christmas Day already – can't you hear the herald angels singing?'

'The first Christmas of hundreds we shall spend together, because I intend to outlive Methuselah and so must you!' He leaned over to kiss her mouth, and then looked thoughtful. 'With only nine hundred and twenty-nine years left – I've used up forty of them already – it seems mad to waste a single night; but we're in Edward's house and I feel obliged to do no more than escort you to your bedroom door.'

'Thank you,' she said softly, wondering how many other men nowadays would have shown the same self-restraint. 'I'll go to the morning service with Edward, but there's no need for you to come.'

'Of course I shall come. I'm sure that Lucia would expect it of me, and in any case I *want* to sing out loud. I'm even sorry she's not here to sing beside me! Can any man far gone in love say fairer than that?'

Clio's transfiguring smile reappeared. 'I don't believe he can,' she said with great contentment.

Costello pulled her upright and held her close for a moment; she was home at last, and need not fear the future.

'Time for bed, sweetheart,' he said. 'We can at least climb the stairs together.'

She was kissed good morning at her bedroom door, and

then he smiled at her. 'My mind is not *entirely* on the book at the moment, but, with your help, I think it's going to do what I intended – tell the true story of the people who lived and loved and suffered and survived through some terrible times. I'm inventing names for them so that no one still alive gets hurt; but I want us to dedicate the book to the memory of Antonia. Do you think Edward will mind?'

Clio reached up to kiss Costello's cheek. 'It will be the best Christmas present you could give him – and the most eloquent epitaph she will ever have.'